D0908209

The Water Hole

OTHER FIVE STAR WESTERNS BY ZANE GREY:

Last of the Duanes (1996)
Rangers of the Lone Star (1997)
Woman of the Frontier (1998)
The Great Trek (1999)
The Westerners: Stories of the West (2000)
Rangle River: Stories of the West (2001)
Open Range (2002)
The Desert Crucible (2003)
Tonto Basin (2004)
Riders of the Purple Sage: The Restored Edition (2005)
Cabin Gulch (2006)
Shower of Gold (2007)
Dorn of the Mountains (2008)
Union Pacific (2009)
Desert Heritage (2010)
Buffalo Stampede (2011)
War Comes to the Big Bend (2012)
Silvermane: A Western Quartet (2013)

The Water Hole

A Western Story

Zane Grey™

FIVE STAR
A part of Gale, Cengage Learning

Detroit • New York • San Francisco • New Haven, Conn • Waterville, Maine • London

GALE
CENGAGE Learning

LIBRARY OF CONGRESS CATALOGING-IN-PUBLICATION DATA

Grey, Zane, 1872–1939.
The water hole / Zane Grey.
p. cm.
ISBN-13: 978-1-4328-2760-1 (hardcover)
ISBN-10: 1-4328-2760-X (hardcover)
1. Archaeologists—Fiction. I. Title.
PS3513.R6545W373 2014.
813'.54—dc23 2013031781

First Edition. First Printing: January 2014
Published in conjunction with Golden West Literary Agency
Published by Five Star™ Publishing, a part of Gale, Cengage Learning
Find us on Facebook– https://www.facebook.com/FiveStarCengage
Visit our website– http://www.gale.cengage.com/fivestar/
Contact Five Star™ Publishing at FiveStar@cengage.com

Printed in Mexico
1 2 3 4 5 6 7 18 17 16 15 14

ADDITIONAL COPYRIGHT INFORMATION

FOREWORD
BY JON TUSKA

Zane Grey's public image was that of a family man. He fathered three children with his wife, Lina Elise, known familiarly as Dolly. First born was his son Romer, followed by his daughter Betty, and finally by a second son Loren. Loren would pursue a career in psychology, earning a doctorate, teaching and writing on the subject. It was Loren Grey who pointed out to me that his father's fascination with polygamy had its origin in his own personality. Zane Grey was highly critical of Mormonism in 1912 in *Riders of the Purple Sage: The Restored Edition* (Five Star, 2005) in which all three of the principal female characters, although they don't know it, are actually half-sisters and daughters of the same Mormon patriarch. By 1915 when Grey wrote *The Desert Crucible* (Five Star, 2003), the sequel to *Riders of the Purple Sage,* his attitude toward Mormon polygamy had somewhat softened. He observed in this novel: "One wife for one man—that was the law. Mormons broke it openly. Gentiles broke it secretly. . . . Unquestionably the Mormons were wrong, but were not the Gentiles still more wrong?"

Grey's lifestyle changed with increasing affluence and popularity. Two of his girlfriends went along in the Grey party when he visited *Nonnezoshe,* the great Rainbow Bridge of the Navajos, for the first time. Afterward girlfriends almost invariably accompanied him in his travels, a situation that deeply wounded Dolly. Yet his numerous affairs with women seemed to inspire him in his Western romances as much as his discoveries of magical places in the wilderness. Mildred Smith, called familiarly Millicent by Grey, became his personal secretary. She was often attired as actress Lois Wilson would be when she brought Grey's heroines to the screen in Paramount films of the 1920s, and at times Smith went without Zane Grey on location with the film crews in Arizona. It is known that Smith began editing and contributing plot ingredients and ideas for how characters behaved in Grey's fiction as early as 1918 in WAR COMES TO THE BIG BEND (Five Star, 2012). Dolly in her correspondence with Grey often warned him against permitting Mildred to influence his writing. Grey tended to declare her contributions minimal and on one occasion confessed to Dolly: "I did take M's advice about a little of the rewriting. To be honest it helped me to get her point of view."

There was a degree of secrecy in Grey's dealings with women. He was attracted primarily by their beauty. They would communicate by letters with him that were written in code. Grey also used code to record diary entries about what he once described to Dolly as his "inamorata". His daughter Betty recalled to me an incident in which her father remarked to her mother within Betty's hearing that it was Mildred's express desire that he should divorce Dolly and marry her. Indeed, it was this statement that prompted Dolly to move into her own bedroom and not, as Frank Gruber wrote in *Zane Grey: A Biography* (World, 1970), because Grey "worked late at his writing and did not want to awaken Dolly upon retiring." Dolly's defense was to make a life for herself, but she organized Zane Grey, Inc., and acted as conservator for the money Grey's work earned even after Grey's death.

Initially Mildred lived in Grey's home on Catalina Island, before moving into the smaller replica of that home Grey had designed for her on the mainland. If Fay Larkin was a sealed wife of a Mormon kept hidden in seclusion in *The Desert*

Crucible, Mildred Smith was no less so in this home Grey gave her. Through the many years of typing and editing Grey's manuscripts, Smith discovered she had literary ambitions of her own. In the early 1920s she collaborated with Grey on four stage plays. With the exception of the first of these, the plays all had contemporary settings, and traces of Mildred's work can certainly be detected in all of the contemporary stories that Grey wrote during the fifteen years Mildred was with him. The first of these collaborative stage plays was *Amber's Mirage.* When Grey was unable to find any theatrical manager to produce it, he turned it into a short novel, "Amber's Mirage", a three-part serial published in *Ladies Home Journal* (5/29-7/29) and collected in restored form in *Rangle River: Western Stories* (Five Star, 2001). It was at Arizona movie locations that Mildred began her own Western romance with a contemporary setting. When no publisher could be found to accept it, Grey rewrote the story and published it under his own name as "Desert Bound", a six-part serial appearing in *McCall's* (12/25-5/25).

The second of the unproduced and unpublished stage plays on which Millicent Smith and Zane Grey collaborated that Grey subsequently turned into a magazine serial was *The Courting of Stephen.* The play is a romantic farce that shows how the principal female character turns the tables on the man she wants to marry, using variations of Stephen's own courtship techniques. *The Water Hole* was the result, rendering into English the Navajo word *Beckyshibeta* for an area that conceals below ground an ancient Indian kiva and at the same time is a source for water in the midst of the surrounding desert. The holographic manuscript for this serial is in Zane Grey's handwriting, so it is impossible to determine the extent to which Smith contributed to this version, but there is no question that the heroine was her creation and Grey did what he could to embody Mildred's personality even more into the Cherry Winters character in the story. When "The Water Hole" appeared as a twelve-part serial in *Collier's* (10/8/27-12/24/27), all of the character names had been changed. When the serial was posthumously published as *Lost Pueblo* by Harper & Brothers as the 1954 Zane Grey novel, the text was that of the magazine version, and so the numerous excisions the magazine had made from the text as well as the altered character names were retained. The text published here restores what Zane Grey wrote including all the characters as he originally named them. How the enchantment of the desert could change a person physically and spiritually for the better was a theme for Zane Grey certainly as old as *Desert Heritage* (Five Star, 2010), written in 1909. Whether Grey should have tried to write a contemporary 1920s romantic farce, as Mildred continued to urge him to do, and how enjoyable the result was are issues best left to the judgment of the reader. All I can say is that *The Water Hole* is unlike anything else Zane Grey ever published.

Chapter One

Cherry Winters did not see anything of Arizona until morning. The train had crossed the state line after dark. New Mexico, however, with its bleak plains and rugged black ranges, its lonely reaches, had stirred in her quite new sensations. Her father had just knocked upon her door, awakening her at an unusual hour. She had leaped at her father's casual proposal to take a little trip West with him, but it had begun to have a rather interesting significance to her. And Cherry was not so sure how she was going to take it.

They had arrived at Flagstaff late in the night, and Cherry had gone to bed tired out. Upon awakening this morning, she was surprised at an absence of her usual languor. She appeared wide-awake in a moment. The sun streamed in at the window, very bright and golden, and the air that blew in with it was sharp and cold.

"Gee! I thought someone said it was springtime," said Cherry as she quickly got into slippers and dressing gown. Then she looked out of her window. Evidently the little hotel was situated on the outskirts of town. She saw a few scattered houses on each side, among the pine trees. There were rugged gray rocks, covered with vines and brush. The pines grew thicker and merged into a dark green forest. In the distance showed white peaks against the deep blue of sky. Cherry had an inkling that she was going to like this adventure.

She did not care to admit it, but, although she was only

twenty years old, she had found a good deal too dull at her home in the East. Serious thought appeared to be something she generally shunned, yet to her, now and then, it came involuntarily.

While she dressed she pondered upon the situation. She had never been West before. After college there had been European travel, and then the usual round of golf, motoring, dancing, with all that went with them. She was well aware of her father's dissatisfaction with her generation. Despite his attitude he had seldom interfered with her ways of being happy. This trip had a peculiar slant, now that she scrutinized it closely. They were to meet a young archaeologist here in Flagstaff, and probably arrange to have him take them to the Grand Cañon and other scenic places. Cherry had become acquainted with him in New York, where he had been lecturing on the prehistoric ruins of the Southwest. Stephen Heftral had struck Cherry as being different from the young men she played about with, but, insofar as her charms were concerned, he was as susceptible as the rest. Heftral had never betrayed his feelings by word or action. He had seemed a manly, quiet sort of chap, college-bred, but somewhat old-fashioned in his ways, and absorbed in his research work. Cherry had liked him too well to let him see much of her. Not until she and her father had been out West did he mention that he expected to meet Heftral. Then she was reminded that her father had been quite taken with the young archaeologist. It amused Cherry.

"Dad might have something up his sleeve," she soliloquized. "I just don't quite get him lately."

Cherry found him in the comfortable sitting room, reading a newspaper before an open fireplace. He was a well-preserved man of sixty, handsome and clean-cut of face, a typical New Yorker, keen and worldly, yet of kindly aspect.

"Good morning, Cherry," he said, folding his paper and smiling up at her. "I see you've dispensed with at least some of your make-up. You look great."

"I confess I feel great," Cherry responded frankly. "Must be this Arizona air. Lead me to some lamb chops, Dad."

At breakfast Cherry caught a twinkle in her father's fine eyes. He was pleased that she appeared hungry and not inclined to find fault with the food and drink served. Cherry felt he had more on his mind than merely giving her a good time. It might well be that he was testing a theory of his own relative to the reaction of an oversophisticated young woman to the still primitive West.

"Heftral sent word that he could not meet us here," remarked her father. "We will motor out to a place called Mormon Cañon. It's a trading post, I believe. Heftral will be there."

"We'll ride into the desert?" Cherry asked with enthusiasm.

"Nearly a hundred miles. I daresay it will be a ride you'll remember. Cherry, will you wear that flimsy dress?"

"Surely. I have my coat in case it's cold."

"Very well. Better pack at once. I've ordered a car."

"Are there any stores in this burg? I want to buy several things."

"Yes. Some very nice stores. But hurry, my dear. I'm eager to start."

When Cherry went out to do her shopping, she certainly wished she had worn her coat. The air was nipping, and the wind whipped dust in her face. Flagstaff appeared a dead little town. She shuddered at the idea of living there. Limiting her errands to one store, she hurried back toward the hotel. She encountered Indians who despite their white man's garb were picturesque and thrilling to her. She noted that they regarded her with interest. Then she saw a Mexican boy leading several beautiful, spirited horses. There was nothing else in her brief walk that attracted her attention.

In a short time she was packed and ready for her father when he came to her room. He acted more like a boy than her erstwhile staid and quiet parent. The car was waiting outside.

"We're off," declared Mr. Winters with an air of finality. And Cherry bit her tongue to keep from retorting that he could speak for himself.

Soon they left the town behind and entered a forest of stately pines, growing far apart over brown-matted, slow-rising ground. The fragrance was similar to that of Eastern forests, except that it had a dry, sweet quality new to Cherry. Here and there the road crossed open ranch country, from which snow-clad peaks were visible. Cherry wondered why Easterners raved so about the Alps when the West possessed such mountains as these. She was sorry when she could see them no more. Her father talked a good deal about this part of Arizona, and seemed to be well-informed.

"Say, Dad, have you been out here before?" she asked.

"No. Heftral talked about the country. He loves it. No wonder!"

Cherry made no reply, and that perhaps was more of a compliment than she usually paid places. The road climbed, but neither the steepness nor the roughness of it caused the driver any concern. Soon the car, entering thicker forest, dark and cool, reached the summit of a ridge and started down a gradual descent, where the timber thinned out, and in a couple of miles failed on the edge of the desert.

It was Cherry Winters's first intimate sight of any desert. She felt strongly moved, yet whether it was in awe or wonder or reverence or fear, or a little of each combined, she could not tell. The sum of every extended view she had ever seen, in her whole life, could not compare with the tremendous open space before her. First it was silver and gray, dotted with little green trees, then it sloped off yellow and red, and ended in a great hollow of many hues, out of which dim purple shapes climbed.

"That must be the Painted Desert, if I remember Heftral correctly," said her father. "It is magnificent. Nothing in Europe like it. And Heftral told me that this is nothing compared to the Utah country two hundred miles north."

"Let's go, Dad," Cherry replied dreamily.

From that time on the ride grew in absorbing interest for Cherry, until she was no longer conscious of reflection about her impressions. The Little Colorado River, the vast promontory of Kishlipi, the giant steppes up to the Badlands, the weird and sinister rock formations stretching on to an awful blue gulf that was the Grand Cañon, the wondrous flat tablelands called mesas by the driver, the descent into glaring sandy Moencopi Wash, and up again, higher than ever, and on and on over leagues of desert, with black ranges beckoning—these successive stages of the ride claimed Cherry's attention as had no other scenery in her experience.

She was not ready for the trading post. They had reached it too soon for her. It looked like one of the blocks of red rock they had passed so frequently. But near at hand it began to look more like a habitation. All about was sand, yellow and red and gray, and on the curved knife-edged ridge crests it was blowing like silver smoke. There were patches of green below the trading post, and beneath them a wide hollow, where columns of dust or sand whirled across the barren waste. Beyond, rose white-whorled cliffs, wonderful to see, and above them, far away, the black fringed top of an endless mesa.

"What do you think of it, Cherry?" Winters asked curiously.

"Now I understand why Stephen Heftral seemed such a square peg in a round hole, as my friends called him," replied Cherry enigmatically.

"*Humph!* They don't know him very well," declared her father.

They were met at the door of the post by the trader, John

Linn. He was carrying some Navajo rugs. His sombrero was tipped over one ear. He had a weather-beaten face, and was a middle-aged man of medium height, grizzled and desert-worn, with eyes that showed kindliness and good humor.

"Wal, heah you are," he welcomed them, throwing down the rugs. "Reckon we wasn't expectin' you so soon. Get down an' come in."

Cherry entered the door, into what appeared to be a colorful and spacious living room. Here she encountered a large woman with sleeves rolled up, showing brown and capable arms. She beamed upon Cherry and bade her make herself "to home." Then she joined the others outside, leaving Cherry alone.

She looked around with interest. The broad window seat, with windows opening to the desert view, appealed strongly to Cherry. Removing coat and hat, she sat down to rest and take stock of things.

The long room contained many Indian rugs, some of which adorned the walls. On a table lay scattered silver-ornamented belts, hatbands, and bridles. Over the wide fireplace mantel hung Indian plaques, and on top of the bookcase were articles of Indian design, beaded, and some primitive pottery. A burned-out fire smoldered on the hearth.

At this point Mrs. Linn came in, accompanied by the trader, and Winters, and a tall young man in khaki. Cherry had seen him somewhere. Indeed, it was Stephen Heftral. Brown-faced, roughly garbed, he fitted the desert environment decidedly to Cherry's taste.

"Miss Winters, I reckon you don't need no introduction to Stephen here," announced Mrs. Linn, with a keen glance running over Cherry's short French frock, sheer stockings, and high-heeled shoes.

"Stephen? Oh, you mean Mister Heftral."

The young man bowed rather stiffly and stepped toward her.

"I hope you remember me, Miss Winters," he said.

"I do, Mister Heftral," Cherry replied graciously, offering her hand.

"It's good to see you out here in my West. I really never believed you'd come, though your father vowed he'd fetch you."

"Well, Dad succeeded, though I can't understand it," rejoined Cherry, laughing.

"Mister Winters, did you-all have a nice trip out?" asked Mrs. Linn.

"I did. My daughter's rather doubtful yet, I fear."

"Now, isn't that too bad, Miss Winters," sympathized the genial woman. "I saw right off how pale you are. You'll get your health back in this desert."

"My health!" exclaimed Cherry almost indignantly. "Why, I'm absurdly healthy. I've been picked for a health poster. It's my father who is ailing."

"Excuse me, miss," said Mrs. Linn, embarrassed. "You see your father looks so strong. . . ."

"It isn't his body that's weak, Missus Linn," Cherry interrupted. "It's his mind."

Here Stephen came to the rescue, as Cherry remembered he had always done in New York.

"Missus Linn, it's not a question of ill health for anybody," he explained. "Mister Winters was an old friend of my father's. I met him in New York. He wanted to come out West and get Miss Cherry as far away from civilization as possible, to. . . ."

"I'll say he's done it," interrupted Cherry. "It must be a real knockout to live here if you're crazy about miles of nothing but sand, rocks, and sky, and you've committed some crime or other and want to hide."

Mrs. Linn tried to control her amazement.

"Mister Winters, your rooms are not quite ready. Please wait here a little. . . . Pa, see that them lazy cowboys fetch in the baggage."

"Stephen, where are the boys, anyhow?" Linn asked as his spouse bustled out.

"They were lounging in the shade when the car came up. Then they disappeared like jack rabbits in the sage. Sure they're going to be funny. I'll help you find them."

"Folks, make yourselves comfortable," invited Linn, and left the room with the archaeologist.

Mr. Winters sauntered over to Cherry and gazed disapprovingly down upon her.

"Cherry, I don't mind you calling me crazy or poking fun at me. But please don't extend that to my young friend, Heftral. His father was the finest man I ever knew, and Stephen is pretty much like him. . . . Cherry, you'll have to put your best foot forward if you want to appear well to Stephen Heftral. He's not likely to see the sophisticated type with a microscope out here. In New York he had you buffaloed. You couldn't like him because you didn't understand him."

"Darling Father," Cherry replied, smiling tantalizingly up at him. "Your name may be Elijah, but you're no prophet. I liked your young friend well enough to let him alone. But that was in New York where there are a million men. I don't know about out here. Probably he'll bore me to extinction. Can't you see he's as dry as the dust of this desert? He's living two thousand years behind the times. Fancy digging in the earth for things of the past. Well, he might dig up a jeweled corncob pipe and discover there were glamour girls in the old Aztec days."

"Cherry, you're nothing if not incorrigible," returned Winters in despair.

"Dad, I'm your daughter. I don't know whether you've brought me up poorly or I've neglected you. But the fact is all our educators and scientists claim the parents of the present generation are responsible for our demerits."

"Cherry, I'm responsible for your conduct out here, at all events," Winters declared forcefully.

"Oh, you are! Well, my dearest Dad, I'm here all right . . . or else I've been drinking."

"Cherry, there'll be no more of this drinking business."

"Dad, you've got me figured wrong. I admit my crowd hit the booze pretty strong. But I never drank. Honest, Dad."

"Cherry, I don't know whether to believe you or not. But I've seen you smoke."

"Oh, well, that's different. Smoking isn't very clean, but it's a fashionable vice, and restful at least."

"How about all your men?" Winters queried, evidently emboldened for the minute. "Lord! When I think of the men you've made idiots! Take that last one . . . the young Valentino who brags of being engaged to you."

Cherry laughed merrily. "Dad, do you think that's nice? Chauncey Sarland is just too sweet for words . . . also he dances divinely."

"Sarland is a slick little article. Like his social ladder-climbing mama. But I'll see that he doesn't dance or climb into your inheritance."

"To think you separated me from him!" Cherry cried, pretending tragic pathos.

A slim young Indian girl entered. She was dark and pretty. "Meester, you room ees ready."

"Thank you," said Winters, picking up his coat and hat. "Cherry, you've got me right. I did separate you from Sarland. Also from a lot of other fortune-hunters. That's why you're out in this desert for a spell. Except for Linn and Heftral, who you can't flirt with, there's not a man within a hundred miles."

Cherry eyed her retreating parent, and replied demurely: "Yes, kind, sweet, thoughtful Father."

Winters went out with the Indian maid, and at the same moment a young man entered the other door, carrying a valise in each hand. He had a ruddy face, and was carelessly dressed in striped woolen shirt, overalls, and top boots. He wore a big dusty sombrero. When he spotted Cherry his eyes popped wide open and he dropped one valise, then the other.

"Was you addressin' *me,* miss?" he asked ecstatically.

"Not then. I was speaking to my father. He just left the room. . . . You . . . sort of took me by surprise."

"Shore, you tuk my wind."

"Do you live here?" Cherry asked with interest, thinking: *This trading post might not turn out so badly after all.*

"Shore do," replied the young man, grinning.

"Are you Missus Linn's son?"

"Naw. Jest a plain no-good cowboy."

"My very *first* cowboy," murmured Cherry.

"Aw, miss, I'm shore honored. I'll be yore . . . yore first anythin'. Ain't you the Winters girl we're expectin'?"

"Yes, I'm Cherry Winters."

"An' I'm Mojave. The boys call me that after the Mojave Desert which ain't got no beginnin' or end."

As Cherry broke into laughter another young man entered, also carrying a grip in each hand. He was overdressed, like a motion-picture cowboy, and he had a swarthy, dark face. He gave Cherry a warm smile.

"Cowboy, reckon you can put them bags down an' get back for more," blandly said Mojave.

"Buenos días, señorita," greeted this one, dropping the bags and sweeping the floor with his sombrero.

Cherry was quick to see that Mojave suddenly remembered to remove his own wide headgear.

"Same to you," replied Cherry, smiling as teasingly as possible.

"Miss Winters, this here's Lorenzo," Mojave said apologetically. "He's a Mexican. He seen a Western movie once an' ain't never got over it. He's been dressed up all day waitin' for you."

"I'm tremendously flattered," returned Cherry.

"Mees, thees are your bags I carry. I peeck them out weeth your name on."

"Now there, Buffalo Bill, you mustn't flatter me any more," Cherry replied coquettishly.

"Oh, mees! *Señor* Buffalo Beel you call me. I have seen heem in the movies."

Here he drew two guns with an exaggerated motion-picture-drama style. "A-ha! Veelian! Een my power at las'! A-ha! Your time ees come. I keel you!"

He brandished both guns in Cherry's face. In alarm she slipped off the window seat to dodge behind a table.

"Lorenzo, you locoed cowpuncher, get on the job!" Mojave ordered forcibly. "Wess is comin'."

Lorenzo evidently had respect for Mojave. Hurriedly sheathing his guns and picking up his sombrero, he recovered the two valises.

Meanwhile Cherry emerged from behind the table.

"Mees, Lorenzo will act for you again," he announced grandly.

"Ye-es. Thanks. But please make it some place where I can dodge," replied Cherry.

Lorenzo left the room, and Mojave, taking up his load, turned to Cherry.

"Miss Winters, don't trust Lorenzo, or any of these other *hombres.* An' perticular, don't ride their horses. You'll shore get throwed an' mebbe killed. But my pet horse is shore gentle. I'll take you ridin' tomorrow."

"I'd love to go with you," returned Cherry.

Then Mojave made swift tracks after Lorenzo, just in time to escape being seen by a third cowboy, who entered from outside, carrying a trunk as if it had been a feather. He set it down. He was bareheaded, a blond young man, not bad-looking, in size alone guaranteed to command respect. And his costume struck a balance between that of Lorenzo and Mojave.

Cherry gazed at him and exclaimed: "Well, Tarzan in cowboy boots, no less!"

Wess stared, then walked in a circle to see who she meant. But as there was no other man present he seemed to divine the truth, and approached her straightaway.

"Wal, for gawd's sake," he broke out in slow sepulchral tones.

"Oh, yes, indeed, it's you I mean," Cherry returned, all smiles. "I'll bet when your horse is tired you pick him up and carry him right home."

"Wal, for gawd's sake!" ejaculated Wess exactly as before.

"Are there any more verses to that song?"

"Wal . . . for gawd's sake!"

"Third and last, I hope."

"First time I ever seen an angel or heered one talk," he declared.

"Please don't call me an angel. Angels are good. I'm not. I'm wild. That's why I've been dragged out West. Ask Dad, he knows. Say, that reminds me. I'm dying for a smoke. Dad's old-fashioned and I don't carry them when he's around. Could you give me a cigarette?"

Wess merely stared.

"Please, handsome boy. Just one little cigarette."

"Ain't got nothin' but the makin's," he finally ejaculated.

"Thanks. That'll do," Cherry replied, receiving the little tobacco pouch he handed her.

It fascinated Wess to see Cherry roll her own. He was so absorbed that he failed to note the entrance of a fourth cowboy, who was burdened with hatboxes and more grips. He was the handsomest of the lot. With his fine intent eyes straight ahead, not noticing Cherry, he crossed the room and went into the hallway. Cherry had watched him pass in a surprise that grew into pique. He had never looked once at her. He would have to pay for that slight.

"Wal! Yore shore some pert little dogie," Wess remarked, lighting a match for her.

"Dogie? Say, Mister Cowboy, explain what you mean."

"A dogie is a calf or a colt that ain't got no mother."

"Where did you learn anything about me?" Cherry asked, a bit wary.

"Shore any kid with a ma couldn't ever roll a cigarette an' smoke it like you do."

"Indeed. Wess, are you a desert preacher?" queried Cherry distantly.

"Sorry, miss. Shore didn't mean to hurt yore feelin's. But it kind of got me . . . seein' you smoke like thet. Yore so damn' . . . 'scuse me, I mean yore so shore pretty that it goes ag'in' my grain to see you up to dance-hall tricks."

"You don't like women to smoke?" Cherry returned curiously.

"Perticular, I don't like to see you smokin'."

"Then I won't," Cherry decided, and, walking to the fireplace, she threw the cigarette down.

"Jes . . . jes 'cause I don't like you to smoke?" Wess ejaculated rapturously.

"Jes 'cause you don't like me to."

"An' you'll forgive me fer talkin' like I did?"

"Surely."

"I'm askin' you to prove thet."

"How?"

"Go ridin' with me tomorrow," Wess suggested breathlessly. "You can ride my pet hoss. He's shore gentle. You don't wanna ride any of these *hombres'* horses. You might get throwed an' hurt. They're shore mean."

"I'd love to go with you," Cherry responded dreamily.

At this moment the handsome cowboy returned, and was again crossing the room, straight-eyed and hurried, when Wess hailed him. "Rustle now, you cowboy. Fetch them bags in."

Cherry had taken a few steps forward. The cowboy glided around the table to avoid encountering her, and then bolted out of the room.

"Well, I never!" exclaimed Cherry. "You'd think I was Medusa. He didn't see me. . . . He simply didn't see me! Who is he?"

"Thet's Zoroaster. Mormon cowpuncher. Fine fellar, but awful scared of women. Ain't never seen any but Mormon girls. He'll never look at you."

"Oh, he won't," replied Cherry with a threat in her voice.

"Shore not. An' don't you ever talk to him. He'd like as not drop dead. Last year a girl from the East asked him to dance, an' he run right out of the hall. Didn't show up for a week."

"It's an awful chance to take, but that boy needs reforming," declared Cherry.

Wess stared at her a moment before he took to his defense. "Wal, for gawd's sake!"

Mojave came in with a sly grin on his ruddy face. "Wess, Mister Linn is askin' fer you," he said.

"Where?" Wess asked in both doubt and disgust.

"He's gone out to the post and wants you *pronto.*"

Wess went out grumbling and Mojave approached Cherry with evident profound satisfaction.

"Looks like you're goin' to be as popular as stickin' paper with flies," he said meaningly.

"Mojave, after flies take to flypaper they struggle to get away. That's not a pretty compliment."

"Say! Did you know you called me Mojave?" he asked in

amazement.

Cherry feigned surprise. "Did I?" Then she was electrified at the entrance of still another cowboy.

" 'S-s-scuse me, f-f-folks, w-w-w-where's Wess?"

"Tay-Tay, he's gone to the post an' I wish you wouldn't. . . ."

"Like h-h-hell he has," interrupted Tay-Tay.

"Linn is lookin' fer him."

"L-l-last I saw of Linn he was runnin' the car in the shed."

"Good. Then he won't be right back an' Wess'll have to find him."

Cherry stood fascinated by Tay-Tay's struggle with words.

"B-b-b-bad I'd say. For you an' Wess. The cows are yore job, an' yore both locoed b-by this d-d-dame. It's g-g-goner rain like hell!"

Cherry turned to Mojave. "Perhaps you b-b-better go. . . . Well, I hope to die if I'm not stuttering too."

Here Lorenzo, filling the doorway, struck a dramatic pose and fixed sentimental eyes on Cherry.

"Por ultimo. Señorita mía," he said eloquently.

"Too many languages around here for me," returned Cherry.

"Here's Lorenzo to give a hand. I was jest tellin' Miss Winters how you could ride. An' she's shore ailin' to see you round up the cows."

Lorenzo's look of fiery pride slowly changed to one of suspicion, and Tay-Tay stared from him to Mojave. The next thing to happen was Wess shoving Lorenzo into the room and stalking after him, to transfix Mojave with menacing eyes.

"Wal, for gawd's sake! So you was jest gettin' me out of the way. Said Linn was lookin' for me. Wal, cowboy, he ain't."

"Don't you accuse me of no sneakin' trick," replied Mojave, flaring up.

"Linn was askin' fer you. He's plumb forgot. He's gettin' absent-minded, you know. Ask Tay-Tay here if Linn didn't send him lookin' fer you to fetch in the cows."

"S-s-smatter with you, Mojave?" retorted Tay-Tay. "L-L-Linn didn't send me nowhere. I c-c-came fer myself."

"Tay-Tay, yore tongue's not only more tied since you seen Miss Winters, but yore mind is wuss," complained Mojave.

Then followed a silence that Cherry hugely enjoyed. What a time she was going to have. Wouldn't she turn the tables on her tricky father? Mojave backed away from the threatening Wess. The other boys edged nearer to Cherry, who thought it wise to retreat to the window seat. The suspense of the moment was broken by the entrance of Zoroaster, who swung two pairs of boxing gloves in his hands. Behind him entered the Indian maid.

"Mees, your room ees ready," she announced, and retired.

Cherry was in no hurry to follow. Something might happen here too good to miss.

"Thar you are!" announced Zoroaster, indicating Tay-Tay.

He might be a Mormon, but he is certainly good to look at, decided Cherry.

"W-w-what y-y-you w-w-want me for?" Tay-Tay stuttered rebelliously.

"Yore time's come. I've been layin' fer you. An' right now we *can* have it out," returned the grim Mormon.

"W-w-why right now more'n another time?" asked Tay-Tay.

"Wal," spoke up Wess, "I reckon a blind man could see thet. Lope on outdoors, Tay-Tay, an' get yours."

Lorenzo showed his white teeth in a gleaming smile. "Geeve the gloves to Wess an' Mojave. They're lookeen for trouble."

"It's me who's lookin' fer trouble, an', after I'm through with Tay-Tay, I'll take any of you on. Savvy?"

"B-b-but if I w-w-want to q-q-quit in the m-m-middle of a round, I won't be able to say s-s-s-stop," replied Tay-Tay.

"Aw, yore jest plain backin' out before this lady. . . . Wal, who of you will put them on?"

Zoroaster looked from one to the other. They all appeared to have become absent-minded.

Cherry had an inspiration, and rose, radiant, from the window seat. "I will, Mister Zoroaster," she said.

The Mormon cowboy's face turned redder than his hair. He was dumbfounded, and plainly fought to keep from running. But Cherry's smile chained him. If she saw in the boxing bout an opportunity to get acquainted with Zoroaster, he evidently saw one to outdo the other zealous suitors for her favor. Awkwardly he thrust a pair of gloves at her.

"All right, miss. You're shore showin' these *hombres* up. But I'll be careful not to hurt you."

Cherry was athletic and, as it happened, was the best boxer in her club. Pretending unfamiliarity with boxing gloves, she begged someone to help her put them on.

All save Wess rushed to her assistance. He stared, open-mouthed, and finally ejaculated: "Wal, for gawd's sake!"

"There. Now, Mister Zoroaster, give me a few pointers, please," Cherry suggested winningly.

"It's easy, miss," he said, extending his gloved hands. "Keep one foot forward, an' lead with your left hand. Keep yore eyes on my gloves an' duck."

Cherry affected practice while Zoroaster circled her. Plainly he was not a scientific boxer, and Cherry, who had had many a bout with the club instructor, saw some fun ahead. Suddenly she ceased her pretense and went for Zoroaster, swift and light as a cat, and grasped at once that she could hit him when and where she pleased.

"Ride 'em, cowgirl. Oh, my!" cried Mojave.

"Thet's placin' one, miss!" shouted Wess in great glee.

"S-s-s-soak him fer me," stuttered Tay-Tay in delight.

"*Señorita,* you ees one grand boxer," Lorenzo declared dramatically.

Zoroaster's fear and amazement helped to put him at Cherry's mercy. She danced around the transfixed Mormon, raining taps upon his handsome nose. Finally she struck him smartly with her left, and followed that up with as hard a right swing as she could muster. It landed square on Zoroaster's nose and all but upset him.

The cowboys, instead of roaring, seemed suddenly paralyzed. Cherry, glowing and panting, turned to see what was wrong. Her father stood in the doorway, horrified, completely robbed of the power of speech. Zoroaster bolted out of the front door, followed by his cowboy comrades.

Cherry's mirth was not one whit lessened by the sight of her father's face. Gaily she ran to him, extending the gloves to be untied.

"Weren't they something? I love 'em all, and that handsome red-headed devil best. Oh, bless you, Dad. I'll stay here forever!"

Chapter Two

From that moment events multiplied. Cherry could not keep track of them. She was having the time of her life. And every now and then it burst upon her what really innocent fun it was, compared to the high pressure of life in the East.

She had disrupted the even tenor of the trading post. Linn averred that something must be done about it. His cowboys had gone crazy. If they remembered their work, it was to desert it or do it wrong. They manufactured the most ridiculous excuses to ride away from the ranch, when it chanced that Cherry was out riding. When she was at home, they each and every one fell victim to all the ailments under the sun.

Cherry saw very little of Heftral during her first days at the post. He always left before she got up in the morning, and returned from his excavating work late in the afternoon. She met him, of course, at dinner, when they all sat at a long table, and in the living room afterward, but never alone. Cherry was quite aware of the humor with which he regarded her flirtation with the cowboys. She did not like his attitude, and wasted a thought now and then as to how she would punish him.

On the whole, however, she was too happy even to remember her father's reason for fetching her out to the desert. The actual reasons for her peculiar happiness she had not yet analyzed.

It was all so new. She rode for hours every day, sometimes alone, which was a difficult thing to maneuver—and often with her father, and the cowboys. The weather was glorious; the desert strangely, increasingly impelling; the blue sky and white clouds, the vivid colors and magnificent formations of the rock walls had some effect she was loath to acknowledge.

When had she been so hungry and tired at nightfall? She went to bed very early because everybody did so, and she slept as never before. Her skin began to take on a golden brown, and she gained weight. Both facts secretly pleased her. The pace at home had kept her pale and thin. Cherry gazed in actual amazement and delight at the face that smiled back at her from the mirror. Once she mused: *I'll say this Painted Desert has got the beauty shops beaten all hollow.*

Her father had asked her several times to ride over to Sagi Cañon, where Heftral was excavating. But Cherry had pretended indifference as to his movements. As a matter of fact, she was curious to see what his work was like—what in the world could make a young man prefer digging in the dust to her company? There was another reason why she would not go, and it was because the more she saw of Stephen Heftral and heard about him from the cowboys and Linn—who were outspoken in their praise—the better she liked him and the more she resented liking him.

For the present, however, the cowboys were more than sufficient for Cherry. They were an endless source of interest, fun, and wholesome admiration.

In ten days not a single one of them had attempted to hold her hand, let alone kiss her. Cherry would rather have liked them, one and all, to hold her hand, and she would not have run very far to keep from being kissed. But it began to dawn upon her that despite an utter prostration of each cowboy at her feet, so to speak, there was never even a hint of familiarity, such as was natural as breathing to the young men of her set.

First it struck Cherry as amusing. Then she sought to break it down. And before two weeks were up she began to take serious thought of something she had not supposed possible to the genus *Homo,* young or old, East or West.

Cherry did not care to be forced to delve into introspection, to perplex herself with the problem of modern youth. She had had quite enough of that back East. Papers, magazines, plays, sermons, and lectures, even the movies, had made a concerted attack upon the younger generation. It had been pretty sickening to Cherry. How good to get away from that atmosphere for a while. Perhaps here was a reason why she liked the West. But there seemed to be something working on her, which sooner or later she must face.

One afternoon Cherry returned from her ride earlier than usual, so that she did not have to hurry and dress for dinner. She had settled herself in the hammock when her father and Heftral rode in from the opposite direction. The hammock was hidden under the vines outside the living room window. They did not see Cherry and she was too lazy or languid to call to them.

A little later she heard them enter the living room. The window there was open.

"Cherry must be dressing," said Winters. "She's back. I saw her saddle. We have time for a little chat. I've been wanting to talk to you."

"Go ahead. I'm glad our ride didn't tire you. By the way, what did you think of my Sagi?"

"Beautiful but dumb, as Cherry would say. Quietest place I ever saw. Why, it was positively silent as a grave."

"Yes. It is a grave. That's why I dig around there so much," Heftral replied with a laugh.

Cherry remembered that laugh, though she had heard it very seldom. It was rather rich and pleasant, and scarcely fitted the character she had given him. She had two sudden impulses, one to make them aware of her presence, and another not to do anything of the kind. Second impulses were mostly the stronger with Cherry.

"Heftral, I'm very curious about you. What is there in it for you . . . in this grave-digging work, I mean?"

"Oh, it's treasure hunting in a way. I suppose an archaeologist is born. I seldom think of reward. But, really, if I discovered the prehistoric ruin I know is buried here somewhere, it would be a big thing for me."

"Any money in it?" inquired the New York businessman.

"Not directly. At least not at once. I suppose articles and lectures could be translated into money. It would give me prestige, though."

"Hum. Well, prestige is all right for a young man starting in life but it doesn't produce much bread and butter. Do you get a salary, in addition to your remuneration for articles and lectures?"

"You could call it a salary by courtesy. But besides bread-and-butter fare of the simplest kind, it wouldn't buy stockings for a young lady I know," returned Heftral, and again he laughed, the same nice infectious laugh.

"Now you're talking," Winters responded with animation. "The young lady, of course, being Cherry. . . . Heftral, we're getting to be good friends. Let's be confidential. Did you ever ask my daughter to marry you?"

"Lord, no!" ejaculated Heftral.

"Well, that's a satisfaction. It's good for a young man to have individuality. I'm glad you're different from the many. . . . May I ask . . . forgive my persistence . . . the awful responsibility of being this girl's father, you know . . . weren't you in love with her?"

There was quite a long silence in which Cherry's heart beat quickly and her ears tingled. She had never really been sure of Heftral. That, perhaps, was his chief charm.

"Yes, Mister Winters," replied the archaeologist constrainedly. "I was in love with Cherry. Not, however, as those young men were in the East. But very terribly, deeply in love."

"Fine! Oh, excuse me, Stephen," rejoined Winters. "I mean . . . that's what I thought. That's why I liked you. These young lounge lizards play at love. They make me sick. Between you and me, I've a sneaking suspicion they make Cherry sick, too. . . . Now, Stephen, here's the vital question. Is all that past tense?"

Cherry made the discovery that she was trembling, and imagined it was from the shame of being an unwitting eavesdropper. How impossible now to call out. Yet she might have slipped away. But she did not.

"No. I never got over it. And now it's worse," Heftral said not without a tragic note.

"Stephen, by heavens, you are a loyal fellow. Would it surprise you to know I'm pleased?"

"Thank you, Mister Winters. But I fear that I'm more than surprised."

"See here, Stephen, you want to be prepared for jars, not only from Cherry, but also me. I'm her Dad, you know. . . . Listen, I brought Cherry out to your desert with bare-faced deliberate intent. To marry her to you and save her from that pack of wolves back there. Incidentally, of course, to make both of you happy."

"My God!" gasped Heftral. He was not the only one who gasped. Cherry in her excitement nearly fell out of the hammock.

"It's an honest fact and I'm not ashamed," Winters went on, getting earnest.

"But, Mister Winters . . . you do me honor. You are most wonderfully kind, but you are quite out of your head."

"Maybe I am. I don't care. I mean it. I love Cherry and I'd

go to any extreme to save her. Then I like you immensely. Your father was my dearest friend in college and until he died. I'd get a good deal of happiness out of putting a spoke in your wheel of fortune."

"Save her!" ejaculated Heftral.

"For God's sake, Heftral, don't say you think it's too late," Winters appealed in sudden distress.

No quick response came, and Cherry's heart stood still as she waited for Heftral's answer. What did that fool think, anyway? She was getting a little sick with anger and fear when Heftral burst out: "Winters, you're crazy. I . . . I meant . . . what did you mean when you said save her?"

"I meant a lot, my boy, and don't overlook it. . . . Tell me straight, Heftral. This is a serious matter for us all. Do you think Cherry is still a good girl?"

"I don't think. I *know,*" Heftral returned ringingly. "Your question is an insult to her, Mister Winters."

"I wonder whether or not any question is that, in regard to young women in this age," Winters went on soberly. "I gave you credit for being a brainy clear-eyed fellow, for all your grave-digging propensity. I saw how you disapproved of Cherry . . . her friends and habits."

"Yes, I did . . . deplorably so. But nevertheless. . . ."

"Love is blind, my son," interposed Winters. "You think more of Cherry than she deserves. All the same I'm glad. That'll help us out. I regard you as an anchor."

"Mister Winters, I . . . I don't know what to say. I'm overwhelmed."

"Well, I dare say you've reason to be. But all the same you listen to me patiently. Will you?"

"Why, certainly."

"You were justified in being shocked at my question about Cherry. But I wouldn't blame anyone for a pretty raw opinion of modern girls. I have it myself. . . . To be brief, they have gotten under my skin, if you know what that means. Cherry's generation is beyond my understanding. They have developed something new. They are eliminating right and wrong. They have no respect for their parents, and so far as I can see very little affection. They have a positive hatred for all restraint. They will not stand to be controlled. They have no faith in our old standards. As a rule they have no religion. They wear indecent clothes, or I might say very few clothes at all. They dance all night, drown themselves in booze, pet and neck indiscriminately, and most of them go the limit."

"Mister Winters!" Heftral expostulated, somewhat taken aback by the elder man's outburst.

"Stephen, I'm telling you straight. This is not my theory. I know. I've got this young crowd figured that far, at least. I have no patience at all with the fatuous mamas and papas who claim the young people are all right. They are *not* all right. They are a fast crowd and the nation that depends on them and can't change them is slated for hell. These wiseacres who say there is no flagrant immorality are far off the track. Those who claim young women of today are no different from yesterday are simply blind. They *are* different, and I don't mean wholly the emancipation of women since the war. I was always for woman suffrage. . . . Well, I'm not concerned with the causes, as whether or not we parents are to blame. I've done my damnedest for Cherry and it hurts to think maybe I've failed. I'm honest in believing I've not been a bad example for my child. But sometimes Cherry makes me crawl into a dark corner and hide. . . . I'm concerned with the facts of what I'm telling you. I want to see Cherry married to a good and straight and industrious young man. Cherry says he doesn't exist. . . . Her mother was like Cherry, though not so beautiful. She was willful, intelligent, bewildering. But she had no vices. Now I take it Cherry is about as fascinating as a young woman could be. Perhaps she is all the more so because of this complexity of modern times. She knows it. I wouldn't call Cherry conceited. She's not really vain. She's rather a merciless gay modern young woman who takes pleasure in wading through a mob of men. If she heard her friends speak of a man who was not likely to fall for her, as they call it, Cherry would yell . . . 'Lead me to him!' Despite all this I feel and hope Cherry can be saved. Lord, fancy her hearing me say that. To my mind, if she drifts with her crowd, she'll never amount to anything. She would probably divorce one husband after another. I don't like the idea. Cherry's mother left her something that she will have control of in another year. And then of course she'll get all I possess, which isn't inconsiderable. Her prospects then, and her beauty, make her a mark for the men she comes in contact with, and their name is legion. I have tried to keep her away from the worst of them. But it's impossible."

"Why impossible?" broke in Stephen tersely.

"I gave up because when I'd tell Cherry a certain young fellow was no fit acquaintance for her I would only stimulate interest. She'd say . . . 'Dad, you think you know a lot, but I'll have to see for myself' . . . and you bet she would."

"Then Cherry wouldn't obey you?" asked Heftral.

"Obey?" Winters echoed in surprise. "Most certainly she would not."

"Then indeed you are to blame for what she is."

"Ha! I'd like to see you or anybody else make Cherry obey."

"I could and I would," declared Heftral.

"My dear young Arizona archaeologist, may I ask how?" returned Winters, not without sarcasm and amusement.

"I'd take that young lady across my knee and spank her soundly."

"Good Lord! You don't know what you're saying. . . . Why, if

I subjected Cherry to such indignity she'd . . . she'd . . . well, what wouldn't she do? Wrecking the place where it happened would be the least. Yet, oh . . . how I have wanted to do that same little thing."

"Mister Winters, your daughter is a spoiled child," Heftral asserted in a tone that made Cherry want to shriek.

"Spoiled . . . yes . . . and everything else," agreed Winters helplessly. "But with it all she is adorable. Have you noticed that, Stephen?"

"Why, come to think of it I believe I have," he answered with dry humor.

"Well, we are agreed on a few things, anyway. We can dismiss her demerits by acknowledging that, and her intelligence, truthfulness, and other cardinal virtues that she has in common with all the young people today. It may be that they are too advanced for us of the older generation to understand. It might be that something wonderful will come of such a paradox. But I can't see it, and my problem is to check Cherry's mad career. . . . Ha! Ha!"

"If I may presume to advise you, Mister Winters, you are undertaking a perfectly impossible task," said Heftral.

"No! Why, Stephen, I am sometimes damn' fool enough to believe Cherry might do all I ask just because she loves me. I know she does. But I always put things to her in a way that makes her furious. So I've quit it. . . . This is my last card . . . my trump."

"This?" Heftral asked with curiosity.

"This trip, and the plan I've decided upon. Here it is. I'm going to marry Cherry to you."

There was an absolute blank silence. Cherry felt what a shock this must have been to Heftral. It was no less a shock to her.

"Now I know what's the matter," Heftral said finally in a queer voice.

"What?"

"You really *are* out of your mind."

"Well, that may be," Winters returned with good humor. "But I'll stand by my guns. I've sense enough to understand that you will at first indignantly refuse such a proposition. Won't you?"

"I certainly do," replied Heftral bluntly.

"Heftral, no young man who knew and loved Cherry could refuse for any other reason than he thought it preposterous. . . . That she didn't care two straws for him?"

"Exactly. In my case one straw."

"The only weakness in my proposition is the hope, the dream, that Cherry might love you someday. You must remember I know her as I knew her mother. Cherry, too, is capable of the most extraordinary things."

"It surely would be that for her to . . . to. . . . Oh, Winters, the idea is ridiculous," Heftral returned, beginning in bitterness and ending in anger.

"Hear me out. If you don't, I'll think you, too, are just like the rest of this generation. . . . I base my hopes on this. Cherry likes you . . . respects you. She makes all manner of fun of you, but underneath it there's something deep. At least it's deep enough to keep her from adding your scalp to her belt. You'll forgive me, Stephen, for saying that any fancyfree girl would learn to care for you . . . under favorable circumstances."

"What are they?" queried the archaeologist.

"Never mind details. But I mean the things that make a man. I'll swear I don't believe Cherry has ever met a real man. . . . Well, to go on. I save my conscience in this case by believing she could care for you. And my plan is simply to give Cherry a terrific jar, and then human nature, with such a favorable start, will do the rest."

"Believe me, it would have to be a terrific jar, all right," Heftral said with another of his resonant laughs.

"Believe me, it *is.* And it's simply this. Be as nice as pie to Cherry. Then at an opportune time just throw her on a horse and pack her off to one of your ruins in the desert. Kidnap her. Keep her out there a little while . . . scare her half to death . . . let her know what it is to be uncomfortable, hungry, helpless. Then fetch her back. She'd have to marry you. I would insist upon it. Then we'd all be happy."

"Mister Winters, the only sane remark you've made is that epithet you applied to yourself a few moments ago."

"It is a most wonderful opportunity. You are ambitious. This would make you."

"No."

"I will make you a most substantial settlement. You will be independent for life. You can follow up your archaeological work for the love of it. You. . . ."

"No!"

"Now, Stephen, I can apply that epithet to you. May I ask why you refuse?"

"You . . . I. . . . Oh, hell! Winters, it's because I really *love* Cherry. I couldn't think of myself in such a case. If I did I'd . . . I'd be as weak as water. Why, Cherry would hate me."

"Don't be so sure of that," replied Winters sagely. "You can't ever tell about a woman. It's a gamble, of course. But you have the odds. Be a good sport, Stephen. Even if you lose you'll have gained an experience that you'll remember a lifetime."

"Mister Winters, you're taking advantage of human nature," Heftral replied with agitation.

Cherry could hear him pacing the room, and she felt sorry for him. It pleased her that he had refused. But she knew her father, his relentless ways, and she held her breath.

"Certainly I am," agreed Winters, growing warmer. "Stephen, look at it this way. Consent for Cherry's sake."

"But, man, I can't believe that wonderful girl is going to hell. I *can't.*"

"Naturally. You're in love with her. To you she's an angel. All right. Think of it this way then. You admitted she was adorable. You just said she was wonderful. You know how beautiful she is. Well, here's your chance to make her yours. Maybe it's a thousand-to-one shot. Remember, you'll do her good in any case. And you've that one chance in a thousand. Her mother was the most loving of women. Why, Stephen, if Cherry loved you . . . you would be entering the kingdom of heaven. She might."

"My God!" gasped the young man.

"I am her father. I worship her. And I am begging you to do this thing."

"All . . . right. I . . . I'll do it," Heftral replied in a queer strangled voice. "It will be my ruin. But I can't resist. Only, understand . . . I couldn't accept money."

"Fact is, I didn't think you would," replied Winters quickly. "And your refusal makes me sure you are the right man. Come, shake on it, Stephen. I'll be forever grateful to you whether we win or lose."

Cherry heard him rise and cross the room. Taking advantage of this, she slipped out of the hammock and ran around to the back of the house, and, entering the long corridor, she arrived at her room in a more excited and breathless state than she had ever been in all her life. Closing the door she locked it and then relaxed against it, with a hand over her throbbing breast.

"If that wasn't the limit!" she exclaimed, and succumbed to conflicting emotions, among which such rage as she had never felt assumed dominance.

Not long afterward her father knocked on the door. Cherry did not answer. He knocked again, and called anxiously: "Cherry?"

"Yes."

"Dinner is ready. We're waiting."

"I don't want any," she replied.

"Why, what is the matter?"

"I've a headache."

"Headache! You? Never heard of the like before."

"Maybe it's a toothache."

"Oh," he returned, and discreetly retired.

When Cherry's anger had finally subsided so that she could think, she found she was deeply wounded. Things for her had come to a very sad pass indeed, if her father could go to such extremes. But were they so bad for her? How perfectly absurd. There was not anything wrong with her. Yet all the same an awakened consciousness refused to accept her indignant assurance. She knew she was the pride and joy of her father's life. He was a trying parent, indeed; nevertheless she could not seriously say he had neglected her or given her a bad example. He was just thick-headed, and too much concerned about her affairs. Cherry, however, dodged for the present any serious thought concerning her friends and acquaintances at home. They were as good as any other crowd.

Heftral. She could overcome her shame and resentment enough to feel sorry for him. What chance had he against her father, especially if he was genuinely attracted to her? Cherry blushed in the loneliness of her room. Heftral had saved his character, in her estimation, by scorning her father's opinions, by resisting his subtle attack, by refusing any consideration of a material gain in his outrageous proposals.

Then Cherry happened to remember what Heftral had said about spanking her. In a sudden fury she leaped up and began to pace the little room. There was not very much in the way of disgust, contempt, amazement, pride, wrath, that did not pass through her mind. What an atrocious insult! He had been in earnest. He talked as if she were a nine-year-old child. Her cheeks burned. She refused in the heat of the moment to answer a query that knocked at her ears.

"Oh, I won't do a thing to Stephen Heftral," she said under her breath, and, as she said it, she caught sight of her face in the mirror. When had she looked like that? Only the other day she had fancied she wore a tired bored look. At least she was indebted to Heftral for a glow and a flash of radiance.

A hundred thoughts whirled through her mind. One of them was to run off from her father and punish him that way. Another was actually to be what he feared she was or might become. The former appeared too easy on him and the second unworthy of her. It stung her acutely that she was compelled to prove to him how really different she was. But revenge first. She would show them. She would play up to their infamous plot. She would walk right into their little trap. Then—she would frighten her clever parent out of his wits. And as for Heftral. She would reduce him to such a state of love-sick misery that he would want to die. She would be ten thousand times herself and everything else she could lend herself to. She would help him on with the little scheme, make him marry her, and then, when he and her father were at the top of their bent and ridiculously sure of her so-called salvation, she would calmly announce to them that she had known all about it beforehand. She would denounce them, and go home and divorce Heftral.

The next morning Cherry saw Heftral and her father ride away on their horses, evidently well pleased with themselves over something. Then she went late to her breakfast, finding it necessary to play the actress with the solicitous Mrs. Linn. She would have to be a brilliant actress, anyway, so she might as well begin. She might develop histrionic ability, and make a name on the stage.

She did not ride that morning. Part of the time she spent in her room, and the other walking in the shade of the cotton-woods.

After lunch Cherry tried to read. All the books and magazines she had appeared to be full of humor or tragedy of the younger generation. One after another she slammed them on the floor.

"This business is getting damned serious!" ejaculated Cherry.

All the preachers, editors, physicians, philosophers were explaining either how horrible the young people were, or else how misunderstood, or abandoned by money-mad parents to their dark fate. Even college boys and girls were writing about themselves. Something was wrong somewhere, and, as the thought struck Cherry, she found herself reaching for a cigarette. With swift temper she threw the little box against the wall. She would have to quit smoking—which meant nothing at all to Cherry. She could quit anything. She remembered, however, that in accordance with the plan to avenge herself upon her father and Heftral, she must smoke like a furnace. So she took the trouble to pick up the cigarettes. Still, she did not smoke one then.

The afternoon slowly waned. It had been an upsetting day for Cherry. She had changed a hundred times, like the shifting of a wind vane. But the thing most permanent was the stab to her pride. Not soon would she get over that hurt. She did not realize yet just why or how she had been so mortally offended, but she guessed it would come to her eventually.

For the first time in years Cherry missed her mother. Was she self-sufficient as she had supposed? She certainly was not, for she fought an hour against rather strange symptoms, and then succumbed to a good old-fashioned crying spell.

CHAPTER THREE

That evening a little before suppertime, when Heftral walked into the living room, Cherry made it a point to be there. She had adorned herself with a gown calculated to make him gasp. She perceived that he had difficulty in concealing his dismay. The day of mental stress, without the usual exercise and contact with the open, had left her pale with faint purple shadows under her eyes. Cherry thought she could take care of the rest.

"I'm sorry you were indisposed," Heftral said solicitously. "I see you haven't been out today. That's too bad."

"It has been a lonely, awful day," replied Cherry pathetically.

"I hope you haven't been very ill. You looked so . . . so wonderful yesterday. You're pale now. No doubt you've overdone this riding around with the cowboys."

"I guess I'm not so strong as Dad thinks I am. But I'm really not tired . . . that is, physically."

"No? What's wrong then?"

Cherry transfixed Heftral with great melancholy eyes. "I'm dying of homesickness. This place is dead. It's a ruin. You could dig right here and find a million bones."

"Dead? Oh, yes, indeed, it is rather quiet for a girl used to New York," he returned, plainly disappointed. "I rather expected you would like it . . . for a while, and, really, you seemed to be enjoying yourself. I know your father thinks you're having the time of your life."

"I was. But it didn't last. Nothing happens. I imagined there'd be some excitement. Why, I can't even get a kick out of a horse," complained Cherry.

"Take care about that," Heftral said seriously. "Linn has seen to it that you've had only gentle horses. I heard him rake the cowboys about this. None of their tricks."

"Mister Heftral," returned Cherry, sweetly explaining, "I didn't mean that kind of a kick. I'd like a horse to run off with me . . . since there's no man out here to do it."

Cherry was blandly innocent, and apparently unconscious of Heftral's slight start and quick look. She was going to enjoy this better than she had expected.

"I . . . I daresay the cowboys . . . and all Westerners . . . couldn't understand you, Miss Cherry," rejoined Heftral. "They will exert themselves to amuse you . . . take care of you. But never dream . . . of . . . how. . . ."

"That a New York girl requires some stimulant," interposed Cherry. "Oh, I get that. These nice dumb cowboys. I thought they were going to be regular fellows. But, do you know, Mister Heftral, not a single one of them has attempted to kiss me!"

"Indeed. From what I know of them, I think that'd be the last thing they'd attempt. They are gentlemen, Miss Winters," said Heftral rather stiffly.

"What's that got to do with kissing a girl?" Cherry retorted, hard put to restrain her laughter. "It'd be fun to see their line of work. And in the case of that handsome Zoroaster . . . well, I might let him get away with it."

Heftral stared at her incredulously, with infinite disapproval.

"Outside of yourself, Mister Zoroaster is the only good-looking man around the place. And as you don't seem to be aware of my presence here, I'd rather welcome a little attention from him."

"Miss Winters!" ejaculated Heftral. "You are complimentary . . . and rather otherwise, all in one breath. It is you who have not been aware of *my* presence."

"What could you expect?" Cherry queried with a bewildering confusion. "I might flirt with a cowboy. But I couldn't . . . well . . . throw myself at a man of your intelligence and culture. All the same I've been hoping you'd take me around a little. To your ruins and interesting places. Maybe amuse me in the evenings, or at least do something to kill the awful monotony. In New York you seemed to like me. I daresay Dad has talked about me . . . queered me with you."

Heftral had been reduced to a state of speechlessness. He actually blushed, and there leaped to his eyes a light that made them very warm and appealing. At this point Mr. Winters came in. He looked unusually bright and cheerful, but at sight of Cherry his smile faded.

"Cherry, dear, you look sort of down," he commiserated, kissing her. "I forgot you had a headache or something."

"Dad, I've just been complaining to Stephen. But he doesn't care whether I'm sick or homesick, or what."

"Stephen? Homesick? Why Cherry!" exclaimed Winters, quite taken aback.

"Dad, will you let me go home?" she asked mournfully.

"Cherry!"

"Don't look like that. What do you think anyway? You've dragged me out to this dead hole. Nothing happens. You said Stephen would be tickled pink to run around with me."

"I didn't say anything of the kind," her father declared, turning a little pink himself.

"Oh, I mean words to that effect," replied Cherry airily. "But, as you've seen, he has studiously avoided me as if I was a pestilence. Left me to the mercy of these cowboys."

"I'm sure there is a misunderstanding," returned Winters, divided between doubt and exultation.

"There certainly is," added Heftral emphatically. "I hope it isn't too late for me to correct it."

"I'm afraid so," Cherry said with eyes on him. "Else how could I *ever* have told you?"

"Nonsense," spoke up her father. "Cherry, you must be a little off your feed or something."

"Dad, I'm not a horse or a cow . . . and I would like a little fruit salad or a lobster." Suddenly she clapped her hands. "I've an idea. Perfectly delicious. Let me send for Chauncey?"

"What? That last faint gasp of the Sarland family?"

"Dad, I'd have a perfectly glorious time riding around with him."

"*Humph!* I don't believe it. You don't know what you do want."

"Please, Daddy. Chauncey would at least amuse me."

"He would. And us, too. But no, Cherry. I can't see it," declared Winters.

"Very well, Father," agreed Cherry. She never called him "Father" except in cases like this. "I've done my best to please you. The consequences will be upon your head."

Winters grunted, gave Cherry a baffled glance, and stepped out the open door to view the afterglow of the sunset. Heftral was perturbed. Cherry enjoyed the assurance that her new line had been effective. No man could resist subtle flattery.

"Miss Cherry . . . if you . . . if I . . . if there *has* been a misunderstanding . . . let me make it right," Heftral began with a sincerity that made Cherry feel villainous. "Frankly I . . . I didn't think you cared two straws about my work, or the ruins . . . or me, either. So I never asked you. You remember I used to try to interest you in the desert. Indeed there is much here to interest you . . . if you will only see. Suppose you ride out with me tomorrow."

Cherry fixed sad eyes upon his earnest face. "No, Stephen. I told you . . . it's too late. You'd never have thought of it, if I hadn't gone down and out. I'm sorry, but I can't accept solicited attention."

"You're very unkind, at least," rejoined Heftral, vexed and hurt. "You've scarcely looked at me, since your arrival. Now you complain of my . . . my neglect. I tell you . . . to accuse me of indifference is perfectly ridiculous."

Then the little Indian maid called them to supper. When Winters followed them in and caught a glimpse of Heftral's face, he threw up his hands, then he laughed heartily. Cherry understood him. It was a return to good humor and the hopelessness of ever doing anything with her. His mirth, however, did not infect Heftral, who scarcely said another word, ate but little, and soon excused himself.

"Say, honey, what'd you do to Stephen?" Winters inquired genially.

"Nothing."

"Which means a whole lot. Well, tell me."

"I let him know I *did* like him very much . . . that his indifference has hurt me deeply . . . and that now. . . ."

"Ah, I see. Now, in the vernacular of your charming crowd there's nothing doing," interrupted her father. "Cherry, dear, if I were Stephen I'd be encouraged. I remember your mother. When I was most in despair my chances were brightest. Only I didn't know it."

"Dad, I did like Stephen," Cherry murmured dreamily.

"It's too bad you don't any more. . . . What are you going to do tomorrow?"

"Perhaps I will feel well enough to ride a little."

"Good. I'm motoring to Flagstaff. I'll be back before dark, I think. I've got important letters and telegrams to send."

"You won't let me wire for Chauncey Sarland?" asked Cherry.

"Cherry, don't always put me at a disadvantage," returned Winters impatiently. "You know I'd let you have anyone or anything . . . if you convinced me of your need. But, darling, you know Sarland would bore you to death. Be honest."

"I suspect he might, after he got here," acknowledged Cherry demurely. "But, Dad, just think of the fun the cowboys would have out of him. And he'd make Stephen perfectly wild."

"Aha! You've said it, my daughter," Winters declared, clapping his hands. "I had a hunch, as Linn says. . . . Well, Cherry, you must excuse me. I've got to spend the evening writing. You can have a nice quiet hour reading."

"Hour! I can't go to bed for hours."

"Cherry, you look perfectly wonderful, ravishing, and . . . well, indecent in that flimsy white gown. It'd make a first-rate handkerchief for one of these man-size Westerners. But it's wasted on the desert air."

"Yes, I'm afraid my desire to look well for Stephen was wasted," returned Cherry. "Men are no good. You can't please them."

"Perhaps the emancipation of women has peeved us," Winters remarked slyly.

Cherry was curious to see if Heftral would come back to the living room. She hoped he would not, for he appeared to be giving her a taste of something different in masculine reactions. She talked to the Linns about the cowboys and Heftral, learning more and more for her amusement and interest. They regarded the archaeologist as one of the family and were immensely proud of his work. It might have been gold hunting, for all the store they put on it. Cherry began to gather some inkling of the importance of Heftral's discovery of the pueblo claimed by scientists to have existed there for centuries past. She began to hope for his success.

Heftral did not appear again and the Linns retired early. Cherry was left to her thoughts, which she found pleasant. Soon she went to her room, and to bed. Though she would not admit it to her father, the quiet of the night, the comfortable feel of wool blankets, the black darkness appealed strongly to her.

What few words and glances it had taken to upset Stephen Heftral. If Cherry had not been so outraged her conscience might have given her a twinge. Deep within her dwelt a respect for honesty and simplicity. The idea she had given Heftral—that she had expected and hoped for a little attention from him—had completely floored him. After all it was not much of a deceit. She had expected more than a little. There was something warm and sweet in the thought of his really caring for her like that. Cherry believed that no real woman of the present or of the future would ever feel otherwise than stirred at a man's honest love. It was in the race, and the race's progress toward higher things depended upon it. Cherry made the mental observation that the world had not progressed very much lately.

Next morning she again delayed going into breakfast purposely to miss Heftral and her father. Cherry put on her riding clothes, taking her time about it.

After breakfast the only one of the cowboys around the corrals was Wess.

"Mornin'," he greeted her. "When did you come back to life? Us boys figgered you was daid."

"Me? Oh, I never let anybody get tired of me," responded Cherry. "Can I have Patter saddled?"

"I reckon, but I cain't see what for. That cayuse is no good. He's got a mean eye when he rolls it. Now my little roan. . . ."

"Wess, you boys can't fool me any longer about the horses. They're all good. Please saddle Patter for me."

While Wess went to fetch the horse, Cherry walked into the trading post, always and increasingly interesting to her. Linn was selling supplies to the Indians. Cherry liked to hear the low strange voices. One of the Indians was nothing if not frankly admiring. He was a tall, slim, loose-jointed individual, wearing corduroys and moccasins, a huge-buckled and silver-ornamented belt, a garnet-colored velveteen shirt, and a black sombrero with a bright-braided band. He had a lean face like a hawk, dark and clear, and piercing black eyes. Cherry had been advised not to appear interested in the Indian men—that they misunderstood it, and had been known to give Eastern women some rude shocks. As usual Cherry disregarded advice.

She noticed when she left the post that the Indian sauntered out to watch her. Cherry thought if Stephen Heftral would act that way, she would be highly gratified. Patter was saddled waiting for her, a fine little bay mustang.

"What's Smoky followin' you for?" Wess queried gruffly.

"Smoky, who's he?"

"Thet blamed Navey."

"Oh, I see. I don't know, Wess. I certainly didn't ask him to. It's quite flattering, though. But not complimentary to you boys."

"Wal, miss, if you excuse me I'll say thet's not funny an' you ain't ridin' out alone," said Wess.

"Indeed. Wess, you can be most disagreeable at times. It spoils a perfectly wonderful man. I *am* going to ride alone."

"Nope. If you won't listen to me, I'll tell Linn."

"Aren't you just inventing an opportunity to ride with me?"

"Reckon not. I don't care particular aboot ridin' with you, after the deal you gave me last time."

"What was that, Wess? I forget."

"Wal, never mind. . . . Now this Indian Smoky is a bad *hombre* an' it's really because he's not all there. He's not to be trusted. He might foller you around jes' curious. But if you got too nice to him, things might happen. If he annoys you, he'll be a daid redskin damn' quick."

"Thank you, Wess. I'll say that's talking," responded Cherry. "But tell me, what do you do to white men out here, when they insult Eastern girls?"

"Wal, miss, white men . . . that is, Westerners *don't* insult girls from anywhere," Wess returned forcefully.

"But they do. I've heard and read of lots of things. Suppose now, just for example, you were to kidnap me and pack me off into the desert. What would happen to you?"

"If I didn't get strung up to a cottonwood, I'd shore be beat till I was near daid. But, Miss Cherry, you needn't worry none about me. I've learned to fight my natural instincts."

Cherry laughed merrily. Some of these cowboys were full of wit and humor. "Wess, I'll compromise this ride with you," said Cherry. "I want to surprise Mister Heftral at his work. So you take me out and show me where he is. But you must wait some little distance away. But won't I be taking you from your own work?"

"Boss' orders are that I look after you, Miss Cherry," Wess said with emphasis on the personal pronouns. "I'll throw a saddle an' be heah *pronto.*"

They rode out along the fenced ground, where Linn kept stock at times, and came upon Tay-Tay, Lorenzo, and Zoroaster digging post holes. If there was anything a cowboy hated more than that, Wess declared he did not know what it was. The trio doffed their sombreros to Cherry, and grinned because they could not help it, but they were galled at the situation.

"Reckon that's fair to middlin'," declared Wess, eying the post holes. "But you ain't diggin' them deep enough."

Zoroaster glared at Wess and threw down the long-handled shovel.

Lorenzo wiped the sweat from his face. "Say, are you foreman on this ranch?" he asked scornfully.

"G-g-g-go along w-w-w-with you or you'll g-get h-h-h-hurt,"

stuttered Tay-Tay.

"Wal, as I don't care to have Miss Winters see you boys any wuss than you are now, reckon I'll move along," drawled Wess.

Cherry gave each in turn a ravishing smile, intended to convey the impression that she wished he were her escort rather than Wess. Then she trotted Patter out on the desert after Wess.

They climbed a gradual ascent to the level of the vast valley and faced the great red wall of rock that loomed a few miles westward. She rode abreast of Wess for a couple of miles, talking the while, then, reaching uneven ground, she had to fall behind on the rough trail. Wess halted at a clump of cedars.

"Reckon this is as far as you'll want me to go," he announced. "Follow the trail right to where it goes into the cañon. You'll see a big cave in the wall. That's the old cliff dwellin' where Mister Heftral is diggin' around."

"Thank you, Wess. Will you wait for me?"

"Wal, not if you're ridin' back with him," Wess returned reluctantly. "But I want to be shore about it."

"I think you'd better wait. I'll not be long."

Cherry had not ridden a hundred paces farther before she forgot all about Wess. The trail led down into a red-walled wash where muddy water flowed over quicksand, which she had to cross. She had already crossed this stream at a different point, though not alone. Here she had to use her own judgment. She made Patter trot across. Even then he floundered in the quicksand and splashed muddy water all over Cherry. Once he went in to his knees and Cherry's heart leaped to her throat. But he plowed out safely. It was this sort of thing that so excited and pleased Cherry. All so new. And being alone made it tenfold more thrilling. The dusty trail, the zigzag climb, the winding in and out among rocks and through the cedars, with the great red wall looming higher and closer, the dry fragrance of desert and sage, the loneliness and wildness, meant more to Cherry this day than ever before. Not for anything would she let Stephen Heftral and her father into the secret that she was actually learning to love Arizona. The beauty and color and solitude, the vastness of it had called to something deep in her. First she had complained of the dust, the wind, the emptiness, the absence of people. But she had forgotten these. She was now not so sure but that she might like the hardship and primitiveness of the desert.

Presently she rode out of the straggling cedars so that she could see fully the great wall. Cherry threw back her head to gaze upward.

"Oh . . . wonderful!" she exclaimed. "I thought the New York buildings were high. But this!"

It was a sheer red wall, rising with breaks and ledges to a cedar-fringed rampart high against the blue sky. The base was a slope of talus, where rocks of every size appeared about to totter and roll down upon her. Then Cherry discovered the cave. It was the most enormous hole she had ever seen, and she calculated that Trinity Church would be lost in it. The upper part disappeared in shadow; the lower showed a steep slope and ruined rock walls, which Cherry guessed were the remains of the cliff-dwellers' homes. She was being impressed by the weirdness of the scene when she heard a shout and then spotted a man standing at the foot of the cave. It was Heftral. He waved to her and began to descend the slide of weathered rock. As he drew nearer to her level Cherry saw that he had indeed been working. How virile he looked. She quite forgot the object of her visit, and almost persuaded herself that if he was particularly nice she would climb up to see him at his work.

"Howdy, Stephen!" she called, imitating the trader as nearly as possible. It struck Cherry then that Stephen did not appear overjoyed to see her.

"Is your father with you?" he asked.

"No. He went to town."

"I hope to goodness you didn't ride up here alone," he said.

"Sure I did. And a dandy ride it was."

"Cherry!" he ejaculated.

"Yes, Cherry," she returned.

He did not grasp any flippancy on her part. "Why did you do it?" he asked almost angrily.

"Well, come to think of it I guess I wanted to see you and your work," she returned innocently.

"But you've been told not to ride out alone . . . away from the post."

"I know I have, and it makes me sick. Why not? I'm not a child, you know. Besides, there aren't any kidnapers about, are there?"

"Yes. Kidnapers and worse. . . . Frankly, Miss Winters, I think you ought to have a good stiff lecture."

"I'm in a very good humor. So fire away."

"You're a headstrong, willful girl," he declared bluntly.

"Stephen, you're not very kind, considering that, well . . . I relented a little, and rode out here to see you," she replied reproachfully.

"I am thinking of you. Somebody has to stop you from taking these risks. The cowboys let you do anything, though they have been ordered to watch you, guard you. If your father can't make you behave, somebody else must."

"And you've got a hunch you're the somebody?" inquired Cherry laconically.

"It seems presumptuous, absurd," he answered stubbornly. "But I really fear I am."

"We're both going to have a wonderful time," Cherry said with a gay laugh. "But before you break loose on this reforming task let me confess I came alone only part way. I left Wess back down the trail at that gully."

"You did? But you told me . . . you lied. . . ."

"I wanted to see how you would take it," she said as he hesitated.

Heftral sat down on a slab of rock and regarded her as one baffled. "That's the worst of you," he asserted. "A man can't quite give you up in despair or disgust. There always seems to be something wholesome under this damned frivolity of yours."

"I'm glad you are so optimistic," returned Cherry.

"No need to ask you how you are feeling," Heftral observed. "Yesterday you were pale, drooping. Your father was really worried. And I. . . . But today you look like a sago lily."

"Sago? That's the name of your cañon, isn't it? And what kind of a flower? Is it pretty?"

"I think it the most exquisite in the world. Rare, rich, vivid. It blooms in the deep cañons in summer. I daresay you'll not stay long enough to see one."

"Stephen, I never guessed you could be eloquent, or so good at blarney," she said, studying him gravely. "I'm beginning to believe there are unknown possibilities in you for good . . . and maybe evil, too."

"Sure. You can never tell what a man may do . . . or be driven to."

"Aren't you going to ask me to get down and come in?" she asked archly.

"You must pardon my manners," he said, rising.

Cherry slipped out of the saddle without accepting the hand he offered, and, leading Patter to a nearby cedar, she tied the bridle to a branch.

"I want to see your cave."

"It's pretty much of a climb."

"I suppose yesterday will stump you for some time," she replied. "Can't I have an off day once in a while without being considered a weakling? Come on, let's go."

Cherry soon found that it was indeed a climb. Distances deceived her so strangely here in Arizona. There was a trail up to the cave, but it wound steep and rough, with many high steps from rock to rock. She was glad to accept Heftral's hand, and when they surmounted the slope, she was breathless and hot. Heftral held her hand longer than necessary.

"Oh-h gee!" Cherry panted, flopping down on a rock in the shade. "Some climb."

"You made it without a stop," Heftral returned admiringly. "Your heart and lungs are sure all right . . . if your mind is gone."

"Mister Heftral!"

"That's your father's assumption," Heftral said dryly. "I don't exactly share it."

"Maybe I am . . . just a healthy . . . moron," Cherry laughed, removing her sombrero. "Wouldn't it be fine if the desert and you developed me into a real woman?"

"Morons don't develop," he replied, ignoring her intimation.

Cherry now took stock of the archaeologist's cave. It was an amazing cavern. She sat at the lower edge of the slope of its back wall, yet the vaulted roof, far overhead, reached out into the cañon. A dry, dusty, musty odor, not unpleasant, permeated the place. The débris from the walls and slopes was red and yellow. Far up, Cherry discerned the remains of walls. In the largest section a small black window, like a vacant eye, stared down at her. It gave her a queer sensation. Human eyes had gazed out of that window ages ago. She saw a trench near her, with pick and shovel lying where Heftral had thrown them.

"Mister Heftral, were you in the war?" Cherry asked suddenly.

"Yes, a little while. Long enough to learn to dig. That's about the only real good the service did me," he replied somewhat bitterly.

"You should be grateful. My friends who went to France came back *no* good. You certainly seem free of any injury."

"I am, I guess, except a twist in my mind. I only knew of it recently . . . last winter in fact."

"Indeed. And how does it affect you?" Cherry asked doubtfully.

"I think it developed a latent weakness for beauty."

"In Nature?"

"Oh, no. I always had that. It must be in . . . woman."

"*Any* woman. Well, that is no weakness. It's a very commendable thing, and gives you a kinship with most men."

"Miss Winters, I didn't say in any woman," returned Heftral sharply.

"Didn't you? Very well, it doesn't matter. Now, show me around the place and tell me all about your work."

Heftral had something on his mind. He did not seem natural. It was as if he had been compelled to be someone he was not. Cherry half regretted that she had not encouraged him to tell more about the woman he had a weakness for. So far she was inwardly elated with the success of her machinations.

"You wouldn't make much of a hit as a guide for lady tourists," remarked Cherry after Heftral had shown her the several trenches he had dug, some bits of pottery, dry as powder, and the ruined walls.

"On the contrary, I was a decided success for a party of schoolteachers who visited me here last summer," declared Heftral.

"Oh, then I have some inhibitory effect upon you," remarked Cherry.

"Probably. I don't seem to care a . . . *er* . . . anything about archaeology, geology, theology, or any other kind of 'ology'," Heftral returned ruefully.

"I'm sorry. I must not tax your mental powers so severely,"

said Cherry.

"You think you're being sarcastic. But as a matter of fact you have taxed all my powers to the limit. Powers of patience, resistance, faith . . . and I don't know what all."

"What a dreadful person I am," Cherry interposed, really in earnest. "Please, if you can't forget it, at least you needn't rub it in. Where do you expect to uncover this buried pueblo? Dad said you had set your heart on discovering it."

"You don't care two whoops for any ruin . . . unless it is the ruin of a man."

"Maybe I didn't at first. But I do now. Can't you credit me with change or growth or something worthwhile?"

"I don't know what to think about you," he returned almost dejectedly.

"Assuredly you don't. Well, I'm quite capable of coming out here and finding that ruin for you."

"Please don't. I'm perfectly miserable now," he retorted grimly.

But there was a light in his eyes that belied his words. Cherry knew he was saying to himself he must not have faith in dreams.

"It would mean so much to you . . . finding this pueblo?" she asked.

"Yes. There's only one thing that could mean more."

"I don't suppose I'd look very well digging around in this dirt," mused Cherry. "But as you haven't any use for me in up-to-date evening clothes perhaps you might like me all dusty and red and hot. So here goes."

Cherry began to clamber down into the deepest trench, and when she got up to her shoulders, she grasped the pick.

"Miss Winters, can't you be serious?" burst out Heftral. "You're not a bit funny. And that talk about me. . . ."

"I'm serious about making you admire me, at least," Cherry laughed, brandishing the pick.

"Please come out of there. You're just soiling your clothes."

"Nope. I'm going to dig," rejoined Cherry nonchalantly. "*¿Quién sabe?* I may have to marry an archaeologist someday."

"Come out of there!" Heftral called peremptorily.

Cherry began to dig in the red earth. She dragged up stones, and presently what looked very much like a human bone. "*Ugh!* I declare. What's that thing?" ejaculated Cherry.

"It's a leg bone, of course. You're digging in a grave. I told you that."

"You didn't," Cherry retorted.

"Never mind about that. You come out of there."

"Mister Heftral, you might send me to my own grave, but you can't make me get out of this one."

As she brandished the pick again, he reached down to grasp it. Cherry held on. Heftral slipped his grip down the handle until he caught her gloved hands. Whereupon he forced the pick from her and dragged her, not at all gently, up out of the trench. He let go of her rather abruptly, probably because of the look she gave him, and Cherry's impetus, being considerable, caused her to stumble. It was a little downhill on that side. She fell right upon Heftral who caught her in his arms. The awkwardness of her action made Cherry more indignant than ever. Her sombrero fell off and her hair covered her eyes. She raised her face from his shoulder and sought to catch her balance. Suddenly Heftral bent to kiss her full on the lips.

Chapter Four

Cherry broke away from Stephen and started back. For a moment she was too conscious of unfamiliar and disturbing agitations to remember that she had adopted the rôle of actress.

"Cherry . . . Miss Winters," stammered the young archaeologist. "I . . . I didn't mean that. I must have been out of my head. Forgive me."

"Now you've done it!" exclaimed Cherry. She was not sure yet what he had done, but it was certainly more than he felt guiltily conscious of.

"I was beside myself," Heftral said hurriedly. "You must believe me. I . . . I had no such intention. I'm . . . I'm as . . . as shocked as you are. You fell right into my arms. And I . . . I did it involuntarily."

"You may tell that to the marines," Cherry replied, recovering and getting back to the business of her part.

"You won't believe me?" he demanded, getting red in the face.

"Certainly not," Cherry returned coldly, as she smoothed her disheveled hair. "I wouldn't put it beyond you to treat every girl that way, especially if she was fool enough to visit you alone out here."

He glared at her in mingled wrath and distress. "I never kissed a girl before," he asserted stoutly.

"Well!" exclaimed Cherry, in simulated contemptuous doubt, when really she was thrilled with what seemed the truth in his eye and voice. "You must have a poor opinion of my intelligence. If you had come out like a man and told me straight that you couldn't resist such an opportunity and were glad of it, I might have forgiven you. It's nothing to be kissed. But you've pretended to be so self-righteous. You've scorned my young men friends. You've deceived me into thinking highly of you . . . respecting you. And I honestly believe I did like you. Now I'm quite sure I ought never ride out alone."

Heftral groaned. Then he leaped into the trench, and, seizing the pick, he began to dig with great violence, making the stones fly and the dust rise. Cherry spoke again, but either he did not or would not hear her, whereupon she recovered her sombrero and turned to find her way down the slope. She had just reached the rough part, and was searching for the trail when she heard Heftral behind her.

"I quite forgot. I can't let you attempt getting down here alone," he said.

"Mister Heftral, I'd fall and break my neck before I'd let you help me," Cherry returned loftily.

"I warn you not to fall again within my reach," he declared grimly.

Cherry started down, aware that he followed closely. She was glad she had her face turned away from him. When she got to the broken sections of rock, she performed apparent feats of balancing that would have put a tightrope walker to shame. She would sway this way and that, and almost fall. Then she leaped the fissures, and took some chances of hurting herself. But she descended the jumble of rocks safely, and then the rest of the slope with ease. Heftral had halted about a third of the way from the bottom, and when Cherry looked over the saddle of her horse, she saw him sitting on a stone, watching her.

"Good bye, wild woman!" he called.

"Good bye, cave man," she retorted.

Mounting, she rode away without looking back, which was an act that required willpower. Once in the cedars, out of sight and alone, she reveled in the unexpected turn and success of her venture. Heftral was simply an honest boy, very much in love, and at the mercy of his feelings. He had helped along her little plan by placing himself at a disadvantage. How astounded he had been, then furious at himself and her. Cherry remembered that he had winced when she said it was nothing to be kissed. Well, she had lied in that. It was a great deal to be kissed, as she began to realize now. She had chosen to lead him to believe kissing was merely a casual and familiar thing in her young life, when in reality she had preserved the sanctity of her lips except when her own indiscretion forced the attenuation upon her.

Cherry believed she was angrier than ever with Heftral, a great deal more so now than at her father. Yet there was a tempering voice she would not listen to. It was piercing her armor to some extent when she rode right upon Wess, so abruptly that she was surprised. That ended her meditations, for Wess appeared to be curious and keen about her visit to the archaeologist. It did not occur to Cherry to tantalize Wess, or to stop and torment the cowboys at their fence-post digging, a fact that dawned upon her with peculiar significance. By the time she was again at ease in her room, she realized the cowboys had begun to fade out of the picture. Cherry did not regret it, though she wondered at herself. Naturally, however, if a girl was going to be abducted against her will, and maltreated, and finally married, she must be quite interested in the man who was daring to do all this.

At lunch she was outspoken about her visit to Heftral's cave. The Linns were much pleased. Plain indeed was it that they were fond of Heftral and proud of his archaeological work.

"Wal, if you liked that Sagi hole you shore ought to see *Becky-shibeta*," remarked Linn.

"*Beckyshibeta.* Goodness, that's a jawbreaker," replied Cherry with a laugh. "What and where is it?"

"*Beckyshibeta* means cow water. It's Navajo for a water hole. I never saw it when it wasn't muddy an' shore tastin' of cows. Reckon it's about sixty miles by trail, nearer across country. Wild rocky place where the Indians seldom go. Heftral thinks they've a reason for avoiding it, same as in the case of *Nonnezoshe,* the great Rainbow Bridge. He has a notion there might be a buried pueblo at *Beckyshibeta.* There are cliff dwellin's still in good state of preservation, an' many ruins. We seldom recommend *Beckyshibeta* to our visitors. It's far off. The cowboys hate the rocky country because they have to pack hoss feed and water. An' shore there are places interestin' enough near at hand, an' comfortable for camp. But before you an' Mister Winters leave, you want to see both *Nonnezoshe* an' *Beckyshibeta.*"

"I'm sure I'd love to," responded Cherry.

She did not meet the cowboys again that day until after supper when she walked out to see the sunset, and to look for her father. This was always an attractive hour at the post. Indians were riding up and departing; the picturesque cowboys, mostly through with work for the day, were lounging about on the bales of wool and blankets. The moment Cherry arrived they became animated as one man. Cherry did not take much notice of them, despite their transparent acts and words. Strolling a little way, she halted at the hitching rail to watch the pageant in the gold and purple West.

"Mighty cool evenin'," remarked Mojave in a voice that came clearly to Cherry.

"Say, fellars, did anythin' hit you in the eye, kinda like a chunk of ice?" drawled Zoroaster.

"S-s-s-some of y-y-y-youse *hombres* has done s-ss-somethin'," Tay-Tay stuttered belligerently.

"Our gracious *señorita* is in one of her grand moods," Lorenzo said.

"Aw, you 'punchers are locoed," Wess added scornfully. "Cain't you tell when to get off and walk?"

Cherry moved on out of earshot of her loyal cavaliers. It was the first time she had not been vastly interested in one or all of them. What had happened to her? But she soothed both conscience and concern with former arguments.

In the west the bulge of desert waved black as ebony against the intense gold flare of sky. Above this belt, a broken reef of purple clouds appeared beaten upon by contending tides of silver and rose. Through a ragged rent the sinking sun sent shafts of radiant light down behind the horizon.

In the east the panorama was no less striking and beautiful. The desert sent its walls and domes and monuments of red rock far up into the sky of gorgeous pink and white clouds.

Cherry drew a deep full breath. Yes, Arizona was awakening her to something splendid and compelling. How vast and free and wind-swept this colored desert. She had learned to recognize a faint fragrance of sage, which came only in a north breeze. It was sweet and cool now in her face. Then up over a nearby ridge came a black silhouette of an Indian and mustang, wild and lovely. Next the hum of a motorcar broke her absorption. No doubt it was the trader's Studebaker returning with her father.

"Look here, peaches," quizzically remarked her father, when they had gotten indoors. "Anyone would think I'd been absent a month. What's the bright idea?"

"Oh! Did I make such a fuss over you . . . as that?" Cherry asked merrily.

"You sure did. Fact is you never welcomed me like that, even on my returns from Europe. Have you been lonely and blue again? Is that why?"

"Not today," returned Cherry. "No, I was just happy . . . and unconscious of it, Dad. I guess maybe I did miss you a lot."

"Well, you can bet I'm glad, whatever it is."

Cherry left him in the dining room, too hungry for conversation. Then she delved a little into her mind. She had absolutely forgotten her new rôle, as she had been quite unlike her old self. In truth she was very angry with her father, another fact that had slipped her memory. She had not been in the least lonely for him or homesick. In reality she had skipped about ten years of her life and had met him as a child. Cherry's relentless deductions took her back through the eventful day to the tift with Heftral, and then she got no further. It was rather confusing. But at length she assuaged her wounded vanity by accepting her remarkably fine spirits as due to the way she was turning the tables on Heftral and her father.

"Maybe I'm jollying myself," murmured Cherry with a snicker. "Good heavens on earth. Could I have been so happy because *he* kissed me?"

Cherry was wholly at ease again when her father joined her in the living room. He was full of his trip to town, and claimed the ride in—looking the opposite way to that in which they had come—was even more beautiful. Telegraph communications from New York had been eminently satisfactory.

"How's your day been?" he queried, when he had concluded about his own.

"Mine? Oh, rich, immense," replied Cherry.

"I hope you haven't played any more hob with these cowboys."

"Oh, dear, no. I've scarcely seen them, but once or twice. . . . I did take Wess, and rode out to see Heftral's cave. Surprised him. I left Wess below a little way and went on alone."

"You did!" exclaimed Winters, surprised and pleased. "That was nice of you. What did you think of Stephen's cave? I've been there, you know."

"An awful hole! Just suits him to a T. He's a cave man. Don't you overlook that, darling Papa."

"Cave man? Stephen Heftral? Why, he's the gentlest and mildest of men."

"Not so you'd notice it. At least for me," Cherry replied, giggling. "No, Dad, you're vastly mistaken in Stephen's character. He's a bad *hombre.*"

"Did you quarrel?" queried Winters, his curiosity overcoming his doubt of her.

"Oh, we scrapped as usual. He wasn't at all tickled to see me. Made some idiotic remarks about being a lover of beauty in woman . . . one woman. Naturally I kidded him, and when he got wise to that, he was sore. Well, finally, to prove my interest in his old cave, I climbed down in one of his graves. I took the pick and began to dig. Do you know, Dad, he didn't like that a bit."

Winters let out a hearty laugh. "Cherry, you are incorrigible. No wonder he wasn't tickled to see you. Why, he wouldn't let even me dig in one of those holes. Said I might break a piece of precious pottery. Besides, in your case he wouldn't like you to soil your clothes and blister your hands."

"I should think he would have liked that," returned Cherry. "Once he called me fastidious and elegant. Another time one of the idle rich. He held my hand once and had the nerve to say it was a beautiful useless thing. Well, to go on, he ordered me out of the grave. I paid no attention to him. Then he took hold of the pick, pulled me up till he could reach me. Next he yanked me out. Gentle? You should have seen him. But he let go of me too quick and I stumbled. Like a ninny in the movies I fell into his arms. Did he gently set me upon my feet? I should snicker not. This paragon of yours, this nice quiet Westerner, grabbed me and kissed me smack on my mouth . . . like I never was kissed in my whole life!"

Whereupon Cherry's father exploded with mirth. Recovering and seeing her face, he apologized contritely. "Cherry, it's just too good," he added. "I think a lot more of Stephen for having the nerve to do it. I wonder, now, did *that* make you so happy?"

"Rot!" exclaimed Cherry with hot cheeks. "It wasn't nerve in him. He just went loco. Then he swore he'd never kissed any girl before. Fancy that? Well, I've told you. I don't quite know what to do about it."

"I shall congratulate Stephen on punishing you properly."

"I don't take punishment easily," said Cherry, with menacing hauteur.

"Lord. Be easy on the poor chap, Cherry."

Linn interrupted them at this point and asked if they would require any or all of the cowboys for any especial trip the next few days. "I want to drive some cattle out, an' reckon this is about the best time," he added. "I've got some tourist parties comin' soon, an' the boys will take them to *Nonnezoshe.* After that the rains will be here."

"Thanks, Linn. We can do very well without the cowboys," Winters returned brightly. Cherry guessed why her father felt so chipper about that news.

"Do you have a rainy season here on this desert?" inquired Cherry, aghast.

"Nothin' to concern you, miss," replied the trader. "Reckon you'll like the thunderstorms, the clouds, an' rainbows. But for us the rains are sometimes bad, because the washes get full of water an' quicksand, so we can't move the stock."

"Thunderstorms? I love them. It will be great to be out in one here," said Cherry.

Cherry was lying in bed reading when she heard Heftral come in and go to his room. The hour was rather late for him. She wondered if he had gone supperless.

Next morning when she went in to breakfast, her father and Heftral were there. If Cherry had expected him to be downcast or embarrassed, she had reckoned without her host. He was neither. He greeted her as if nothing unusual had occurred and he gave her a cool steady stare. Cherry's quick intuition grasped at the imminence of the catastrophe. Heftral had burned his bridges behind him. It did not seem likely that her father could have had much to do with this late decision in Heftral. Cherry had bidden him good night at his door, and he was not an early riser. So she concluded Heftral had fought out something with himself and the die was cast. It stirred Cherry as had nothing she could recall. She was ready, even eager for the adventure. And she would react to it at Heftral's provocation.

"When is Linn sending out the cowboys?" inquired Heftral.

"Today," replied Winters, with a meaning glance at his young friend. "It'll be terrible for Cherry to be left without anybody to pick on. Heftral, suppose you knock off work and stay home to amuse her."

"Very happy to," returned the archaeologist. "I'm sure I can think up something that will amuse even the blasé Miss Winters."

"You needn't concern yourself about me," Cherry said spiritedly. "And I'll have you know I'm not blasé. Did you ever see me look old or bored?"

"Certainly not old, but bored . . . yes indeed, and with your humble servant, myself."

"You don't bore me any more, Stephen," Cherry replied deliberately, giving him an inscrutable glance. "You have become a mystery. Your possibilities are unlimited."

"Much obliged," rejoined Heftral with nonchalance. "I hope I can live up to your idea of my development."

"When will you start amusing me?" inquired Cherry with a provoking little smile.

"There's no time like the present."

"Very well, begin. You have only to be perfectly natural."

"That is what I thought. So I need not exert myself. After breakfast come with me for a walk. I know where to find some horned toads."

"How far is it?"

"Quite near. In the big wash over the ridge. But I advise you to change that child's dress for something comfortable and protecting."

"Goodness. This is a tennis skirt and blouse."

"Who'd guess it," Heftral returned dryly. "Be ready in about an hour."

Cherry went to her room, prey to not a little inward excitation. Mr. Heftral had been quite business-like. She had fancied he would take her for a long ride someday, which would give him better opportunity to make off with her. Surely he would not attempt the abduction while on a short stroll near the post. But she felt uncertain about him. She had best be prepared. To this end she considered what it would be best to wear. If she donned riding clothes and boots, which she heartily wanted to do, it would rouse Heftral's suspicions. Outside of that all her clothes were unsuitable for the kind of a jaunt she was likely to have. She gave Heftral about one day and one night before fetching her back to the post. That, however, was long enough for his purpose, though she remembered her father hinting otherwise. Cherry searched among her things, and finally found an old woolen outing skirt, absurdly short, as it had been made when style called for the most abbreviated dresses for girls. It would do despite that drawback. She selected as heavy stockings as she could find, which were thin at that, tennis shoes, a shirt waist with high collar and long sleeves. She put on a soft felt hat and gloves. Then as an afterthought she slipped a vanity case into the pocket of her short sport coat, and tried to choose among many other articles she would need badly, in case she were kidnaped. But pocket space was limited. Thus equipped, and full of suppressed mirth, yet not free from other agitation, she sallied forth to meet Mr. Heftral.

Cherry knew she had occupied more than an hour, yet she was surprised to find he was not waiting for her. Nor was her father to be found. "Nigger in the wood pile, all right," soliloquized Cherry. She went out to see the cowboys ride away with Linn. They were a disconsolate lot, and gazed at her from afar.

Upon her return to the house she encountered Heftral. His boots were dusty, and his face heated from exertion. He looked too grim and tense for the mere prospect of a little walk. Unless he meant to propose to her. Or else carry out her father's plan. Cherry knew it was one or the other, and she trembled. But Heftral seemed too concerned with himself to note that she was not wholly at ease. And in another instant Cherry regained composure.

"Here you are," he said as he met her. "Glad you're a little more sensibly dressed."

"I thought maybe you'd have me digging around in the sand after horned toads," she replied.

"Daresay you'll be digging around for more than that before we get back."

He led her out the side exit of the yard, where the foliage of peach trees and the house obscured their departure from anyone who might have been looking from the post.

"Horned toads are really one of the wonders of the desert," he said as he walked briskly out toward the rise of ground. "They have protective coloration. It is very difficult to see them. They are beautiful, with eyes like jewels. At rare times when angry one will emit blood from its eyes."

While he talked, he was leading Cherry up the ridge. Then in a few moments they were over and going down on the other side, out of sight of the post. He talked horned toads until manifestly he had exhausted his fund of natural history, then he switched to desert scenery. Cherry knew he was only marking time, endeavoring to absorb her so that she would scarcely notice the distance they had come and that it was still far to any break in the floor of the desert. She helped him by listening intently. It was a full ten miles to the wash.

"Stephen, didn't you say it was only a little walk?" she asked innocently.

"Why, yes. Isn't it?"

"If you'd ask me, I'd say it was long. Where do we go from here?" returned Cherry, gazing down into the sandy void. There was no trail she could see, though in the sand just below she espied horse tracks.

Heftral jumped down off the bank to the slope, which was several feet under the level. "Come," he said, and Cherry detected a slight change of tone.

"Gee. I can't get down there," she replied fearfully.

"If you won't let me lift you down, why, slide."

"Slide! Mister Heftral, I'm not a baseball player."

Quick as a flash, then, he reached for her, clasped her knees, and lifted her so that she fell over his shoulder.

"Oh!" Cherry cried in a surprise that was not feigned. How powerful he was. She might have been a sack of potatoes. He carried her several strides down before Cherry began to protest and squirm. She would have kicked if her legs had been free. At any rate her struggle and the steep soft slope of sand caused Heftral to lose his balance and fall sidewise. Cherry rolled off his shoulder and sat up. Heftral floundered erect and, seeing her sitting there, wide-eyed and blank, he burst into laughter. Cherry could not help following suit.

"Mister Heftral, is this how you hunt horned toads?" she queried.

"No. But why did you overbalance me? I could have packed you down to the bottom."

"My position was scarcely dignified. In the future if it is necessary to pack me, as you call it, please give me a moment to prepare."

"All right. Come on. Let's see if you're any good on seven-league boots," he said, and strode down with giant steps.

Cherry engaged to do likewise, succeeded admirably, and reached the bottom of the wash in good time. "My shoes are full of sand," she announced, and sat down to remove them.

"Don't let a little thing like that fuss you. It may happen again."

"You're quite gay, all of a sudden," Cherry remarked as she shook the sand out of her shoes.

"Yes. Why not? It's something to see Miss Cherry Winters as she is this moment," he responded, eying her with a glint of admiration.

"I suppose you mean me in this short skirt. It is indecent," she returned calmly. "But you needn't look. It was the only old thing I had."

Soon she was following him down the wash. It appeared to be quite deep, with a dry streambed of rock and gravel at the bottom. Desert plants grew sparsely along the banks. Heftral did not look back or speak, and he walked a little too swiftly for Cherry who lost a few paces. Presently they turned a corner, and Cherry espied what she had been expecting—two saddled horses. There was more, in shape of a mule carrying a pack.

Cherry plodded on, pretending not to see them. In fact, on the moment, she was conscious of hot and cold sensations, of an emotion that recalled childhood. It was fear. How foolish! Nevertheless she was aware of a palpitating heart, of a rush of blood, of prickling skin. A quick glance showed Heftral had halted beside the horses. If Cherry had not been in on the secret of this affair, she would have been mystified by the man's look. He was pallid and grim, under strong restraint. Cherry strove to find nerve to meet this situation as she had planned. Where was her anger? It had oozed out of her trembling fingertips. But that was only momentary. Sight of Heftral rallied her courage. She would deceive him, punish him and her father if it took all the spirit and endurance she could muster.

"Whose horses?" Cherry inquired as she reached Heftral, and sat down on the slope of sand. She did not look at him directly. "It's pretty warm . . . for a short walk. When do we hunt horned toads?"

As he did not answer, she glanced up at him. Assuredly he was laboring under some deep emotion. Cherry suddenly divined that despite what he had undertaken, he was afraid of her and of the outrageous indignity he had been persuaded to attempt. That acted as a spur to her. It was the stimulus she needed.

"What's the matter, Stephen? You look strange. Your eyes. You're staring at me. I can't complain of lack of attention right now the second time."

"Better late than never."

"Come here, Mister Archaeologist. I won't hurt you," said Cherry, beckoning.

"You want me? Over there?"

"Ah-huh!"

"You're taking a chance. I've become a . . . a bad man," he returned doggedly, as if he needed to convince himself.

"Since when? Since that episode at the cave? Well, if you repeat that, your end will be near. . . . I asked you who these horses belonged to?"

"They're mine."

"Yours! What are they doing here . . . saddled? And that pack animal?" Cherry queried in surprise. "Surely we don't need this outfit to hunt horned toads."

"Cherry, that about the toads . . . was a lie," he returned haltingly. "It was a trick to get you away from the post."

"A trick? How thrilling! Well, now you've so basely deceived me and got me here . . . what are you going to do with me?"

"I've . . . kidnaped . . . you," he declared huskily.

Cherry uttered a merry laugh. "Oh, I remember. You were to amuse me. Fine, Stephen. I suppose you planned a little ride and picnic for me. But, my dear man, I can't ride in this skirt."

"You can't walk, so you'll have to ride," he returned.

"*Have* to? Say, Stephen, this is getting to be more than a joke. I can stand a lot of fun. But horseback in this knee-high skirt? Nothing doing!"

"It's not a joke, Cherry. I'm in deadly earnest. You're going with me willingly . . . or otherwise."

"Indeed! Isn't that sweet of you? Lovely little all-day party, eh?"

"We will not return tonight."

Cherry rose with a divinely startled movement. "*Mister* Heftral!" she exclaimed in cold amaze.

That was the crucial moment for Stephen Heftral. He turned white to the lips.

"Are you drunk or mad?" she added icily.

"Both! Drunk with your beauty . . . mad for love of you," he replied hoarsely.

"It would seem so," said Cherry. She turned her back upon him in contempt and started to walk away. She heard his footsteps thud in the sand. Then he seized her by the shoulders, whirled her around, and forced her back to the shade.

"If you run, it'll only be the worse for you," he warned, releasing her.

"You ruffian!" cried Cherry, wheeling. "Let me pass."

Heftral confronted her, and, when she tried to get by, he put his hands on her shoulders and gave her a good hard shove. Cherry staggered backward. The sand was soft and deep. She lost her balance and suddenly sat down upon the slope, thus losing coat and sombrero. The feelings she called upon were reinforced by genuine ones. This was most undignified. Yet Cherry wanted to laugh. She sat there, blazing up at him, in a gathering might of wrath.

"Ruffian or anything you like," Heftral said darkly. "But you go with me, if I have to throw you on that horse."

"Father will beat you for this."

"No doubt. But it will be too late."

"And the cowboys will do worse."

"Yes. But I shall have queered you with them."

Cherry got to her feet and stepped close to Heftral. There was now a dangerous gleam in his eye—a wild dark light. He had gotten by the most difficult part for him—the announcement of his intention. Cherry saw that he did not expect any serious trouble with her. How she would fool him!

"Don't you dare lay a hand on me again," she said passionately.

"I hope it won't be necessary. But you get on this horse."

"No!"

"I tell you. . . ."

Cherry rushed to pass him, yet was not quick enough. He caught her arm. As he swung her around, she gave him a terrific slap on the side of the face. Heftral dropped her arm. His hand went to his cheek which was as red as fire. It seemed realization was upon him, augmenting shame and fury. Cherry divined that but for her blow he might have betrayed himself and given up this outrageous affair.

"You . . . you struck me," he said hoarsely, and suddenly

snatched out and caught her left arm.

"Sure I did, Mister Hoodlum," rejoined Cherry. "And I'll do it again. Did you think you'd get away with this so easy? There!" And she struck him quick and hard, this time with a tight little fist.

"Wildcat!" shouted Heftral, roused to battle, and then he closed with her. Cherry was strong, lithe, supple as a panther, and she fought him fiercely. It was no longer pretense. The rough contact of his hands and her own violent action brought her blood up, gushing and hot. He was endeavoring to subdue her and she was struggling to get away. At the same time she beat and tore at him with all her might. She scratched his face. She got both hands in his hair and pulled. Naturally the fight could not last long, for he was overpowering her. When he got his left arm under her right and around her waist to grasp her left, he had her nearly helpless. Then he put his other arm under her knees and lifted her.

His hair stood up like the mane of a lion; his face was bloody from the scratches; his eyes gleamed with fire.

"My God!" he panted. "Who'd have . . . thought it in you."

"Let me down!" cried Cherry, straining and writhing.

"Will you get . . . on that horse?"

"No . . . you Wild West boob!"

The epithet pierced his mind. "Boob? Ha! Ha! You've hit it," he replied wildly. "Very well . . . my Eastern princess . . . take this from the Western boob."

He bent his head and kissed her quickly—then again, crushing his hot lips on hers.

"I'll . . . kill . . . you!" gasped Cherry, when she could speak.

"Kill and be damned. I wish you would," he returned passionately. Then he surrendered to the contact and possession of her. Clasping her tightly, he rained kisses on her lips and neck. Cherry felt the wet blood from his scratched face on her cheek.

Her muscles grew rigid. She was like bent steel about to spring. Suddenly she sank limply. His passion had overcome her where his strength had failed. But Cherry did not lose her wits. It was as if she knew she had to keep playing her part. Yet her collapse and the shaking of her relaxed body had nothing to do with reasoning. He had surprised her into the primitiveness of a savage. The change in her reaction struck him, and he released her.

Cherry slipped down, as it chanced, to her knees. The thing could not have happened better.

"I . . . I . . . understand now," gasped Cherry. "You mean . . . to. . . ."

"My God!" cried Heftral, staggering back in horror.

"Mister Heftral," went on Cherry piteously. "I . . . I'm not the brazen girl I . . . I've made you believe. This is as much . . . my fault . . . as yours. But have mercy. Don't be a brute."

"Shut up!" shouted Heftral, his face changing to a dusky red. He backed against a stone and sat down, to cover his face with his hands, deeply and terribly shaken.

Cherry sank back herself, to rest a moment, and to straighten her disheveled apparel. Her rage had died a sudden death. She was still conscious of disturbing unfamiliar sensations, which, however, were gradually subsiding. Much had happened that had not been down on the program. She divined that Heftral had not intended even the least insult, let alone his assault on her lips. And certainly in her plan Cherry had not dreamed of making him think she believed him capable of the basest things. Even at that troubled moment Cherry realized that more could come of this incident than had been expected. Both of them were trifling with deep and unknown instincts. They might pass from jest to earnest. But Heftral had not the slightest inkling of Cherry's duplicity.

"You've blood on your face," Heftral said suddenly.

"Yes, it's yours. If I had my way, I'd have your blood on my *hands,*" returned Cherry murderously.

"Wipe it off," he ordered, getting up.

Cherry produced a wisp of a handkerchief. "Where is it?" she asked.

"On your cheek . . . the left one. Here, let me rub it off. That inch-square rag is no good." He had a silk scarf, which he used to remove the blood from her cheek. He applied considerable force, and his action was that of a man trying to remove a stain of guilt.

"You scratched me like . . . like a wildcat," he said harshly.

"Did you expect me to purr?" she returned with sarcasm. Then she rose to her feet. "You tore my sleeve half off. I hope you happen to have a needle and thread."

Ignoring her facetiousness, he picked up her coat and sombrero, and handed them to her.

"Get on that horse," he ordered.

Chapter Five

Without comment and as one subdued Cherry went up to the horse and mounted. Her skirt slipped halfway above her knees. She stood in the stirrups and pulled it down, but at best it was so short that it exposed several inches of bare skin above her stockings.

"Is this supposed to be a movie or a leg show?" she queried bitingly.

"I can't help it if you've no decent clothes," he replied.

"Why didn't you suggest I wear my riding clothes?"

"I didn't think of that. But you'd have suspected something."

"Me? No. I'm much too stupid. If I had been capable of thinking, I'd have known you were a villain. . . . To force a girl to ride a horse with her dress up to her neck!"

"I don't care how you look," he flashed hotly, stung at her retort. "At that you don't look *much* worse than usual." He picked up Cherry's coat, which she had dropped, and hung it on the pommel, and draped it over her knees. "That'll keep you from sunburn, at least."

"You're very thoughtful and kind, Mister Heftral," said Cherry sweetly. "Where do we go from here?"

"Up the wash," he rejoined gruffly. "You take the lead."

"Want to watch me, eh? You think I might run off? I note you've given me a plug of a horse that probably never ran in its life."

"You might do anything, Miss Winters," he said.

"What wonderful trust you have in me!" exclaimed Cherry.

Whereupon she rode on up the deepening gully. Heftral followed her, leading the pack horse.

So the great adventure was actually on. Cherry could not have believed it but for the bruises she had sustained in the fight with Heftral, and her torn blouse, and this ridiculous skirt that had begun to have resemblance to a ballet dancer's.

After she had taken stock of her physical state, she delved a bit into the mental. She found she was still trembling ever so slightly. Her heart beat high. And her mind was racing. She was stirred by bitterness toward her father, and resentment toward this man who had been led to believe she was no good and needed this kind of a lesson. They thought they had her number, mused Cherry defiantly. Pretty but vain. Intelligent, yet too languorous to think or work. Adorable though probably immoral. Modern, still there were hopes.

An alarming thought struck her that she had experienced vaguely before. It was barely possible that these accusations were justified. Cherry swore, and refused to listen to such a treacherous voice.

Something more pleasant to dwell upon was a genuine pity for Heftral. He had been a perfectly straightforward, fine, and promising young man until he encountered her father. He was now in line to become a first-rate villain. No doubt when Cherry finally divorced him there would be no hope whatever. She decided, in order to make it impossible that he ever could recover, she would delay the divorce proceeding for a time—and meanwhile be very sweet and sorrowful and might-have-been-loving to him, so that he would be abjectly crushed.

Her meditations on this phase of the experience were decidedly pleasant. And it was most agreeable to be on horseback again. She had been rather unjust to the horse, for he was turning out to be docile, easy-gaited, and willing. He had struck into a trail that wound up the gorge.

The walls were perceptibly higher and changing their character somewhat. The sand slopes were disappearing. Presently this wash turned at right angles and opened into a cañon. It was deep, yellow-walled, and rugged, and through the center of it meandered a thin stream of water. Cherry believed this creek was the Sagi, which she had crossed a number of times above. But she had not seen this cañon. The very sight of it was exciting and disturbing. There was sure to be quicksand. Cherry hoped she would have some narrow escapes, so that she would find out what Heftral was made of. If no risks came along naturally, she would make some.

The sand in the creekbed, however, was disappointingly solid. In the next hour Cherry crossed this water a dozen or more times, without a mishap. Her horse was a good deal better judge of places than she. Meanwhile the cañon grew wider and deeper.

It also grew hot. Cherry began to feel the burn of the sun. And as the movement of the horse often jolted her coat from its protective service, her knees began to get red. This was a novelty, and she was divided between concern and a satisfaction that she could presently show Heftral more objective proofs of his cruelty.

Unobtrusively, at moments when the trail made a short turn, she saw Heftral in the rear. He did not look in the least like a bold bad man. He drooped. Apparently he did not see her, let alone watch closely against any attempt she might make to escape. Perhaps he was disgusted now with the case and hoped she would run off. This was embarrassing. Cherry did not want to escape. She was getting a tremendous kick out of being kidnaped. But she would not let him know that. She considered the advisability of attempting to get away. It did not strike her favorably. If Heftral did not or would not catch her, there would be something of a different predicament. She would be lost, unless she could go back as they had come.

Cherry rejected the idea. Too much risk. And she adopted another, equally feminine, and very much better. When a turn of the trail hid her from Heftral's sight, she selected a soft place in the sand and slid off her horse, careful to make it look as if she had fallen.

Presently she heard the hoofs of Heftral's horse padding closer. Then Cherry made herself look as much like a limp sack as she could. From under the brim of her sombrero she saw him come into sight. He gave a violent start. Leaping out of the saddle, he ran to her. His action, his look were unaccountably sweet to Cherry. It was hard to close her eyes.

Evidently he stopped to gaze down upon her a moment, for there was a silence, then he kneeled to lay a hand on her shoulder.

"Now, what's the matter?" he inquired with more doubt than sympathy.

Cherry stirred and sat up. "I fell off my horse," she said.

"What for?"

"Guess I got dizzy or something. You must have hurt me internally. Or I wrenched my side . . . anyway I had a terrible pain."

"That's too bad. I'm sorry. I never calculated on *any* weakness, physical or mental." He was studying her face with deep inscrutable eyes, and despite his words he was not sympathetic.

"Weak! Why I'm bordering on nervous collapse right now," returned Cherry.

"Yes, I observed how weak you were . . . physically," he said. "You could probably throw me in a catch-as-catch-can wrestling match. And when you hit me on my nose . . . with your fist . . . well, you came very near being alone for a while."

Cherry gave him a searching look. "Will you take me back to the post?"

"Certainly not."

"But if I'm hurt or ill."

"You're going to *Beckyshibeta* in any event."

"*Beckyshibeta?* Why, that's a long way, you told me."

"Sure. It's far away, and lonely, too, believe me. No one will find us there."

"How long do we . . . do you mean to keep me prisoner there?"

"I have no idea how long it will take for you to change . . . or die."

"Oh! Very well, you can bury me at *Beckyshibeta,*" concluded Cherry, getting up wearily.

She refused his proffered assistance, and made a fine effort at mounting, as if some of her bones were broken. And she rode on, thinking that the weak-sister stuff would not do with Stephen Heftral. She must slowly recover her strength and become a veritable Amazon. Perhaps there would occur some accident that might be calculated to frighten even her, though she could not imagine what it could be. Then she would try the clinging vine. Even Stephen Heftral would fall for that. But it must be something over which a modern girl could safely lose her nerve. A terrible storm or a flood. Cherry prayed for both. Stephen Heftral must be reduced to a state of perfect misery.

Cherry rode on, gradually recovering her poise in the saddle. The cañon opened wide, with the walls far away. There were flats of green grass and cedar groves to cross. In one place she saw several deserted hogans. Indians had lived there. She had a desire to peep in at the dark door, facing the east.

The trail came to a point where it forked. Cherry waited for Heftral to come up.

"Which way, Sir Geraint?" she inquired.

"Left," he said. "And I don't think you're a bit like Enid. She was meek. Besides, she was Geraint's wife."

"Well, Geraint drove Enid ahead, so she would encounter all the risks and dangers first. No doubt the similarity of our ride to theirs ends right there."

"The only danger here, Miss Winters, is the one I'm incurring. And it's too late to avoid that."

Danger! What did he mean? Perhaps the wrath of the cowboys, for it was certain they could not have been let into the secret. How would they take this stunt of Heftral's? Cherry began to wonder why she had not thought of that before. True, they had ridden away with a herd of cattle, but they must return sooner or later, and find out. Here was a factor her father had not considered. Even if he did have to tell them, she knew the cowboys, especially Wess, would not stand for it. On the other hand, perhaps Heftral had meant the danger to be love of her. And he had said it was too late to avoid it. She was very glad, and, if it were actually true, she would see to it that he suffered more and more.

They took the left-hand fork of the trail and entered an interconnecting cañon, which narrowed until the crumbling walls seemed ready to tumble down upon her. Soon the trail became so rough that Cherry had to pay heed to it and have a care for her horse. The ascent increased until it was steeper than any Cherry had ridden. As she climbed, the trail took to a zigzag course up the slope and often she could look directly down upon Heftral, who was not having the best of luck with the pack animal.

Presently it took Cherry's breath to gaze down and she quit it. The trail sometimes led along a ledge so narrow that she wondered how the horse could stick to it. But he never made a misstep or a slip, and appeared unconcerned about the heights. Cherry christened him Surefoot.

At last the trail led up to a level again, from which Cherry gazed back and down at the red slope, the huge rocks, the slides of weathered stone, the cedars, and the winding dry streambed at the bottom. Cherry had to look quite a while to locate Heftral. It was no trail for a pack horse, or rather the horse was not one for such a narrow steep obstructed trail. Heftral was walking, dragging at the animal. When he finally reached the summit, he was red-faced and panting.

"I note the way of a transgressor is hard," observed Cherry.

"Why . . . didn't you . . . run off?" he asked.

"I'd only have got lost. Besides, I think it'd be unwise to leave the commissary department. Also, I have an absorbing desire to see what is going to happen to you."

"That'll be nothing compared to what's coming to you," he returned as he mounted again. "Oh, by the way, how is that internal injury I gave you?"

"It's better. But I can bear it for your sake, Stephen. I want so much to help you make a success of this cradle-snatching stunt."

"Say, you flatter yourself," he retorted.

"Well, yes, I'm not exactly an infant. But I'll be good practice for you, so that later, when the tourists come, you may be able to manage some flapper pretty well."

"Would you mind riding on, and not talking so much," he said with asperity.

"I certainly wouldn't have waited for you, if there'd been any trail. But it's disappeared."

"Ride straight toward those red rocks," he returned, pointing.

Cherry did as she was bidden, glad to be able once more to let her horse look out for himself, so that she could attend to the surroundings. The sun was slanting westward, toward a high wall that ran away to the northward. The desert stretched level ahead of her, with a horizon line notched by red rocks. Not far in front, a growth of purple brush began to show sparsely and to thicken in the distance. It was very fragrant and beautiful.

Presently Cherry recognized the fragrance of sage.

Huge clouds had rolled up, and except in the west they were black and stormy. Dark curtains hung down from them to the floor of the desert. They must be rain. The afternoon was hot and sultry, without a breath of wind. By and by the clouds hid the sun and turned duskily red.

Cherry was somewhat surprised to have Heftral catch up and pass her.

"Better trot your horse, if you're not too weak to hang on," he said. "It's going to storm and we must reach the shelter of the rocks."

"How lovely. I hope it rains cats and dogs," she returned amiably.

"Don't worry. You'll be scared stiff when night comes, if it gives."

Cherry was about to laugh him to scorn, but happened to remember that she really was afraid of storms.

"Are desert storms bad?" she inquired anxiously.

"Terrible. You can't see. You get half drowned. Rocks roll down the cliffs and floods roar down the washes."

"How lovely. . . . I imagine one of your brilliant ideas to keep me interested."

Surefoot had an easy trot, for which Cherry was devoutly thankful. She had begun to realize that she was not made of leather. And the faster gait had a business-like look of getting somewhere.

Meanwhile, the sun disappeared wholly behind massing clouds, and thunder rolled in the distance. Drops of rain began to fall, and the warm air perceptibly cooled. Cherry put on her coat, and was once more reminded of the annoying brevity of her skirt. What a picture she must make. How her Central Park riding friends would have howled to see her mounted in this rig. She wondered what Heftral would do if it rained heavily.

Cherry had a sneaking suspicion that he would let her get as wet as if she were under Niagara. But after all a warm rain would not be such a hardship. Thunder and lightning, however, made her nervous, even indoors.

The storm quartered slowly across the desert, a wonderful sight to eyes used to close walls and crowded streets. Cherry breathed deeply. The sage fragrance seemed to intoxicate her. The misty rain felt sweet on her hot cheeks. The growing breeze brought a breath of wet dust.

Heftral was trotting his horse at as fast a clip as the pack animal could keep up. Cherry set Surefoot to a lope. Then she experienced an exhilaration. She was astounded that she was not thinking about the possibility of being wretchedly wet and uncomfortable.

It turned out, however, that they beat the gray pall of rain that moved behind them across their trail. Heftral led down among the strange scrawled rocks Cherry had seen for so long into the shelter of a shelving cliff. Clumps of cedar and patches of sage dotted the slope in front, and, opposite, a high wall of rock shut out the horizon.

"Throw your saddle," Heftral said practically, as he dismounted.

When Cherry had accomplished this, Heftral was at hand to hobble her horse and turn him loose.

"If there isn't a water hole in this cañon, there sure will be one *pronto,*" he said.

"You think it will storm?" she asked dreamily.

"Storm? You're to see your first real storm. Say, are you any good at camp work?"

"You mean chopping sticks, cooking stuff, and washing dishes?"

"Well, not exactly. We don't chop sticks. . . . But you have grasped my meaning."

"I'm perfectly helpless," Cherry assured him, which was a lie.

"Fine wife you'll make," he replied.

"Mister Heftral, I'm used to being waited upon," said Cherry, elevating her chin. "And I didn't coax you to fetch me on this . . . this camping trip."

"Good heavens!" he expostulated, spreading his hands wide. "I know that. . . . But I didn't figure on what we're up against."

"You should combine study of weather conditions with your archaeological and girl pursuits."

"Damn it," he returned doggedly. "I can't get rid of the idea that you'd be a thoroughbred . . . a real sport in any kind of a fix."

Heftral turned away then, unconscious that he had brought delight to Cherry's heart. She hoped she had deserved what he had said. And there appeared to be signs that she would be tested to the utmost. She decided, however, to allow him to labor under doubts for a while longer.

Finding a seat where she could lean against the wall, Cherry watched her captor with interest. He unpacked with swift hands. Then he strode to the cedars and fetched back an enormous load of firewood, which he threw down with a crash. His next move was to start a fire, and wash his hands. Following this, with a speed and facility that astonished Cherry, he mixed biscuit dough in a pan. There were several canteens full of water, and a number of canvas sacks, all bulging. He had two small iron ovens in the fire and a coffee pot. If Cherry had been blind, she would soon have been pleasantly aware of steaming coffee and frying bacon. Presently Heftral straightened up and glanced in her direction.

"Of course you can swear you'll starve to death. But you won't do it. And you can save your face by not making the bluff. . . . Will you have supper?"

"Yes, Professor Heftral, I'm hungry. And besides, I'm curious to see if you can cook. You have such varied accomplishments."

He brought her supper and laid it on the level rock beside her. Cherry had told the truth about being hungry, but she did not tell him how good everything tasted. The hot biscuits, well-buttered, were delicious. And when had she tasted such coffee? For dessert she had a cup of sliced canned peaches. And altogether the meal was most satisfying. Cherry was ashamed to ask for more, but she could have eaten it.

Meanwhile, the afternoon had waned, and twilight shadows were filling the hollows below. A steady rain set in. The campfire lighted up the shelving roof of the cliff. Cherry walked to and fro, around the corner of projecting wall, and explored some of the niches. She felt pretty tired and sore. Her knees burned from their exposure to the sun. Her cheeks felt pleasantly warm.

Heftral was packing loads of firewood. He did not appear to mind the rain, for he certainly was wet, and did not take the trouble to put on his coat. It was seeing him in a different light. Cherry remembered a good many of her gentlemen friends and acquaintances who could dress and talk and dance and grace social occasions in the great city, who she doubted would have been her selection for service and protection in the desert.

She walked to the campfire and held her hands to the blaze. The night air had begun to have a little chill. The hot fire felt pleasant.

"You got your hair wet," said Heftral disapprovingly.

"So I did," Cherry replied with her hand to her head.

"Well, there isn't very much of it, so it'll dry quickly. . . . You must have had beautiful hair once."

"Once?"

"Yes, once. Women have sacrificed for fad and comfort. The grace, the glamour, the exquisite something natural to women disappeared with their long hair. It's a pity. In your case it fills me with despair. Why did you want to look like a man?"

"Gracious. I never did."

"Why did you cut your hair then?"

"To be honest I don't know. My reasons would sound silly to you. But as a matter of fact women are slaves to fashion. They used to be slaves to many things . . . men, for instance. But we've eliminated that."

"I wonder if women are eliminating love, also?" he inquired gloomily.

"They probably are, until men are worthy of it."

Heftral stalked off into the darkness, and stayed so long that Cherry began to grow anxious. Surely he would not leave her alone. It was pitch dark now; the rain and wind were augmenting; the solitude of the place seemed accentuated. Cherry gazed out into the dark void, and then back at the caverned cliff. There might be all kinds of wild animals. Snakes and other reptiles. It was delightful for a woman to be alone on occasions, but here was one when there seemed need of a man. To her relief Heftral emerged from the gloom, packing another load of firewood.

"Are you going to stay up all night?" he asked. "Tomorrow will be the hardest day you ever had. You need sleep and rest."

"Where am I supposed to get them?"

"I made your bed up there," said Heftral, pointing to a ledge. "It's easy to climb up from this end. You'll be dry. . . . I'll spread my tarp and blankets here by the fire."

Cherry did not show any inclination to retire at once. She was tired enough, but did not choose to be sent to bed like a child. She stood by the fire until she was thoroughly dry. Then she sat down on a stone just the right distance from the red crackling logs. Heftral stood on the other side, looking down, with his hands outstretched. He seemed to have the burden of the world upon his shoulders. Then he turned his back to the fire, and stood that way for a long time. The wind whipped in under the shelving rock, cool and damp; the rain pattered steadily outside; the fire sputtered and cracked; the fragrant smoke blew this way and that. At last Heftral turned again to face the fire. And he looked more troubled than ever.

"Mister Heftral, you seem gravely thoughtful for a man who has accomplished his purpose," observed Cherry.

"I was just thinking," he replied, giving her a strange glance, "how jolly a picnic would be . . . if we were good friends."

"Yes, wouldn't it?" Cherry returned flippantly.

"Very unreasonable of me, I know. I didn't and couldn't expect you to enjoy being dragged off this way. But being here made me think how . . . how wonderful it would be if . . . if. . . ."

He did not conclude the sentence and his closing words were full of regret. Quite evidently he felt that he had sacrificed a great deal to her father's whim. Cherry had an uneasy consciousness that sooner or later he would betray her father and explain this unheard of proceeding. She did not want Heftral to do this and must prevent it coming about. The only way, she repeated to herself, was to give him such impression of her that he would carry the thing out through sheer anger and disgust. As an afterthought Cherry reflected that she could correct the terrible impression she was likely to give him. But suppose she could not? She dismissed that as absurd.

"I'd prefer you had kidnaped me in a limousine," she said lightly. "I'm used to being whisked off . . . and kept parked in some outlandish place."

"Good God!" he ejaculated. "I've begun to believe your father!"

"What did he say?"

"Never you mind. But it was enough. . . . And . . . will you oblige me by keeping your . . . your habits to yourself."

Cherry tittered. "If that isn't just like a man. A lot of thanks I get for trying to make it easy for you."

"Make what easy?" he asked belligerently.

"Why, this stunt of yours. . . . Now you've got me off on your old desert, I should think you'd be glad to find I'm not . . . well, an innocent and unsophisticated little dame."

"Cherry Winters, you're a liar!" he almost shouted at her, starting up, bristling. Then with a pale face he wheeled and strode off into the darkness along the cliff wall.

He left Cherry with a heart beating high. In spite of her bald remarks he was struggling to keep alive his ideal of her. Cherry thought she might go too far and stab it to death. But the truth was that her father had grossly misrepresented her, and that she had aided and abetted it by falsehood. Love was not easily killed, certainly not by a few fibs. She would carry on. And the revelation of her true self to Heftral would be all the sweeter. Gazing into the opal heart of the campfire, Cherry lost herself momentarily in a dream, from which she awakened with a start. A coyote had wailed his dismal wild cry. It made Cherry shiver.

She left the campfire, and climbed up the slanting rough rock to the ledge where Heftral had made her bed. What a nice snug rock, high and dry. Cherry would feel reasonably safe when Heftral came back. She sat down on the tarpaulin covering her bed, and her sensation roused the conception that it would not be a featherbed or a hair mattress by an exceedingly long shot. Suddenly she realized she would have to sleep in her clothes for the first time in her life. How funny. Then without more ado she took off her coat, made a pillow of it, and, removing her shoes, she slipped down into the blankets, stretched out, and lay still.

The bed consisted of two thicknesses of blankets and the canvas under and over them. Hard as a board under her. Yet what a relief, warmth, and comfort the bed afforded. The fire cast flickering fantastic shadows upon the roof of this strange habitation. Gusts of wind brought cool raindrops to her fevered face and the smell of wood smoke. Above the steady downpour of rain she heard a renewed crackling of the fire. Rising on her elbow, she saw Heftral replenishing it with substantial logs. The night afforded Cherry satisfaction. She dropped back, laughing inwardly. Stephen Heftral was in quite a serious predicament.

Cherry settled herself comfortably to think it all over. But she did not seem to be able to control her mind as usual. Her eyelids drooped heavily and though she opened them often they would go shut again, until finally they stuck fast. A pleasant warmth and sense of drowsy rest were stealing over her aching body. She had a vague feeling of anxiety about snakes, tarantulas, scorpions, but it passed. She was being slowly possessed by something vastly stronger than her mind. The rainfall seemed to lessen. And her last lingering consciousness had to do with the fragrance of smoke.

Cherry half awoke several times during the night, in which she rolled over to try to find a softer place in her bed. But when she thoroughly awoke it was daylight. The rain had ceased. Sunrise was a stormy one of red and black, with a little blue sky in between. When she sat up with a groan and tried to straighten, she thought every bone in her body was broken. She sat on her bed and combed her hair, and slyly cleaned her sunburned face with cold cream. Over the edge of rock she espied Heftral, brisk and whistling around the campfire. Whistling! Cherry listened while she put on her shoes. Then she got to her knees. Never had she had so many sore muscles. The arm Heftral had wrenched was the worst.

"Hey, down there!" called Cherry. "What was the name of that robber baron who ran off with Mary Tudor?"

Heftral stared up at her, almost laughing. "Bothwell, I believe," he replied constrainedly.

"Well, good morning, Mister Bothwell," added Cherry.

He returned her greeting with the air of a man who had almost forgotten something unpleasant. He did not whistle any more, and eyed Cherry dubiously as she limped and crawled down the slope to a level.

"How are the eats?" she asked brightly.

"I was just about to call you," he said. "Breakfast will be ready soon as the coffee boils."

"What kind of a day is it going to be?"

"Bad, I fear. It's let up raining, but I think there'll be more."

"Gee, how sore I am. You nearly broke my arm. And that slab-stone bed finished me."

"I hope the internal injury is better," he rejoined dryly.

"Oh, that. I guess that was hunger, or else a terrible pang of disappointment to find you such a monster. Call me when you're ready to give me something to eat."

Cherry walked about to stretch her limbs. The overhanging sky was leaden and gray, except where a pale brightness had succeeded the ruddy sunrise. She heard a roar down in the cañon and concluded it was running water. Little muddy streams were coursing down the shallow ditches. Beyond the cliff she saw water in sheets running off the rocks above. The cedars were green and fresh, and the sage had an exquisite hue of purple. Cherry ventured to the edge of the cedar grove, and saw down into the cañon where a red torrent swirled and splashed. She recalled hearing the trader tell of sudden floods pouring down the dry washes. This was one of them, and she understood now why heavy storms impeded desert travel.

A shout turned Cherry's footsteps campward. Heftral had breakfast ready, and it was equally as appetizing as the supper the night before.

"Evidently you're not going to starve me into submission, anyway," she observed.

"I don't know about submission, but you'll be starved into

something, all right," he declared.

"Do we have to cross this cañon?"

"We do, and *pronto,* or we won't cross at all."

"Why, there's a regular torrent."

"It's not bad yet."

"Then we must hurry?"

"Yes. If we rustle along . . . and are lucky . . . we may make *Beckyshibeta* tonight."

Not for worlds would Cherry have importuned Heftral to turn back. But the serious nature of desert travel under unfavorable conditions now dawned upon her, and her mood of levity suffered a sidetracking. She had no more to say. Hurrying through breakfast, she proceeded to assist Heftral with the camp chores. He objected, but she paid no attention to him.

"Where are the horses?" she asked suddenly.

"They'll be near somewhere. They're hobbled, you know, and wouldn't stray from good grass. I'll fetch them in."

He was absent so long that Cherry began to worry.

At last he showed up, riding his horse bareback, and leading the other two. Surefoot looked fat. Cherry undertook the job of saddling him. As she swung up the heavy saddle, she observed Heftral watching her out of the corner of his eye. When her horse was ready, she turned to Heftral. He was loading the pack animal. Cherry had watched the cowboys throw what they called the diamond hitch—an intricate figure-eight knot that held the pack on—and she now saw Heftral was as expert as any of them. Nevertheless some assistance from her was welcome to him. He made only one remark, which was about the way she pulled on the rope. When the pack was on tight, Heftral saddled his own horse.

"I've left my chaps out for you to wear," he said, indicating a pair of worn leather chaps lying on a rock.

"How can I wear chaps in this dress?" queried Cherry.

"I don't know. Stuff your skirt down in them. Reckon there's not much to stuff."

Cherry overlooked his facetiousness, and, picking up the chaps, she stepped into them. They were too long and too large. From the expression on Heftral's face she gathered that she must be a funny-looking object.

It was when Cherry essayed mounting her horse that she came to grief. The chaps were stiff and heavy, and she could not reach the stirrup with her foot. Heftral offered to lift her up, but she declined. Finally she made a violent effort, a sort of spring. She missed the pommel with her hand and the stirrup with her foot, and fell flat. Cherry scrambled up, quite enraged. If there was anything she hated it was to look clumsy.

Heftral's face had a strained look. He was holding in his laughter. "I . . . I suggest you try to mount from the rock there," he said.

"I'll get up here or die," replied Cherry furiously.

Next time she lifted her left foot with both hands and got it in the stirrup. Then she leaped, sprung from her right foot, and, catching pommel and cantle, she dragged herself up into the saddle.

"Not so bad for a tenderfoot," observed Heftral. Whereupon he rode off, leading the pack horse.

Cherry followed down the slope of wet red earth, by some scrawled rocks, into the cañon. They rounded a corner to come upon the muddy swift stream. It was silent here, but from below came up a dull roar. Cherry had never seen such heavy-looking water. It was half silt. What a terrifying place to venture in.

Heftral crossed a flat sandbar, and urged his horse into the water. He spurred, and yelled, and dragged at the pack animal. They set up a great muddy splashing. Cherry gathered that the more speed used here, the easier and safer the crossing. Her heart simply leaped to her throat. Heftral's horse went in to his flanks. What a tremendous floundering the two horses made. Cherry almost lost sight of them in the splashing. They reached shallow water, heaved up, and waded out safely on the bar opposite. Heftral halted his horse and turned to look. For a moment he merely looked.

"Well, Central Park!" he called in a tone that challenged Cherry.

"Coming, fossil hunter!" she replied defiantly.

Surefoot naturally would rather have turned back. Cherry had to kick him to start him at all. And then she could not make him go fast enough. He splashed in to his knees, slowed up, and began to flounder.

"Come hard!" yelled Heftral.

Cherry urged her horse with all her might. It was too late for good results. Surefoot struck the deep water at too slow a gait, and the current carried him off his feet. Cherry's distended eyes saw the red flood well to her hips. How cold, angry, strong. Heftral rode madly down along the opposite bank, yelling she knew not what. In the presence of real peril Cherry's sense and nerve rose to combat her terror. She kept her seat in the saddle. She pulled Surefoot diagonally downstream. He was half swimming and half wading. Fifty yards below where Heftral had crossed, Cherry's horse struck shallow water and harder bottom and made shore just above a place where the stream constricted between steep banks, and began to get rough.

Heftral had waded his horse in to meet hers.

"You should have ridden in fast," he said almost harshly. But the fact that his face was white caused Cherry to forgive his rudeness.

"You told me a little late," replied Cherry coolly.

"I apologize. I . . . I thought you would follow suit," he returned with an effort.

Cherry did not need to be told what a narrow escape it had

been. She effectively concealed her real feelings.

"Pray don't apologize. I didn't expect much courtesy from you," she said evenly.

The blood leaped to Heftral's pale cheek and he stifled a retort. Then he rode back to the pack animal and took up the halter again. Cherry rode on behind him, pondering over the possibilities of this eventful day.

Chapter Six

Five hours later, and fifteen miles farther on over this awful desert, Cherry had experienced sensations never before known to her except by hearsay.

She had been wet to the skin for hours. It was not rain but a deluge. She had forded so many gutters and wastes and gorges that she could no longer remember the number. She had fallen off her horse into the mud. She had been compelled to dismount and climb up steep wet sand slopes, where every step seemed the last one before she flopped down to die. She had been pulled across raging creeks by Heftral, and rescued from certain death at least twice. And the wonder of it all was that she had kept the true state of her misery and terror from her captor. She vowed nothing would ever make her show yellow and crawl—to give this man and her father the satisfaction they craved. She would prove one thing anyhow—that a modern girl could have more nerve than all the old-fashioned dames together. Lastly she was unable to decide whether she would end by passionately hating Heftral or loving him. Certainly he could not have planned such opportunities as had come up. He treated her almost precisely as if she had been a young man. Indeed it was because of this in two instances that she had nearly drowned. Yet he was amazingly cool, indifferent to her and danger as well. But when necessary he had the quickness, the judgment, and the strength to drag her to safety.

The rain let up now and then, so that Cherry could see the

desert. If it had ever been level, it was no longer so. It was turned on end, broken into ragged pieces, upheaved and monumental, a wild world of walls, cliffs, rocks, cañons, and water. Cherry thought it had probably rained likewise for Noah and the ark.

There was not a dry stitch on her, and she appeared to be red mud from head to toe. Sand and water were mixed inside her shoes. When Heftral trotted his horse, or dismounted to descend into some gully and climb out, Cherry grew hot and breathless from the unusual exercise. When they rode slowly, which fortunately was not often, she grew cold. And now she began to get hungry.

She remembered she had wrapped up a piece of meat and a biscuit, and deposited it in her pocket. With dismay she found the biscuit wet and soggy. But she ate it anyhow. Then the piece of meat. She had never before known anything to taste so good. And she reflected on how little she had ever appreciated food. A person must starve to realize that.

The rain poured down again, so thick and heavy that Cherry could only dimly discern the pack horse scarcely fifteen paces ahead. Cherry's saddle held a pool of cold water. It rained down inside her chaps into her shoes. What a miserable sensation that was. It pelted her back and ran in a stream off the brim of her hat. Patiently she waited, praying for a lull. But none came. And her state became one of utter wretchedness. All she asked now was to live long enough to choke her father and murder Heftral.

Cherry was to learn something undreamed of—the latent endurance of a human being. She managed to stick on her horse, to keep up without screaming. But she knew another gorge, if they encountered one, would be her finish. She would just fall off her horse and sink out of Heftral's sight. Maybe that would touch the indifferent brute.

No more cañons were met with, however, though the rock

walls grew mountainous. All at once Cherry seemed to realize the dull gray light was darkening. The day was ended, and the storm appeared to increase in fury. At times the great walls afforded protection, but largely they rode in the open. Surefoot now kept on the heels of the pack horse. When Heftral at last halted, Cherry had an overpowering sense of huge black walls, and a roaring of wind or water.

"It's been some rotten day," said Heftral as he reached to take her from the saddle.

Cherry could see his face dimly in the gloom. When she tried to get out of the saddle, she simply slid off into Heftral's arms. He carried her a few steps and set her upright on a rock.

"You're a game kid, anyway," he muttered as if speaking to himself. Then he disappeared. Cherry found she could lean back against a wall, which she did in unutterable relief. Evidently they were under some kind of shelter, for it was dry. She smelled dust that had never been wet. The blackness above was split by a pale band, which must have been the sky. Sounds of wind and water filled the place with hollow roar. She was very cold, miserable, inert, and hungry, but had arrived at a state where she did not care. If she could only sleep or die. Her wretchedness was a horror. She could scarcely lift a hand. Every bone in her body seemed broken, every muscle bruised. And she was so wet, she knew presently she would melt.

Suddenly a light pierced the blackness, and she heard a crackling. Heftral's figure showed in a dim flare. He had kindled a fire. Wonderful man to find dry wood in a deluge. She saw a blue-gold blaze leap up through a tangle of brush and sticks. In a moment the place was illumined by a roaring fire. It had a subtle effect upon Cherry. She saw sheer walls of rock on three sides, and a black void on the other.

Heftral approached her, and drew her to the fire. "Get dry and warm. It'll make a difference," he said, and he placed one of the canvas packs for her to sit upon. But Cherry, weak as she was, stood up to the blaze, extending cold trembling hands.

"It feels good," she replied.

Indeed she wanted to walk into that blazing pile of sticks. What had she ever known about a fire? Of its singular beauty, its power to cheer, its wonderful property to warm cold flesh. It was the difference between death and life. She understood the barbarians who first invented, or found it. She knew now why she loved the sun.

Her wet clothes began to steam. She turned from one side to the other, as long as she could stand the burn.

"Sit down and let me pull off the chaps," suggested Heftral.

When he had accomplished this task, which was not easy, in view of the fact that Cherry had to hold desperately on to the pack to keep from being dragged off, she felt almost as if she were undressed. The short skirt of woolen material had shrunk and wrinkled until it was a spectacle that made Cherry shriek with laughter, despite her woes. Heftral laughed with her, but evidently avoided looking at her. After wringing the water out of her skirt as best she could, Cherry approached the fire, standing as close as she dared. She turned around and around, sat down upon the pack until she rested, then repeated the performance. It was amazing how quickly her clothes dried. And equally amazing was the effect upon her spirits.

Meanwhile Heftral was cooking a meal with an extreme celerity that suggested lack of firewood or some other reason for haste.

"What's the rush?" asked Cherry. "Looks as if we'd have to stay here tonight, anyhow."

"Aren't you hungry?"

"Famished."

"Well, that's reason enough."

"You're awfully good to me. . . . Where are we?"

"Beckyshibeta."

"So soon!" Cherry exclaimed, gazing around her. The flare from the fire showed yellow walls, dark caverns, cracks, and in front a space of rock-strewn ground leading to dimly outlined trees, and then a blankness.

"So it was your life's ambition to fetch me here?" Cherry said incredulously. "Gee, men are queer. You might have accomplished much more by taking me to the Ritz!"

"Any man could do that," replied Heftral. "At least you'll remember this trip."

"I'll say I will."

The rain had ceased and there appeared to be a cessation of wind. Cherry heard a low, dull rumble. Heftral informed her it was thunder and that they were in for the very deuce of a storm.

"But we're safe and dry, unless we get flooded out. That's happened here before."

"Indeed. Interesting place."

"Are you dry?"

"Just about, I guess. And burned to a crisp."

"Come to the festal board, then," he concluded.

The wants of primitive peoples must have been very few. Shelter, warmth, food, and something to wear. Yet what cardinally important wants these were. Cherry was so grateful for the former that she almost reconciled herself to the lack of the last. She reflected that if her skirt shrunk any shorter she would have to don Heftral's chaps permanently or else look like one of the chorus girls in the Follies. She did not care, after all. It would only be more to the sum of Heftral's iniquity.

Cherry was thinking along that line, and eating prodigiously, when something happened. All went dazzlingly, blindingly white. She lost her sight. Deep blackness again, then an awful terrific crash. The great walls seemed to be falling. Cherry screamed, yet did not hear her own voice. A tremendous boom and bang resolved into concatenated thunder, which rolled away, leaving Cherry weak and paralyzed with fear.

"W-what was . . . th-that?" she faltered.

"Just a little lightning and thunder," he replied. "They'll get bothersome presently, when the streaks of lightning come down like the rain. Better finish your supper. Then you can crawl under your blankets and shut out the flashes, anyhow."

Cherry's appetite had been effectually checked, but she swallowed the rest of her meal, every moment dreading another earth-riving crash. But it did not come at once. She had surprise added to dread. The stillness and darkness became most oppressive.

"Where's . . . my bed?" asked Cherry, rising.

"I haven't unrolled it yet," replied Heftral, jumping up.

Just then a sudden silver-blue blaze struck Cherry blind. She stood as one stricken, every muscle, nerve, and brain cell in abeyance to the expected crash. Such a shock came that it knocked Cherry flat. And when she became conscious of sound again a mighty rumbling of thunder boomed at the walls. Heftral was trying to lift her. Cherry opened her tight-shut eyes and clung to Heftral. He had got her to her knees when another white flash and awful clap made her collapse in his arms.

Heftral carried her a few steps back and put her down. But she still clung to him. "It's only a storm . . . just lightning and thunder," he was saying most earnestly. "We're safe. We can't be struck or hurt. There's only one danger . . . that of being caught here in a flood. But it'd have to rain a long time. . . . Cherry, don't be such a child. Why. . . ."

It did not do any good, so far as comforting Cherry. She knew it, too. She had been worn out physically. And from childhood she had always dreaded a storm. That fear had been born in her. And never had she seen or heard anything to compare with this lightning and thunder. They were blinding, deafening, nerve-racking, and absolutely stunning. That was why Cherry had her face on Heftral's breast and clung to him with all the strength she had left. She was aware that he tried to disengage himself—that he kept on talking, but both action and voice augmented her terror. They would come again, and she wanted to be hidden, to be held. They did come, and Cherry, even with her eyes shut and face pressed hard against Heftral's breast, saw the intense white light. Then followed the stupendous crash. The earth shook under her. The whole world seemed full of staggering sound. It clapped back and forth from wall to wall, and rolled away like a mountain of stone.

Cherry had a last lingering recollection of the part she had meant to play, of a wicked hope for this very opportunity.

"Y-you've taken m-me from m-myself," she faltered.

Heftral's reply was drowned in another explosion. But Cherry felt him take her closely in his arms and hold her tightly. Then it seemed the storm broke into incessant flash and crash, until there was no darkness or silence again. That period, long or short, was the worst Cherry had ever experienced by a most exceeding degree. When the storm passed, she seemed dazed. But she felt Heftral lay her down and cover her with blankets. And that was the last thing she knew.

When she awakened, the sun was shining somewhere, for she saw a gold-crowned rim of lofty wall. She remembered instantly where she was and how she had gotten there. Yet the place was as weird and magnificent as any dream. Great walls and columns of colored stone rose above her. Only a narrow strip of blue sky could she see. She heard a sullen roar of waters and smelled wood smoke.

"So this is Paris . . . I mean *Beckyshibeta,*" Cherry murmured wonderingly. And she tried to rise so that she could look about her. But with the movement such a pang shot through her body that she fell back, uttering a sharp little cry. She was so cramped and stiff that the slightest sudden effort caused pain. Whereupon she moved her aching limbs very cautiously and stretched her sore body likewise.

Cherry was swearing softly to herself when she espied her muddy shoes on a rock beside her bed. She did not recall taking them off. Heftral had done that. Her coat, too, was under her head. Then she ascertained with relief that these two kindly services constituted the extent of Heftral's activities as lady's maid.

She heard a step grate on rock. Then Heftral appeared to gaze anxiously down upon her.

"Did you call?" he asked quickly.

"I just squealed," she replied, gazing up at him, careful to draw the blankets close to her chin.

"Good morning," he went on as an afterthought.

"Good morning," returned Cherry sweetly.

"How are you?"

"I'm not sure, but I think I'm dead."

"You're sure a live and handsome corpse," he said bluntly. "Lord, I wonder if anything could mar your beauty."

His tone was one of exasperating resignation, as well as reluctant admiration. To Cherry it was like a drink of wine.

"Stephen, are you calling on the Lord?"

"I sure am."

"Well, I think it's a sacrilege, blasphemous. What a nerve you have."

"In extreme cases the most degraded of men might naturally express himself so. I own it was silly of me. I can't expect any succor," he said solemnly.

"You shouldn't expect mercy, either, from the Lord . . . or *me*."

"Probably you'll be more inclined to be merciful if I fetch you a nice hot breakfast," he said tentatively.

"Yes. Your cooking is your one redeeming virtue."

"Thanks," he replied, and turned to go.

"Stephen, wait!" she called. "What did I do last night?"

"Do? Why, nothing in particular."

"I remember being knocked flat by a stroke of lightning. That must have dazed me, for the rest seems a sort of dim horror."

"It was a bad electric storm even for this desert. No wonder you were shocked. You see it's very much worse when you're walled in by cliffs. The echoes crack from cliff to cliff . . . truly terrific."

"Was I frightened?"

"Rather."

"Did I scream or . . . say anything?"

"You told me I had taken you from yourself," he replied gloomily.

"Heavens! What did I *do*?" she exclaimed, intensely curious.

"I fear it would embarrass you."

"No doubt. That's why I insist. I want to know."

"Well, I picked you up, intending to carry you up here, where it's more sheltered. But you grabbed me . . . hid your face . . . and hung on as if for dear life. So I just held you till the storm was over."

"What do you mean by 'hung on'?"

"To be frank you hugged me outrageously."

"Indeed! Did the storm last long?"

"Hours."

Cherry gave him an inscrutable glance and smile. "I presume you would have a storm like that every night."

"Yes. I would . . . if I had the power," he said intensely.

"You would be worse than cruel," she rejoined gravely. "My mother was a very highly organized and sensitive person. Inordinately afraid of lightning and thunder. I was marked before my birth. And prematurely born after a storm. . . . One of the recollections of my childhood is that Mother used to take me into a dark hallway during a storm."

"I'm sorry I said that," he replied, and left. Presently he fetched up her breakfast and retired rather hurriedly, without speaking again. Cherry struggled to a sitting posture, and applied herself diligently to the ham and eggs, toasted biscuit, well-buttered, and coffee. Truly Mr. Heftral was astounding. Where did he get fresh eggs? Of course he had fetched them. But how? Perhaps he believed that the way to a woman's heart lay through her stomach.

Cherry had intended to stay in bed and rest. But one look over the bulge of rock up at lofty golden rims and down into a wilderness of bright green cañon put idleness out of the question. She would explore *Beckyshibeta* if she had to drag herself around. Consulting her little mirror, she saw that her face had been sunburned, but not unbecomingly so. And the other sunburn did not matter, even if it did hurt, any more than her shriveled and shrunken garments. There was no danger of any critical and supercilious woman seeing her. Suppose Chauncey Sarland's mother could see her in this rig! Cherry giggled. It would be rich. Nevertheless she did not care for that catastrophe.

She got up groaning. Muscles and bones were no doubt essential to the human frame, but this morning she would rather have dispensed with them. She was weak, lame, sore, and burned. The band of sunburn above her knees was particularly annoying. She reflected that it was a new-style scarlet garter, and would have created a sensation at Atlantic City.

"Oooo!" moaned Cherry as she tortured herself erect. "Why did I leave home?"

It was serious business, this treatment she had given her body. She could not have stood much more without being totally incapacitated. Heftral had called her a game kid, which was an appellation that gave her extreme pride, both because it was natural it should, and secondly because it had been reluctantly wrenched from the archeologist. That was one reason why she did not go back to bed, instead of suffering excruciating pangs.

Finally she wore off the stiffness to the extent of being able to navigate, then she laboriously climbed down to a level and gazed about her. The place appeared to be simply an enormous cavern with a dome higher than that of the Grand Central Station, which was going some, Cherry admitted. It opened on a level bench that extended out over a green cañon, perhaps half a mile wide and twice as long. How refreshing and colorful the different kinds of foliage. It contrasted beautifully with the red and gold of gorgeous colossal cliffs that sheered up as if to the very sky. A sullen roar of water greeted Cherry's ears. She heard the twitter of birds in the cedars and cottonwoods. All appeared bright and clean, with a warm sun shining after the storm. Thin yellow waterfalls were dropping over the cliffs, and at the apex of the cañon, its upper end, a heavy torrent was tumbling down over the broken masses of rocks.

These were Cherry's first impressions and sensations. She walked out of the shade into the sunshine. Every step was an effort, but fetched wonderful reward in an enlargement of her view of the weird and magnificent surroundings. The stone walls were higher than the Singer Building. They were full of great caverns and hollows near their base, and above were cracked and stained and covered with moss, with niches and ledges where green growths grew. Cherry stood spellbound. *Beckyshibeta!* What a marvelous place! It was majestic, grand, and increased in beauty and wonder as she grasped its true perspective. The cañon stunned her, too, with its shut-in solitude.

"Oh, glorious," murmured Cherry. "I had no idea it was like this. He never said so. Mister Linn didn't lead me to expect much. But this!"

Cherry sat down in the sun, and time was as nothing. She might have been there minutes or an hour. It was long, however, for cramped muscles told her so. She breathed it all in. Her eyes feasted. Something seemed transformed within her. What had she missed all these idle years? Never, except in a highly colored romance or two, had she read of such places as this, and she had believed them merely fiction. But no pen, no brush could do justice to the truth of *Beckyshibeta.*

Cherry felt that she would be unutterably grateful to Heftral always. Still she could not let him know. He was a terrible scamp, but. . . . Where was he anyhow? For a sheik who had made off with a maiden, he was certainly elusive.

She went in search of him. Owing to her crippled condition and the awesome nature of the place, Cherry did not make much progress. She got around an immense corner of wall, below the cavern he had chosen for their camp, and found another cave higher and larger than the first one. It was full of the ruins of sections of wall that had fallen. Cherry threaded slow passage between blocks of rock and over weathered slides to another projecting corner that she thought hid the mouth of the cañon. The roar of water grew louder. Her way was so beset with obstacles that she was long in reaching her objective. But at last she got around the corner.

If she had gazed and gaped before, what did she do now? All the details she had seen were here repeated and magnified. In addition, was a wicked red stream down in a series of rapids. The cañon opened into a larger one, bewildering to Cherry's eyes.

Next she descried Heftral digging with a pick. He stood just around the jutting point of wall, and it had been the cracking of his pick that attracted her attention. Cherry made her way to him. Strange he did not see her. He was shamming or absorbed, not improbably the latter. He dug like a man who had found the foot of the rainbow.

Cherry hailed him with: "Hey, there, subway digger!"

Heftral was startled. He whirled and dropped his pick. Cherry did not need to be told that he had actually forgotten her.

"Why . . . Miss Winters . . . you . . . I. . . ," he stammered.

"Fine morning on the avenue," she returned.

"It is fine," he said, recovering himself, and reaching for the pick.

"Stephen, you forgot me, didn't you?"

"I'm afraid I did."

"Left me alone to be eaten by grizzly bears or run off and get lost or anything!"

"There are no bears. And you can't run off until the creek falls. Nor can anybody get across to frighten you."

"Very well, but that doesn't explain your leaving me alone."

"No, it doesn't. To be honest, I just plain forgot you."

"Can you beat that! You're a funny captor. As you evidently didn't intend to maltreat me, I certainly expected to be taken care of, amused, and instructed. And you forget me!"

"I always forget everything, when I come to *Beckyshibeta,*" he replied apologetically. "Everything except that here, somewhere in these caverns, is buried the lost pueblo of *Beckyshibeta.* I know it. I have read the signs. . . . I daresay if I had run off with the Queen of Sheba or Helen of Troy, I'd have forgotten."

Cherry seemed again struck with his singular simplicity and passion. The man was so keen, so sincere, so strong and hopeful that he deserved to find the treasure upon which he set such store.

"I'll find *Beckyshibeta* for you," she said impulsively.

He stared, then laughed. "I suppose that'd be woman's revenge. To heap coals of fire upon my head. To flay me with remorse. . . . But, fun or no fun, please don't find *Beckyshibeta* for me."

"Why not? It seems to be your driving passion. Most men I know are driven by other motives. Money, power, fame."

"*Beckyshibeta* would give me all these. But I've never thought of them."

"Then why don't you want me to find it?"

"I'm quite mad enough over you now. If you found *Beckyshibeta*, I. . . ."

"Oh. So that's it? That would be a calamity."

"I agree with you. Therefore be careful not to go digging around in these caves. As to that, you stay in camp and stop following me."

"I'll follow you if I want to . . . but I don't," retorted Cherry.

"I don't approve of you gadding," he said severely. "I thought you'd rest all day."

"Take me back," returned Cherry imperiously.

"You found your way here alone. Now go back and stay there," he ordered.

Cherry did not know whether to swear or laugh at him. He was most decidedly in earnest. It might be well to save the profanity for a more fitting time. So she laughed.

"My Lord, I go," she said. "When will it please you to return to our castle?"

"I'll be along later," he rejoined, quite oblivious to her levity. "You can fix yourself some lunch."

Whereupon Cherry left him to his explorations and turned back, pondering the interview. Every encounter with Heftral left her unsatisfied, but she could not figure out why. It took her a good half hour, resting frequently, to retrace her steps, and all this while she divided her thoughts between Heftral and *Beckyshibeta.* At last she reached camp and found a comfortable slab. She was exhausted, yet the exertion had been good for her.

"Dad was not such a damned fool, after all," soliloquized Cherry. "I like Stephen Heftral. . . . It's up to me to find out why. I'm sorry Dad picked *him* to abduct me. Because I want to hate him and foil him utterly. But thank God I've run into one man who isn't drunk with alcohol, money, or women."

Cherry found resting so good that she went back to her blankets, and did such an unheard-of thing as to fall asleep in the daytime. When she awoke, it was the middle of the afternoon. She felt better. Heftral had not returned. The fact that he stayed away from her, on any pretext, astonished Cherry. She was unaccustomed to that in men who had the entrée to her society. She had scarcely believed that he would remain away all day. "He's mad about me, I don't think," she told herself emphatically. She was puzzled, piqued, amused, resentful, and something else she did not quite realize yet. It was, however, having a salutary effect.

Cherry contented herself with watching the changing afternoon lights in the cañon, and toward sunset, which came early, owing to the high walls, she thought she had been transported to some enchanted world. She saw the top of a distant mesa turn bright gold—exquisite rays of indescribably pure and beautiful light streamed down over the rims—in the distance, far through the gateway of the cañon, she saw purple of so royal a hue that she exclaimed in delight—walls were shrouded in pink haze, and near at hand the amber air seemed to float over the soft green foliage.

"I'm glad to be here," sighed Cherry. And she began to discover hidden depths in herself. It might be possible that she could be self-sufficient for a while. There was something incalculably strong working against the habit of mind that had been hers. Clothes, luxury, amusement, idleness, the theater, the dance, the ever-present necessity of unlimited money, the attention of men—these were most astonishingly unnecessary here. Cherry shook off the spell. *Beckyshibeta* was only a hole in the rocks. Beautiful, strange, wild, yes, but it was not a place to change one's soul. And she resented the awakening, insistent tearing at her mind.

CHAPTER SEVEN

The sun had set and the sky was full of rosy clouds when Heftral returned, dusty and tired, wiping his tanned face. He seemed different to Cherry, or she saw him with different eyes. There was something proven about him.

"How's my fair prisoner?" he asked.

"If I'm better in body and mind, I can't thank you for it," she replied.

"*¿Quién sabe?*" he returned. "Do you like *Beckyshibeta*?"

"This terrible shut-in lonely hole in the rocks? Heavens!" she ejaculated languidly.

"Cherry, be honest," he said.

"Why, Stephen, honest is my middle name," she averred.

"No. It might be game, but it's not honest. You are as crooked as a rail fence . . . mentally. . . . Please be honest *once,* Cherry."

"Why?" she inquired, curious, in spite of her frivolity.

"Because I have always connected you somehow with *Beckyshibeta.* Strange, but it's so. I believed you would like it . . . be inspired, perhaps softened."

"Stephen, am I hard?"

"Hard as these rocks."

"You are not flattering."

"Maybe not. But I'm honest," he said stoutly.

"No, you're not. You're not straight about this stunt of yours. Dragging me off here." And she bent penetrating eyes on Heftral.

"You will find me honest in the end," he replied, the dark red blood staining his cheek.

"Ah-huh," returned Cherry doubtfully.

"Are you going to be honest or not?" he inquired sharply. "I still have faith left in you . . . enough to believe you're not utterly lost to . . . to the dream of glory of Nature."

"Ain't Nature grand?" rejoined Cherry with simpering impudence.

"Cherry Winters, if you don't love *Beckyshibeta,* I shall despise you," he declared hotly.

There was no doubt about this, Cherry saw. Heftral was at war with the world—backing his faith in her against the materialism and paganism of the modern day. It thrilled Cherry—quite robbed her of her contrariness.

"Stephen, I'd like to make you despise me, but I can't honestly. I do love *Beckyshibeta* and I am glad you dragged me here," she said with a rich note in her voice, and turned away her face.

"Thank you. That will help," he replied with emotion.

Cherry watched him go down to the creek with the water bucket. It would hardly do, Cherry considered, for her to think seriously about him just then, so she dismissed the gravity of the situation, not by any means easily. But she realized she must, sooner or later, have a reckoning with herself. For the present, she must stick to her part, and not let any earnestness or eloquence of Heftral's betray her into honesty again.

Heftral returned whistling. Besides the brimming bucket, he carried a log of wood big enough to crush most men Cherry knew. She leisurely approached the camp and watched him swing an axe. He started a fire, put on the oven, and then went for more wood. This time he brought such a big load that Cherry objected.

"You'll break your back," she said in alarm. "Stephen, you

may not be the most desirable of companions, but you're better than a cripple. Please be careful."

"Say, I'm not half a man. You ought to see an Indian pack in firewood. He fetches a whole tree. . . . But come to think of it, if that causes you concern, I'll try a big load next time."

Cherry did not answer this. She sat down close by and watched him get supper.

"Stephen, how long will our supplies last . . . grub, as the cowboys call it?" she asked.

"I packed enough for three weeks, but did not allow for your unsuspected capacity. I daresay, if I stint myself, it'll last ten days."

"And then what?"

"Sufficient unto the day. We can subsist on rabbits, or I can ride to an Indian camp over here and get more. Or . . . we can return to the post."

"What! You'd take me back there . . . to face my father, the Linns, and the cowboys, knowing me ruined, disgraced?" she exclaimed.

"Sure, I will," he replied cheerfully.

"Stephen, if any other man had done this thing to me, and fetched me back . . . what would you do?"

"Do? A whole lot. I'd kill him."

"Exactly. But it's all right for *you* to do it?"

"Cherry, my intentions are honorable."

"Do you imagine you can make the cowboys believe that?"

"I confess I'm a little worried on that score," he replied ponderingly. "As a rule cowboys are obtuse and inclined to be bullheaded. Then they were so absurdly infatuated, and each of them thought he owned you. Stupid, conceited jackasses! Still they had ample encouragement."

Cherry relapsed into silence, the better to enjoy the ever-increasing humor of this situation, and the deliciousness of another sentiment that seemed hard to define. Presently Heftral began to talk, as if she were the most interested of comrades, as indeed, if the truth were admitted, she was.

"I followed another blind lead today, all to no avail. Eight hours of digging for nothing. How often have I done that here? But I know *Beckyshibeta* is buried here somewhere. If I only had unlimited time. But the department insists on definite rewards, so to speak. I have to find things . . . bones, pottery, stone utensils and weapons. In short, I am forced to dig where they tell me to and not where I want to. Elliott, head of our department, was out last year. I think I told you. Awful pill . . . Elliott! He's only a surface scratcher. Well, he belittled my theory. He said there was little sign of an ancient pueblo here at *Beckyshibeta*. . . . And so I can get only snatches at work here."

"Suppose we tell Elliott to go where it's hot," suggested Cherry.

"I wish I could. But I must have bread and butter, and some clean clothes occasionally," he returned, and without pathos.

"Stephen, do you always expect to be poor?" she asked.

"I hope not. I have my dream. But I suppose I really always will be."

"Too bad. But I don't know. Money is a curse, they say. Personally I don't see it. . . . Do you know I am rich?"

"No. Your father, of course. But are you, too?"

"Yes, disgustingly rich. My mother left me seven hundred thousand dollars when she died."

"Good Lord!" ejaculated Heftral, both astonished and startled, pausing in his work to gape at her. "Your father never told me that."

"Well, it's true. And Dad tells me it has nearly doubled. You see I can't touch the whole principle until I'm twenty-five. I have only the income from it . . . fifty thousand or so a year . . . and I confess I'm broke half the time. I'm always borrowing from Dad."

"Cherry, are you honest now?"

"Assuredly. I certainly wouldn't string you so vulgarly."

"Damn him, anyway," Heftral declared forcefully with a violent gesture.

"Who? Dad?" she asked innocently.

But Heftral did not answer and there was an immediate change in his demeanor. He prepared supper in silence, and remained glum during the eating of it. Cherry let him alone. She partook heartily of the good meal, and then left Heftral to himself. By this time the early twilight was creeping under the walls and it would soon be night. Cherry strolled a little on the edge of the bank. She saw one lone star come wondrously out of the paling pink. Fair as a star when only one was shining in the sky! She had read that somewhere. Wordsworth, perhaps. What would he or Tennyson or Ruskin make out of *Beckyshibeta*? There was nothing in Europe to compare with the cañon country. Cherry felt proud of that.

As it grew dark she returned to the campfire. Heftral had disappeared. She looked into the opal heart of the embers and saw beautiful disturbing visions there. Then she climbed up the rock to her bed.

As she sat down on it, she was surprised to find it high and soft. Upon examination she discovered a foot layer of cedar boughs under it. How fragrant! Heftral must have done that right after supper. He was a paradox. He had handled her roughly, had driven her to the limit of endurance, yet he was thoughtful of her comfort. But the new bed certainly was a relief and a joy. Cherry sighed for some soft woolly pajamas. But she had to sleep in her clothes. After removing her shoes, she decided she would take off her stockings, too.

She crawled in between the blankets, and knew in her heart she would not have exchanged them for silk sheets. Weary, aching as she was, she could not wish it otherwise. She had never actually experienced rest. She had never been sufficiently aware of comfort, ease. They had been habits, with no reason for them. Here they served a wonderful blessing, a reward.

Where had Heftral gone? It had upset him to learn she was rich. Cherry could not figure out just why. No one would take him for a fortune-hunter. It would be more embarrassing, of course, to compromise a wealthy girl than a poor one, simply because marriage would not have such a sacrificial look. Every hour of this adventure had enhanced its romance, augmented its possibilities for delight as well as pain. What would the new day bring?

Chapter Eight

Cherry had been alone all morning. For several hours she had welcomed the solitude. She had not seen Heftral, who had called to her that he was leaving her breakfast on the fire. If anything she was more stiff and sore than ever, but the pangs wore off more quickly with the use of her muscles. About noon she began to feel relief.

She simply could not get over Heftral's leaving her to her own devices. *Beckyshibeta* was more to him than she was. That both irritated and pleased Cherry. But of course she would not stand for it. So she set out to hunt him up.

The day was lovely, although when she got out in the sunshine, which was seldom, it was hot. The fragrant smells of summer wafted down into the cañon, mingling the sweetness of sage with wildflowers and fresh green verdure. The creek had run down and was no longer a roaring torrent. Cherry thought she could wade in it if she wanted to. It would have been nothing for a horse.

When she walked away from camp under these magnificent walls, she became somebody else. She grew pensive, dreamy, absorbed, and happy. No use to deny! Only she did not want Heftral to see it. A confusing thing, too, was the fact that under its spell she had to force herself to be true to her old inclinations. Therefore she refused to realize, or at least to seek to understand, the elevating power of this strange cañon wilderness. She could not help sensation. She had to see, to feel, to smell the place, and even to taste the sweetness of the dry desert air.

By the time she had worked her way around the second jutting wall, where Heftral had been digging, she was warmed by the exertion and free of stiff joints. In truth she felt fine. Heftral had abandoned this cavern. So Cherry went on, to encounter the most difficult and hazardous climbing over rocks that the kidnaping escapade had led her to. There was a thrill in it. How gratified she felt to surmount the last rock pile. She espied Heftral about on a level with her. But the cañon jumped off deep below him and zigzagged in wonderful hair-raising ledges beyond.

Heftral did not see her, which fact tickled Cherry. She had opportunity to approach him by way of a dangerous ledge before he would be aware of her presence. High places did not bother Cherry. She was level-headed and cool, and reveled in taking risks.

When she got about halfway to him, however, she had to halt. She was getting in trouble and faced inclines that made even a girl of her bravery quail. So she sank down to rest and gaze.

The cañon opened wide. It was much vaster and wilder than that part of *Beckyshibeta* where Heftral had pitched the camp. Cherry felt something pull at her heartstrings. Was not this desert fastness simply marvelous? But to look down now made her shiver. She had been aware of the gradual height she had attained. Below, a hundred feet or more, spread a slope of talus, a jumble of broken rock that fell roughly down to the green thicket. She almost forgot Heftral and her mission in a realizing worship.

Heftral's pick, ringing steel on stone, brought Cherry back. She espied a ledge above her where no doubt Heftral had crossed to the wide area beyond. Coming to a narrowed point, she got on hands and knees, and began to crawl out. She knocked some loose rocks off the ledge. They rattled down. Cherry swore. Heftral heard the rattling and turned to look up.

Flinging aside his pick, he ran forward to the end of the bench. "Stop!" he shouted.

Cherry obeyed, more from suggestion than anything else. She gazed across the void at Heftral. "Howdy, Stephen!" she called gaily.

"Didn't I tell you not to follow me?" he queried angrily.

"I don't remember."

"Yes you do."

"All right, then I do."

"You turn around very carefully and go back," he ordered. "Be careful. . . . You'll turn my hair gray."

"That'd make you very handsome and distinguished-looking," replied Cherry.

"Go back!" he shouted sternly.

"Not on your life!" retorted Cherry, and started to crawl again. She was approaching the narrowest part. It might have daunted her before, but now she could have managed a more perilous place.

"Stop! Turn back!" thundered Heftral.

This was pouring oil upon the flame.

"You go to the devil!" Cherry replied, and kept on crawling. She passed the risky point without a tremor or a slip, and presently, reaching the bench, she stood up before Heftral in cool triumph.

"If you do that again, I'll . . . I'll . . . ," he choked.

"That was a cinch," replied Cherry coolly. "My stockings are thin, though, and the rock hurt my knees." She rubbed them ruefully, quite unabashed by Heftral's staring.

"You'll fall and kill yourself," he stormed.

"No, nix, never, not little Cherry. I was a trapeze performer in my class at college. That amble across there was easier than taking candy from a baby."

"I tell you it was extremely dangerous," expostulated Heftral.

"We'll always disagree, Stephen. I imagine life together for us will be one long sweet hell."

"No, it won't. I might have entertained such an idiotic idea once, but it's dispelled."

"We needn't discuss the future now. I've begun to reconcile my- . . . myself to this and you. Don't spoil it. . . . Did you have a nice dig this morning?"

"Come. I'll help you back over this ledge. Then you go to camp and stay there," he said peremptorily.

"No, I won't. I want to be with you."

"Very sorry, but I don't want you here."

"Why? I'll sit still and watch you, and be quiet."

"No."

"Please, Stephen," she pleaded.

"I couldn't work with your big eyes mocking me. You make me remember I'm only a poor struggling archaeologist."

"But you brought me here."

"Yes, and I'd . . . I'm damned sorry for it. Someday I'll tell you why I did it."

"Are you repudiating your . . . your, well, your interest in me?" she queried with hauteur.

"Call spades spades," he returned. "You mean my love for you. No, I don't repudiate that. I'm not ashamed of it, though it has made me a fool."

"Oh! Then there's another reason why you brought me to *Beckyshibeta*?" she went on gravely. It seemed to Cherry that there was no use in trying to stall off the inevitable. Things tumbled over one another in a hurry to drive her. Pretty soon she would get sore and face them.

"Yes, there's another, and of *that* I am ashamed. But come, get out of here and leave me in peace."

"Mister Heftral," Cherry said, now haughtily, "has it occurred to you that I ought not to be left alone . . . entirely aside from my loneliness?"

"No, it hasn't," he returned, clenching his hands, and gazing helplessly down at the river.

"Well, you're rather dense. Some Indian or desperado . . . anybody might come. They could get across now, I think."

"No one ever comes here. At least, very seldom, and then I know they're coming. You're quite safe. And certainly you don't want my society."

"It is rather dreadful. But I'll stand it a while. I'll stay here until you get ready to go back to camp," replied Cherry airily, and she promptly sat down.

Heftral took her hand and pulled at her. "Come," he said, trying to control his temper.

"Let go, or we'll have another fight," she warned. "The other time I didn't hit below the belt, or bite."

He gave up. "Very well, if you're that mulish, stay. But you look here, you spoiled child . . . if you cross this dangerous place again, you'll be sorry."

"Why will I?" asked Cherry, immensely interested.

"Because you'll get what you should have had . . . long ago and many a time."

"And what's that, teacher?"

"A blame' good spanking."

Cherry could not believe him serious, yet he looked amazingly so. But that was only temper—a bluff to rout her utterly. It was so preposterous that she laughed in his face. "Mister Heftral, pardon my laughing, but you are so crude . . . so original," she said, and here the Cherry Winters of New York spoke in spite of herself. Perhaps nothing else she could have said would have stung him so bitterly.

"I have no doubt of it. All the same, I meant what I said. We are in Arizona now. And if you can't see the difference between real life and modern froth, I'm sorry for you. Most of America is too decadent for a good, healthy spanking. It has, I might say, a vastly different kind of interest in a young woman's anatomy. But among the wholesome pioneers in the West, thank God, there are parents who are still old-fashioned. I'm not a parent. All the same I can constitute one, and give you jolly well what you need."

He strode away to his work, leaving Cherry for once flabbergasted. It took some moments for Cherry to recover her egotism to assume dominance of her thoughts. Heftral must truly be laboring under a hallucination. She would put him to the test presently.

Sauntering closer to the middle of the wide bench, where he was plying his pick, she found as restful a seat as appeared available. It would tantalize him to have her so near, watching, as he called it, with her mocking eyes. She confessed to herself, however, that her interest in his work was growing keenly sincere. She truly wanted him to find *Beckyshibeta* even as she had boasted she might find it for him.

"Stephen, how will you know when you strike this buried pueblo?" she asked suddenly. "What will it be like?"

"I'd know the instant I struck my pick in it," he replied with surprising animation. Heftral evidently was quick to recover from anger or slight.

"You would, of course, but how would *I* know?"

He gave her a depreciating glance. "Well, judging by the intelligence you've shown lately, you never would know a pueblo. Not if you fell into a kiva."

"Ah-huh! Gee, I'm a bright girl. . . . What's a kiva?"

"It's a deep circular hole in the ground, covered by a roof, with an entrance. Used by the cliff-dwellers. . . ."

Cherry interrupted him. All she had to do was to ask a question of an archaeological nature and he was off on a tangent.

"Then if you disappear suddenly, I'm to search for your remains in a kiva? Very appropriate end for you, I'd say."

Heftral went back to work, and though Cherry directed sundry queries at him, he apparently did not hear them. She grew provocative. He gave no heed. Then she called him mummy hunter, grave robber, bone digger, and like names. Finally she resorted to cradle snatcher, but that likewise did not penetrate his skull.

"Say," she concluded in disgust, "if I offered to kiss you, would you talk?"

"Yes," he flashed, swiftly facing her with a gleam in his eye.

"Oh! Well, I withhold the offer, but I'm glad you're not altogether a dead one."

"Cherry Winters, you're an unmitigated fraud," he returned. "Also, you are a salamander."

"I don't like the sound of that last word. Salamander?"

"It's a term I heard in New York. I gathered that it was applicable to a young woman who enticed with false smiles and words and suggestions. Who allured with all feminine . . . I should say female powers . . . and never gave a single thing she promised."

"Stephen, you are calling a turn on all women from Eve to Pola Negri. . . . Say," she burst out suddenly, "I'll bet you a new saddle to a pair of gauntlets that I make you swallow your salamander jest."

"You're on, Miss Winters," he declared. "I'll enjoy riding that saddle, and remembering this winter, while you are back in New York. . . ."

"Doing what?" she interposed as he hesitated.

But he dropped his head and returned to his interrupted digging.

"I'll finish it for you," she added with scorn. "While I am idling, flirting, dancing, sleeping away the beautiful sunrise hours, wasting money, wearing indecent clothes, drinking . . . and worse!"

She saw him flinch, then his jaw set, but that was all the satisfaction she got. Cherry had an unreasonable longing to hear him passionately deny most of these vices for her. But he did not. He believed them—perhaps now thought the very worst of her. This was what she had desired, yet most inconsistently, she would have preferred him to defend her as he had to her father.

Cherry let him alone for a while, although her contemplative gaze often returned from the lofty crags and wonderful walls to his strong, stooping figure, and his tireless labor.

When the enchantment of the cañon began once more to lay hold of her, with its transforming magic, she had recourse to a very devil of perversity and provocation. Studying the ledges and slopes of all this great section of ruined wall, she at last noted a narrow strip where even a goat might have had difficulties. It led toward another projecting corner of red wall, beyond which another and larger level beckoned with a strange spell. Cherry studied the place a long time. She had reason to believe that Heftral had not worked any farther than where he now stood. She yielded to an unaccountable impulse to gain that level.

Rising, she took occasion to stroll around in front of Heftral, then up to the edge of the amphitheater and in the direction of a rounded wall that led toward the objective point. The ring of Heftral's pick ceased. Cherry missed it with infinite satisfaction.

"Cherry, where are you going?" he demanded. "Didn't I . . . ?"

She crossed the rim of curved wall and gained the near end of the narrow strip. How fearful the depth below.

"Hold on!" yelled Heftral, his boots thudding over the rock.

Then Cherry turned. "Don't dare come another step!" she cried more than defiantly.

Heftral halted short, perhaps a matter of fifty steps from her. "Please, come back."

"I'm going across to the next bench."

"Cherry! That is worse than this other place. I have never risked beyond where you are now. Honest. It is more treacherous than it looks."

"I don't care."

"My God, girl, if you should slip! Have you no heart?"

"You'll have only yourself to blame."

Heftral struggled as if resisting a temptation to leap. He was silent a full moment. Cherry saw his expression and color change.

"You damned little fool!" he roared, at last. "Come back!"

"Nothing doing, Stephen," she taunted.

"Come back!" The stentorian voice only inflamed Cherry the more.

"Say, how'd you get like that?"

Heftral started for her and strode halfway around the curved-rim wall before he halted. Cherry backed upon the narrow strip, an exceedingly risky move, but her blood was up and she had no fear. He saw and stopped as if struck.

"Cherry, darling!" he called with an importuning, almost hopeless, gesture.

This, strangely, came near being Cherry's undoing. She wanted to obey him. Never could she be driven, but she was not tenderness proof. Her sudden incomprehensible weakness roused her to fury.

"Stephen, sweetheart, you've kidnaped the wrong flapper!" she screamed at him.

Heftral deliberately wheeled and went back to the bench.

Facing her then, he called out: "Flap and be damned! You'll find you can't fly. And you'd better stay over there, for, if you ever come back, you'll pay for this."

Thus inspired, Cherry turned to the narrow strip. It would not have frightened her if it had been a beanpole across Niagara. Sure as a mountain sheep she stepped, and never got down on hands and knees until she reached the knife-like edge. Over this she crawled as might a monkey. She stood up again and ran the rest of the way. Gaining the bench, she went for a peep around the vast corner of wall. The most wonderful of all the caverns opened before her. It was stupendous, overpowering. How marvelous to come back again and explore. Whereupon she retraced her steps.

Heftral remained as motionless as a statue watching her. On the return, Cherry exercised coolness where at first she had been daring. She crawled most of the way and never looked down into the abyss once. Breathless and hot she rested a moment before taking to the rim wall, then walked across that to where Heftral stood waiting. She saw that he was white to the lips, but he wheeled before she could get a second look at his face. It seemed silly to follow him, but she did, wondering what he would do or say. He led the way back toward camp.

Cherry had not anticipated this. Had she gone too far? Had she hurt him irretrievably? And now that it was over she reproached herself. What a spiteful vengeful little baggage she was! Still there was the part she had set herself to play.

She had difficulty in keeping up with Heftral. She kept up on the easy level ground, but over the rock slides she fell behind. It seemed a long way back to camp. Excitement and exertion had told on her. When the last corner of wall had been passed, Cherry thought she was pretty well all in.

Heftral had his back to her. How square his shoulders—rigid. He pivoted on his heels, to disclose terrible eyes.

"Cherry Winters, do you remember what I told you?" he demanded.

Swift as his words came a sensation of sickening weakness. Like a stroke of lightning it had come. She imagined she had been prepared, but she was not. She had misjudged him, underestimated his courage. Her subtle mind grasped at straws.

"Re-member?" she faltered, trying to smile. "About being . . . mad about me?"

"Mad *at* you!" he replied grimly. Then he seized her before she could move a hand. Surprise and fear inhibited her natural fighting instinct. Heftral lifted her—carried her.

Suddenly he sat down on the flat rock and flung her over his knees, face down. All her body went rigid. A terror of realization and horror of expectation clamped her mind. He spanked her with such stunning force that it seemed every bone in her body broke to the blow. The pain to her flesh was hot, stinging, fierce. The shock to her mind exceeded the sum of all shocks Cherry had ever sustained. She sank limply over his knees. *Smack!* Harder this time. Her head and feet jerked up. Her teeth jarred in their sockets. Again! Again! Again!

Cherry all but fainted. Intense fury saved her that. She rolled off his knees to the ground and bounded up like a cat. A bursting, tearing gush of hot blood ran riot in her breast.

"I'll . . . kill . . . you," she panted, low and deep.

Heftral was pale, shaken. He realized what he had done. The enormity of it must have flashed over him when she blazed so fiercely her fists clenched, her breast swelling.

"Once in your life, Miss Winters," he said huskily. "It's done. You can't change that. And *I* did it. I shall have that unique distinction among your men acquaintances."

Cherry tried to fly at him, to scratch out his eyes, to beat him before murdering him. But she let him pass. She felt her legs sag under her. Blindly then she groped and crawled up to her bed, sank under the blankets, and covered her face. The tension of her body relaxed. She stretched limply, palpitating, quivering. That numb dead sensation—where Heftral had smacked her—gradually gave place to burning, smarting pain. The physical suffering at first had precedence over the chaos of her mind. The hurt was terrific. Hot tears streamed down her cheeks. And she lay there panting, slowly succumbing, her spirit subservient to her tortured flesh.

It was dark when she had to uncover her head to keep from suffocating. The bright shadows of a campfire flickered on the stone above her.

"Cherry, child!" called Heftral like a fond parent, "wash your face and hands and come to supper."

Her blood leaped and boiled again. Rising on her hand, she was about to give passionate vent to all the profanity she had ever heard, but, as she saw Heftral moving around the fire, she stilled the impulse. She sank back under a compulsion she had never known. Was she beaten—whipped—cowed? Fierce devils of spirit answered that query. She had only been preposterously shamed and humiliated by an educated ruffian. Her pride had been laid low. Her vanity was bleeding to death. Cherry writhed in her bed, only to be made painfully aware again of the maltreated part of her anatomy. The instant there was a possibility of her returning to the old Cherry Winters, that burning pain had to recur. What a strangely subduing thing. Her mind had no control over it or the whirling thoughts it engendered.

She composed herself at last, in as comfortable a position as she could find. Again Heftral called her to supper. Eat! She would starve to death before she would eat anything he had prepared. How terribly she hated him. The revenge she had planned seemed nothing to her wild ragings now. Mere killing would not be enough. Death ended all sufferings. He must be made most horribly wretched. He must grovel at her feet and bite the very dust.

These bitter thoughts had their sway. They did not have permanence. All of a sudden Cherry discovered she was crying. To realize that, to fight it and fail, added to her breakdown. She cried herself to sleep.

Chapter Nine

Her eyes opened upon azure blue sky and gold-tipped wall. Consciousness came as quickly as sight. Her impulse was to shut out the beautiful light of day. She was ashamed to face it. But slowly she moved the blanket aside. Listening, she soon ascertained that Heftral was not in camp. Peeping over the rock, she saw a smoldering fire, and the steaming coffee pot and oven on it.

Cherry got up. If she had needed anything to remind her of the insufferable outrage she had sustained, she had it in sudden pains, more excruciating than any she had yet endured. The brute! He had not realized his strength. Maybe he had, though. How coldly and calmly he had gone about the chastisement. To wait until they had come all the way back to camp. In the light of another day his offense seemed greater.

There was her breakfast on the fire. Cherry remembered that she had sworn she would starve before she would touch Heftral's food again, but she did not see any sense in that now. As a cook she was not a genius.

"If there was a mantelpiece here, it's a cinch I'd eat my breakfast off it this morning," she said mirthlessly.

Dark, brooding thoughts attended the slow meal. Afterward it occurred to Cherry to wash the few utensils Heftral had left for her use. There was a pan of hot water at hand. This she did and not without an almost conscious gratification. Then she stared a while into the fading red coals of the fire. Next she walked in the sun, and could not shut out a sense of its warmth, of the sweet songs of wild birds, of the fragrance of sage and cañon thicket, of the glorious light under the walls.

What was she going to do? There were a thousand things. But first, and of absolutely paramount importance, was the fact dawning upon her that she had to repeat the foolhardy act of yesterday. A new, vague, sweet self raised soft voice against it, but was howled down by Cherry Winters proper. She had to show Heftral that this so-called cave-man dominance of the past, as well as the masculine superiority of the present, were things abolished, obsolete, blazed out of the path by modern woman. This was no part she was playing. She had ceased to be an actress. That fun, that desire to turn the tables upon her father and Heftral had vanished in the night.

Heftral was at work higher up than the day before and close to the amphitheater around which Cherry had crossed to the next bench.

She walked right past him, casually glancing in his direction. How could he guess that her heart was beating fast and that contending tides of emotion warred within her?

If she ever saw a man surprised it was then. The last thing Heftral would imagine was that she would come back. What sweet healing balm to Cherry's crushed vanity. He leaned on his pick and watched her. Would he order her back? Would he plead with her again?

Cherry was not foolish enough to underestimate the risk of this slanting narrow trail. She had accomplished it under high power by which almost she could have run on the air. This time, her nerve and caution, and lightness of foot, balanced the audacity of yesterday. She crossed without a slip.

Heftral stood leaning on his pick, watching. Not a word had come from him. Cherry would have given considerable for his thoughts. She could guess, of course, that he was completely routed, and probably most exceedingly furious. But was he disappointed? That she was an irresponsible child! Cherry tossed her head. What did she care? Something hot seared her and she accepted it as hate.

Once around the huge buttress of wall, out of Heftral's sight, she forgot him. Here was an amphitheater that dwarfed the Coliseum at Rome, and it was set against a background of magnificent forbidding walls. How silent! Cherry felt that she was alone in a sepulcher. Her steps led her high, so high she marveled and thrilled, and trembled sometimes at the gigantic fissures and the leaning cliffs.

Suddenly she espied what appeared to be little steps cut in the rock. She was astounded, could not believe her eyes. But there they were, one after another, worn, scarcely distinguishable in the smooth stone. They had been cut by hand. Intensely absorbed, Cherry followed them, forgetting the fear of high places and crumbling walls.

Presently she lost the little steps. She halted, breathless and flushed. Evidently she had climbed far. Before her spread a level bench most wonderful in its location and isolation. To look back and down made her gasp. How would she ever descend?

Her quick eye grasped at once that this wide protected bench could be reached only by the slope up which she had climbed. All at once it dawned upon her that the predominating feature of this place was its inaccessibility. These little steps had been cut by cliff-dwellers. Her heart beat faster than ever. She had discovered something. If Heftral had known of this place, surely he would have told her.

Cherry began to explore. In the smooth rock she found round polished holes where grain had been ground centuries before. She found the stone pestles lying as if a hand had laid them aside only yesterday. She found the edge of a wall buried in débris. Little red stones neatly cut and cemented. High up she sighted a cliff dwelling pasted like a mud wasp's nest against the shelf of rock. She had thought this amphitheater level, but it was anything but that. It began to look as if a great space had been buried by avalanche or the weathering processes of ages. It would take days to explore it.

Cherry stepped into a hole up to her knee. It appeared to her the ground had given way under her. Pulling her leg out, she was overcome to discover that she had stepped through a roof over something. Carefully she brushed aside the dirt and dust. She found poles of wood, close together, and as rotten as punk.

"Ah-huh! That's something," she ejaculated.

The hole made by her foot stared at her like a black eye. It spoke. Cherry began to thrill and shake. She dropped a little stone in it. No sound. She tried a large stone. She heard it strike far down. Then this was a kiva. Well? Then Cherry's mind bristled into action. *"Beckyshibeta,"* she whispered in awe.

She sat down, suddenly overcome. She had discovered the ancient pueblo Heftral had been searching for so diligently. It stunned her. How strange! What luck! There seemed a destiny in the willfulness that had led her to this place. It must be more than chance.

Then she remembered boasting to Heftral that she would find *Beckyshibeta* for him. She had done so. She had not a single doubt. And suddenly her joy equaled her amazement and transcended it. What a perfectly wonderful thing for Heftral. She was so happy she laughed and cried at once. It was not a delusion. Here opened the black mysterious eye of a kiva.

Cherry was consumed with only one desire. To tell Heftral. She climbed, she ran. The little steps cut in the stone slope had no terror for her now. In bad places she sat down and slid, unmindful of her dress or skin. Yet how long it took to get down. Once on the bench below she could not go fast. It was too rough. And at that she got more than one knock from a rock. At last she got around the last corner of wall, out of breath, panting so that she had to rest a moment.

Heftral was there, digging, digging, digging. Presently he would have something to dig for. With her breast heaving, Cherry watched him. The moment was somehow rich, sweet, beautiful, far-reaching, and inscrutable. Then she cupped her hands and called through them piercingly.

"Mister Heftral!"

He heard her, for he straightened up, looked, and then resumed work with his pick.

"Come! Come over!" called Cherry. He looked again, but did not reply. "Stephen. Come over!"

Here he quit his labors and leaned upon his pick, evidently nonplussed.

"Stephen! Please come!" shrilled Cherry.

"No. Not. Never. Nix!" he called, imitating her.

"Stephen, I want you," she went on.

"Nothing doing."

"If you come over . . . you . . . you . . . you'll have the surprise of your life."

"I don't care for your kind of surprises, Miss Winters," he replied after a jarring pause.

"But you will, I tell you."

"Not on your life!"

"Honest. Only come!" she called now pleadingly.

No answer. Heftral stood like a statue. Cherry could hardly contain herself any longer. He was making it so perfectly wonderful for her. What a climax! She must get him across there somehow and make a pretext to lead him to her discovery. In her extremity she was quite capable of going to unheard-of limits to accomplish her purpose. *Beckyshibeta* had changed the world for Cherry. She had no time to stop to analyze the transformation.

"I'll make you happy, Stephen," she trilled persuadingly.

"You've got another guess coming, Miss Winters," he said.

What a mulish creature a man could be anyway. And this one with his heart's desire waiting for him! Cherry had a wild notion that she might include herself in the finding of *Beckyshibeta.* Assuredly there was need of her discovering herself now.

"Stephen, dear. Come!" she called despairingly.

"I told you not to go over there," he answered. "Now you can get back by yourself."

"I'm terribly scared, Stephen. I . . . I've sort of found out . . . something."

"Fly over," he replied mockingly.

"Is that nice . . . when I want you?"

"Cherry Winters, every word you utter is a lie."

"No. I've stopped lying. Come and see."

"I tell you I'm as unmovable as these rocks!" he shouted in a tone that signified considerable strain.

He just imagined he was, thought Cherry, but still he might carry his stubbornness to a point of spoiling her little plan. Nevertheless, if she could not move him now, she would have the pleasure of keeping it secret longer.

"Stephen, dearest!" she called.

"You go to the devil!" he yelled, using her very words, but his tone was vastly different.

"My darling!" cried Cherry at the end of her rope. If that did not fetch him!

Heftral rather desperately jumped into the hole he had been digging. She could see his pick move up and down, with speed that implied tremendous effort. Cherry realized that her plan was useless for the time being, so she decided she had better husband her resources and attack him later. What she could not accomplish at such long range would be easy enough by close contact.

Whereupon she stepped out on the narrow strip. As she did so, for the first time, her eye caught the perilous depth and the jagged rocks far beneath. Cherry stepped back with a sudden cold sensation. Life might have grown singularly full all at once, but death was still only a step away. But she was not one to lose her head during excitement.

She crossed this dangerous bridge with coolness and courage, taking no chances, and unmindful of her sore knees. She made it successfully.

Heftral's back was turned. She approached and, hiding behind a large rock, peeped out at him. For what seemed long moments he did not look. But at last he straightened up and gazed around evidently to see where she had gone. Cherry took good care to keep hidden. She was tingling all over. He concluded that she had passed him and gone on out of sight. Then he sat down on the edge of the hole, removed his sombrero, and wiped his face. It was a most serious one. He sat there idle, lost in thought. How sad his expression. His trouble in this unguarded moment was there to read. Cherry conquered her impulse to rush out and tell him there were at least a couple of reasons why he should be tickled to death. But the moment gave her a glimpse into his heart. And it stirred Cherry so deeply, so strangely, that she wished to escape being seen by Heftral. At length, wearily and without hope, he looked again in the direction he supposed Cherry had taken, and then resumed his work. Cherry slipped away noiselessly and rounded the corner of wall without being seen.

Soon she yielded to a desire to sit down and think about herself. What had happened? She went over it all. Where had vanished the delight, the inexplicable joy she had anticipated? Heftral's sad face had checked her, changed the direction of her thoughts. She felt so sorry for him that she wanted to weep. Resuming her journey back to camp, she went on a little way, then stopped again. Something was wrong. Her breast seemed oppressed, her heart too full. She felt it pound. Surely she had not exerted herself enough for that. No—the commotion was emotional. She had sustained an unaccountable transition. She was no longer the old Cherry Winters. A last time she sat down to fight it out—to face her soul. After all—how easy. Only to be honest. For the first time in her life, she was honestly, deeply, truly in love. No need of wild wonderings, of whirling repudiations. She had fallen in love with this adventure, with the glorious desert, with the lonely soul-transforming cañons, and with Stephen Heftral.

The instant the solution flashed out of her brooding mind she knew it was the truth. It seemed annihilation of self-catastrophe, yet it held a paralyzing sweetness. Cherry received the blow to her consciousness, like a soldier, full in the face, while she was gazing down the cañon, now magnifying its gold and purple, its wonderful speaking cliffs.

Then she heard the thud of hoofs. A horse! Startled, she turned the corner of the wall that separated her from camp. Her alarm vanished in amazement at sight of a dudish young man dismounting from a pinto mustang as flashy as its rider. He wore a ten-gallon white sombrero that appeared to make him top heavy, white moleskin riding trousers, tight at the knees, high shiny boots and enormous spurs that tripped him as he walked. Cherry then recognized this young man, Chauncey Sarland, the darling of many weekend parties, a slick, dark, dapper youth just out of college. Also she heard more thuds of hoofs and voices coming. Anathematizing the luck, Cherry slipped in behind a section of rock that had split from the cliff, and ran along it to the far end, where she crouched down to peep through a crack.

Chapter Ten

Cherry was amazed, curious, resentful at this rude disruption of her rapture. Chauncey was a nice kid, but to meet him here! Where she was alone with Heftral.

Two riders appeared above the bulge of the bench, off to the left. One was an Indian, leading a pack horse. Presently Cherry made out the second rider to be a woman. Mrs. Sarland! No human creature could have looked more out of place, or uncomfortable, or ridiculous. Mrs. Sarland's marked characteristic had been dressing and playing a part to improve the family fortunes. Here, if Cherry had not been suddenly furious, she could have shrieked. They approached camp. The Indian dismounted and began to slip the pack. Chauncey went to his mother's assistance. Manifestly it was no joke to get her off a horse. She was heavy, and looked as if her bones had stiffened.

"Oh mercy! My muscles . . . my flesh!" she wailed.

"Cheer up, Mother. We're here at last," Chauncey replied with satisfaction.

"*This* is the place then?" she asked, peering around in disgust.

"Beckyshibeta."

"It looks like it sounds. I don't see much of a camp. Mister Winters said his daughter was here with some friends."

"Perhaps this is the guide's camp. We'll look around and find them. My word! It'll be good to see Cherry."

"Chauncey, our Indian is riding away!" Mrs. Sarland exclaimed in alarm.

"I understood he was going to see his family."

"Suppose he doesn't come back? Suppose we don't find Miss Winters and party. Here we are in a god-forsaken hole a hundred and ninety miles from a railroad. Nothing but a lot of wild Indians around. We may get scalped."

"You needn't worry, Mother," returned Chauncey. "You'd never get scalped. You can take off your hair and hand it over. I'm the one to worry."

"Chauncey Sarland! How dare you talk that way? You ought at least be respectful after my being good enough to let you drag me out here."

"Pardon, Mother," the youth said contritely. "I'm sore. This beastly trip through all that beastly desert. And no sign of comfort here. It's most annoying."

"Whose fault is it?" queried Mrs. Sarland as she carefully looked around a rock to see if there were snakes or bugs present. Then very wearily she sat down.

"Yours," young Sarland returned, looking at his drooping horse. "I suppose I'll have to remove that beastly saddle."

"My fault? You miserable boy!" exclaimed his mother, highly indignant. "You know I'm doing it all for you. Chasing this worthless Winters girl! I've suffered agonies on this ride. And that horrid place where we tried to sleep last night! Will I ever forget it? And this awful sunburn!"

"Cherry isn't quite worthless, Mother dear," rejoined Chauncey complacently. "Her dad has several millions. And Cherry is pretty well fixed. You know that's why you're here."

"There's gratitude for you," Mrs. Sarland declared witheringly. "Here I am trying to make it easy for you. You who've gone through most of your father's money. Now you make it appear I'm doing this for myself."

"All right. All right," Chauncey said impatiently. "But don't blame me for bringing you on this particular wild-goose chase. I didn't like the idea, believe me. I told you in New York that Winters was taking Cherry to a tourist hotel. That's what I believed then."

"Didn't you say Cherry told you her father was taking her into one of the loneliest places in the world?"

"I sure did. Mother, Arizona looks to me to be about half of the United States. And it's lonely all right. Imagine fine-combing this desert all to hunt up a girl. That fellow who charged a hundred dollars for a car ride that scrambled my insides. I'd like to get hold of him. Mother, I've an idea Winters and that trader Linn were laughing at us up their sleeves."

"*Humph!* That dirty-looking trader laughed in my face," asserted Mrs. Sarland. "And as for the wasting of a whole hundred dollars . . . that's your fault, too. You never knew how to bargain. You just throw money away. It drives me mad. You have no backbone, no stamina. Otherwise you'd have eloped with Cherry before her father ran off with her to this terrible place of rocks."

"Eloped! My dear Mother, you don't know Cherry Winters," returned her son significantly.

"Perhaps we'd better not talk so loud or mention names," remarked Mrs. Sarland apprehensively.

"Didn't you try to tell that Indian guide and the car driver our family history? Hello! Here comes a white man. Tough-looking customer."

"Oh, gracious, I hope he isn't a desperado," Mrs. Sarland replied in alarm.

This last from mother to son tickled Cherry so keenly that she was hard put to it to keep from hearty laughter. She peeped around the edge of her covert. Yes, Heftral was coming. He had spied the visitors, and he was peering everywhere for Cherry.

"How do you do," greeted Heftral as he came up. "Your Indian told me of your arrival."

"Very nice of him to find someone," returned Mrs. Sarland gratefully.

"Whom have I the pleasure of addressing?"

"Missus Percival Smith Sarland, of New York, and her son Chauncey. Of course you've heard of us."

"I regret to say I never have."

Cherry giggled inwardly at this slight, because she had more than once told Stephen about the Sarlands.

"Indeed. I see. You've never been away from this raw crude Arizona," replied Mrs. Sarland, apologizing for his ignorance. "Do many tourists come here to this Becky . . . something or other?"

"Very few. We don't encourage them."

"There, Mother. I told you so," broke in Chauncey, who had been staring hard at Heftral.

"Is there any resort for tourists near?" asked Mrs. Sarland.

"Linn's trading post is the nearest habitation of white folks. But you'd hardly call it a resort."

"I should say not. We stopped there to get ready for this trip. . . . May I ask your name?"

"Stephen Heftral, at your service, madam."

"Heftral? Surely that's the name we heard. You're an archaeologist, I understand."

"Yes, madam," Heftral returned shortly.

"Work for the government, don't you?"

"Yes."

"And you're *the* Mister Heftral. Well, I'm sorry for you. There's a Mister Elliott at the post now. He came the day we arrived. He's from Washington, D.C. I heard Mister Linn say he was furious that you had gone to this Becky-place before the time scheduled, and it would likely cost you your job."

"Mister Elliott at the post? Well, that is a surprise," Heftral returned, quite perturbed.

"I daresay. It's too bad. I'm sorry for you. But you might find decent work somewhere. You look stronger than those bowlegged cowboys."

"Thank you. Yes, I think I am rather strong. You spoke of cowboys. Were they . . . did you see any around the post?"

"Cowboys! I rather think so. They nearly rode us down. Stopped our car to keep us from being killed by stampeding cattle. One of them was tow-headed, and pretty fresh, to say the least."

"Cattle stampede. Oh, Lord," Heftral muttered in distress.

"What did you say?" asked Mrs. Sarland.

"I . . . I was just talking to myself," replied Heftral hastily.

"We are looking for Miss Cherry Winters and her party," Chauncey interrupted with importance. "I'll give you ten dollars to guide us to her camp."

"There you go, Chauncey Sarland, flinging money to the four winds," declared his mother.

"Miss Cherry Winters and party?" echoed Heftral.

"That's what I said," the young man returned testily. "Mister Winters informed me. I'm a very dear friend of Cherry's . . . in fact of the family."

"Did Winters say how many were in the . . . party?" inquired Heftral.

"No. I gathered there were several. People from the post. Where are they camped?"

"Not here. I have not seen any . . . party. Do you mean you've ridden all the way out here to see Miss Winters?"

"Certainly. Do you know her?" Chauncey replied suspiciously.

"I think I've seen the young woman," said Heftral dryly.

"You haven't. Any man who ever saw Cherry Winters wouldn't *think* he'd seen her. He'd never forget her."

"Oh, excuse me, perhaps I'm wrong. The person I saw was about twenty, and acted fifteen, and dressed as if she were ten.

Very coy and vivacious, and wild, I may say. She was not bad-looking."

"Miss Winters is strikingly beautiful, one of the loveliest girls in New York. Why Ziegfeld wanted to put her in the Follies," young Sarland declared grandly.

The expression on Heftral's face was something that made Cherry want to shout with glee.

Mrs. Sarland had been looking at the bits of broken pottery and stone utensils that lay carefully arranged on a flat rock.

"Is this the kind of bric-a-brac you dig for?" she inquired. "You appear to be careless with it."

"It's broken when we find it, madam. I could not be careless with such priceless relics."

"Priceless? That lot of junk!" Chauncey interposed in amazement.

"We would like to see a little of your . . . your place here," said Mrs. Sarland graciously. "Then I will engage you to find Miss Winters's camp for us."

"*Beckyshibeta* is very dangerous," returned Heftral. "You have to climb over rough rocks."

"Excuse me from climbing. But we'll take a look. Come, Son."

"I don't care anything about Bechyshib- or Beckysharp," responded Chauncey. "I want to see Cherry Winters."

"What? After our long journey out here to see this wonderful place?"

"You called it beastly before Professor Heftral dropped in," Chauncey replied scornfully.

"Oh, dear, this young generation. No appreciation of art or love of the beautiful."

"I'll have a look up the cañon to see if Miss Winters . . . and party . . . are camped near," Heftral said, moving away with Mrs. Sarland.

Chauncey at last bent himself to the task of unsaddling his horse, which performance defined his status as a horseman. Cherry, convinced that the Sarlands would find her sooner or later, preferred to surprise Chauncey. So she took advantage of his occupation with horse and saddle to run back the way she had come. Then she boldly turned around the corner. Sarland was sauntering here and there, inspecting the camp, plainly nonplussed. Presently he heard Cherry's step and wheeled.

"Oh!" Cherry cried, starting back.

"Cherry!" he burst out rapturously. "What luck! By heaven, I'm glad to see you!"

"Young man, you frightened me," returned Cherry. "What are you doing here?"

Suddenly his gaze took in her apparel and his eyes popped. Cherry had not realized until that moment what a scarecrow she really was.

"Cherry Winters! Some get-up you've got on. You look like a ballet dancer. Lord, Mother will have a fit. . . . Why, you're showing bared, dirty, red knees!"

"See here, young fellow, you're pretty impudent."

"Why all the bluff, Cherry?" he asked with a laugh. "It's great to see you again, even if you are a sight to make Fifth Avenue weep." He approached her with outstretched arms and unmistakable intention.

"Don't you dare. I'll yell for my husband," cried Cherry.

"Husband?"

"I said my husband."

"Cherry Winters with a husband? Impossible!"

"I'm Missus Stephen Heftral, wife of the archaeologist in charge of the excavation here. You impudent young upstart!"

"Wife? Stephen Heftral? Good God! But you're Cherry Winters. Your father said you were here."

"You're crazy. Who are you and what are you doing here?"

"No, I'm not crazy, but you are."

Cherry pointed imperiously down the cañon. "Take your horse and get out of here."

"Cherry Winters, you can't stall me like that," he replied hotly. "I've come clear across the country to rescue you from your father. This is what I get! This is how I find you! It has a darned queer look!" His eyes held a sharp suspecting glint of anger and jealous doubt.

"Poor boy," Cherry said solicitously. "You must have gotten away from your keeper. There. There. Run along and find him."

Chauncey pointed to Cherry's left hand. "If you're Missus Heftral, where's your wedding ring?"

"In the years I've lived here with my husband, I never saw the like of you," declared Cherry. "Either you're an escaped lunatic or a college freshman trying to impersonate Tom Mix. I'm going to call my husband."

"Go ahead. It'll be great when Mother claps eyes on you. Cherry, it's your wheels that are twisted, not mine." Then he seemed to become genuinely concerned. "You know, Cherry, you do look strained and queer. My God! You might have lost your memory. Cherry, you used to smoke too much!"

Cherry backed away, trying to elude him, but he got in front of her.

"No, you won't escape that way. I'm going to make you remember."

"Let me by!" Cherry cried wildly. She was really possessed with an infernal glee. What would Stephen say to this? "Get out, or I'll have my Stephen decapitate you."

"Cherry, dear, you're strange. Your eyes. Try to concentrate. I'm Chauncey. Chauncey Sarland. Something terrible has been done to you or you'd remember me and how I love you. Why I couldn't hurt a hair of your lovely head."

Cherry kept maneuvering for a loophole to dodge through.

"If you touch me, I'll scream!"

Chauncey made a lunge and captured her, and, before Cherry could thwart his intention, he had grasped her hand and looked at her ring. "There! You *are* Cherry Winters. I know that diamond as well as if it were my own. It was a present from your father."

"Stop mauling me," cried Cherry, breaking free from him. "I don't know you. I never saw you in my life! I'll bet you're one of those movie-mad boys and you're trying to steal my ring."

"You do it well, Cherry, if you're not truly mad. There's a nigger in the wood pile here, young lady, and I'm going to drag him out."

Indeed there was, Cherry thought, and never in her wildest flights of imagination could she have planned anything so good. She almost wanted to hug Chauncey for happening along at this opportune hour. Then voices drew Chauncey's attention and he hurried to meet Heftral, of whom Cherry caught a glimpse among the cedars. She ran up the rock slope to hide in a niche where she could not be easily discovered. When she got herself satisfactorily crouched, she peeped out with eyes that fairly danced. This was better than any comedy-drama she had ever seen. Chauncey and Heftral were approaching. Plain it was that Heftral was extremely annoyed or pretending to be. He had a sort of baffled look. His sweeping gaze about camp explained to Cherry one of the reasons he was so concerned. She wondered what had become of Mrs. Sarland.

Chauncey viewed the desert camp in dismay. "I'll be damned!" he ejaculated.

"Will you please produce the young lady?" demanded Heftral stiffly.

"She's gone."

"My dear young fellow, she was never here."

"I tell you she was," Sarland retorted angrily. "Cherry," he yelled. "You come back here. This has gone far enough."

"I agree with you," said Heftral.

"She was here. I talked with her, though she denied she was Cherry. She looked awful. Her clothes were soiled and torn . . . dress up to her neck. Most disgraceful! And either her reason's gone or she's a clever actress."

At this point Mrs. Sarland appeared, red and puffing, and evidently of ruffled temper.

"Chauncey . . . this Mister Heftral . . . talks strange," she panted. "He left me a few minutes ago most unceremoniously. There's no other camp. Cherry isn't here."

"Yes she is, Mother. Or she was a moment ago," Chauncey asserted positively. "But now she's gone."

"Gone! Where?"

"I haven't an idea. She just vanished."

"Why don't you find her? You've chased her long and far . . . why not a little more? My son, you act queer."

"There you are," interposed Heftral with exaggerated conviction. "Why don't you chase this hallucination of yours? I'm sorry indeed to see a fine young fellow like you, laboring under mental aberration."

"What?" snapped Chauncey.

Heftral turned to Mrs. Sarland. "Have you ever had your son under observation or *er* . . . examined, you know?"

"You . . . you . . . commoner! How dare you!" burst out Mrs. Sarland.

"Really, I don't mean offense. If he *was* all right, then it's the long ride, the heat, the loneliness of the desert. These things act powerfully upon some persons, especially any who are not strong mentally and physically."

Chauncey strode forward to confront Heftral with dark and angry mien. "See here, sir," he said, "cut that stuff. You're trying to string me. But you can't do it. I tell you there was a girl here not ten minutes ago. If she wasn't Cherry Winters then I *am* out of my head. But it was Cherry, and it's *she* who is crazy. She doesn't know who she is. She forgot she's engaged to marry me."

"Engaged to you!" Heftral ejaculated, taken aback.

"Yes, to me. Ask Mother."

Heftral turned bewildered with a voiceless query.

"There was an understanding between my son and Miss Winters," replied Mrs. Sarland. "No formal announcement, but all their friends knew."

Heftral seemed stunned.

"Look here, Heftral," Chauncey spoke up suddenly. "Are you a married man?"

"Certainly not," replied Heftral, surprised into the truth.

"So! That's it!" Chauncey shouted triumphantly. "I've a hunch you're a damned villain. Wait until I find that girl!" He rushed to and fro, and finally disappeared around the corner.

"Missus Sarland, don't you think I had better stop him?" queried Heftral in real concern. "This cañon is a big place. He could get lost or fall off a cliff. He's so slim, he could almost slip down into a gopher hole."

"I don't care what happens," Mrs. Sarland complained. "I'm overcome at this shocking turn of affairs. I'm beginning to think Cherry Winters was here. The fools men make of themselves over that girl. . . . I wish I'd never come to your miserable old ruin. I'll crumble myself before I get away."

"Courage, madam. All is not lost!"

"Stop calling me madam," replied the woman testily. "My name is Missus Sarland."

"Pardon. . . . Shall I endeavor to locate your son before he . . . ?"

Chauncey hove in sight at that moment high up on the shelving rock. Cherry had caught sight of him before the others, and she tried to melt into the niche. But she was a little too substantial. Part of her protruded and young Sarland saw it.

"Aha!" he shouted, leaping down the slope. Cherry wanted least to show her face, because she was fighting a wild laugh, but, as soon as Chauncey laid rough hands on her, she blazed with wrath.

"Here you are. Come out of it," he said exultantly. "Hey, you down there. I've found her."

"Let go of me, you nincompoop!" cried Cherry.

"You shameless thing! No wonder you can't face me. . . . Out you come!"

"Let go! Stephen!" Cherry shrieked as Chauncey dragged her out. She wrenched free to glare at him.

"Sarland, I'll knock your head off!" Heftral called loudly.

"So *he* is your party?" sneered Chauncey in jealous contempt. "I'm on to you, Cherry Winters. This beats any stunt you ever pulled back East. Came out West for a real kick, eh? Won't it sound sweet back home?"

"Yes, and you'll be just about the kind of fellow to blab it," retorted Cherry.

"Come on down here. You've got to face them," he said, snatching at her.

Cherry resisted until he was pulling her off her balance, and then she had almost to run to save herself. Sarland did not release her even when they reached a level. In fact, he dragged her in a most undignified, if not actually brutal way, toward his mother.

"Stephen!" Cherry cried in pain and mortification.

Heftral intercepted Sarland and gave him a resounding slap that was certainly equivalent to a blow. Sarland went down in a heap. His grand sombrero rolled in the dust.

"You blackguard!" Mrs. Sarland screamed. "To strike my son! You'll suffer for this."

Chauncey got tangled up in his long spurs and with difficulty restored his equilibrium.

"Say, you confounded young jackass," Heftral declared coolly. "If you touch this lady again, I'll take a real crack at you."

"Don't hit him, Stephen," interposed Cherry, trying to recover her humor. "I don't want his death on my hands."

Then ensued an awkward silence. Chauncey went from white to red. He brushed the dust from his immaculate riding breeches, and picked up the huge velvet sombrero. Meanwhile, Mrs. Sarland was staring in wide-eyed recognition at Cherry.

"Well, Mother, do you know the young lady? Was I right or wrong?"

"Right, my son," snapped Mrs. Sarland.

Whereupon Chauncey turned to the others. "Cherry, I've got the goods on you," he said. "You needn't take the trouble to keep up the farce any longer. What I can't understand is that your father should tell us you were here."

"I can't understand that, either," Cherry replied soberly.

"He must have guessed it and hoped I'd rescue you," went on Chauncey. "Or else he saw you were gone beyond redemption."

"That probably is it, Chauncey," Cherry said with sweet meekness.

Heftral appeared the most uncomfortable of the four, although Mrs. Sarland was getting ready to explode.

"Anyway, it's too late," concluded Sarland with bitterness. "Heftral, you told me you were not married. 'Certainly not,' you said."

"Yes, I . . . did," Heftral returned haltingly, as if his mind was not working.

"There! Cherry, *you* swore you were Missus Stephen Heftral, didn't you?" went on the accuser, bolder as he recognized he had the whip hand.

"Yes, I did," Cherry returned, bending terrible eyes upon Stephen.

"*Miss* Winters!" burst out Mrs. Sarland in accents of horror. "You're here with this man *alone*?"

"Yes, but not willingly, Missus Sarland," Cherry answered with profound sorrow. "He kidnaped me."

"Kidnaped you? Good heavens! Then he isn't what he pretends to be?"

"Indeed he isn't."

"Desperado . . . Wild West villain sort of man?" she whispered huskily.

"Worse than that."

Chauncey had turned pale at this revelation. His distended eyes, fast upon Heftral, denoted both fear and anger. "Your name isn't Heftral?" he queried apprehensively.

"Looks as if my name is Dennis," Heftral returned, coming out of his stupefaction.

"Chauncey, the truth is he is Black Dick, a notorious character hereabouts," explained Cherry.

"Black Dick! I . . . I heard about him from the driver," rejoined Sarland apprehensively. "But, Cherry, why did you try to deceive me about yourself? Why didn't you tell me in the first place who this man was?"

"It was the shame . . . the ignominy of it all, Chauncey," she said, enjoying Heftral's discomfort. "I knew he'd drive you off and I thought I could get away with that story. I'd rather have died out here than have anyone know."

"And he actually kidnaped you?"

"Well, I just guess he did. Ambushed me when I was in camp with friends on the way here. He caught me alone. Seems he followed all the way from the post where he'd been watching me. He grabbed me. I fought with all my might. But he was too much for me. Tied me on a horse. Oh, it was awful! Look at these black-and-blue marks. These are nothing to others I have that I . . . I can't very well show you. I had to ride a whole day and night in the most terrible storm. When we got here, I was more dead than alive."

"By Jove, it's like a book!" ejaculated Chauncey. "Kidnaped you for ransom? Heard about your dad's wealth, of course?"

"No, Chauncey, it isn't money he's after," declared Cherry. "I imagined that at first. And I offered to give him everything from ten to a hundred thousand dollars. But the brute would only laugh and kiss me again. Swears the minute he saw me at the post he went mad over me."

Chauncey's consternation and fright were strong, but he laughed—hysterically—nonetheless. He rocked to and fro. "Ha! Ha! Ha! Ha! It was coming to you . . . Cherry Winters! Drove him mad? Ha! Ha! He's only one of many. Prefers kissing you to a hundred thousand bucks! By golly, you've finally got the kick you were always longing for!"

"Chauncey, I deserve all I'm getting," Cherry rejoined, sadly resigned.

"Why didn't your father get word of this? What is the matter with your friends?"

"I think they must have been captured by Black Dick's outfit and are being held."

"My God! And . . . and where is Heftral, the archaeologist? They said he was here."

Cherry managed a convincing moan. "There was a Mister Heftral, a wonderful man, but now he's . . . he's gone, and there's nobody but this vicious desperado left."

Chauncey turned white. "You mean . . . ?"

"Hush!" Cherry almost screamed. "Don't remind me!"

All this time Heftral had been standing near, gazing at them and absorbing the fantastic dialogue. He had assumed a most ferocious aspect, and Cherry, after a second glance, thought it was genuine. At this juncture, the Indian guide who had brought the Sarlands appeared riding through the cedars. Heftral strode to intercept him and spoke some Indian words in very loud and authoritative tones. The rider wheeled his horse and disappeared the way he had come.

"Look," whispered Cherry. "I told you. He's driven off your guide."

"Cherry, I'll beat it and fetch a horse back to save you," Chauncey whispered, breathless with the excitement of the idea, and he made for his horse.

"Chauncey! Don't leave me!" screamed Mrs. Sarland, who had been listening, pale and mute up to this minute.

Heftral also espied Sarland, and vigorously called him to come back. But Chauncey only went the faster. Whereupon Heftral pulled his gun and fired in the air.

Bang! Bang!

"Come hyar," roared Heftral, "or I'll make a sieve out of you!"

Mrs. Sarland gave a loud squawk and promptly fainted. Chauncey ran back, very wobbly and livid.

"D-don't kill me . . . Mister Dick," he implored. Plain it was the two shots had brought him realization.

"All right then, but no monkey business," Heftral growled, flipping up the gun and returning it to his belt. "You better look after your mother. I reckon being strong-headed doesn't run in the family."

Whereupon Heftral strode in the direction of Cherry. She saw him coming and went in the opposite direction. Heftral caught up with her at the corner of the wall.

"Something of a mess, isn't it?" he said quietly as he detained her.

Cherry sat down upon a flat rock and fastened solemn eyes upon him. There did not seem to be need of further pretense, for she was really distressed, yet she not only welcomed the facts of the case but also meant to keep on accentuating them.

"Stephen, you have ruined me," she said tragically.

"Oh, Cherry, it can't be as bad as all that," he protested.

"Why didn't you acknowledge me as your wife?" she asked.

"My God! How could I ever dream you'd say that? Sarland asked me if I was married. And I said certainly not. He suspected, of course, and I was fool enough to fall into his trap."

"Chauncey knows many of my friends. He will tell."

"But he said you were engaged to marry him!" ejaculated Heftral.

"Piffle! I never was. How could you believe it?"

"I'm afraid I could believe almost anything of you," he returned in bitter doubt.

"That has been evident all along," she replied, aloof and cold. "But it does not mitigate your offense. . . . It might be possible to keep Chauncey from talking. But not Missus Sarland. She's an old gossip. This little escapade of ours will kill her ambition to see me Chauncey's wife. She will get it through her thick head that it always was impossible. And she'll take her vindictiveness out on me. She'll ruin my reputation."

"How can she?" Heftral asked miserably. "I thought modern girls didn't have reputations to lose."

"That's an hallucination of yours and my father's. Granted a certain freedom and license of modern life, it's true all the same that there are still limits. We've transgressed the most vital one."

"Not you, Cherry. I'm to blame."

"That'll do me a lot of good, I don't think," rejoined Cherry dismally.

"But maybe we can carry out this idea of me being Black Dick. He's well-known on the reservation. Travels around with a half-breed Paiute. They've been known to hold up tourists.

Perhaps I can carry the bluff through."

"You can try, surely. But in my opinion it's a forlorn hope. Besides, the cowboys will trail us. You heard what Missus Sarland said. The cowboys evidently changed their plans."

"Your father . . . *er* . . . or something may put them off the track," Heftral said lamely.

"Father? Why, man alive, he'll *send* the cowboys after me!" exclaimed Cherry. "I declare I don't know where your wits are."

"If I ever had any, they vanished when you appeared on my horizon. So did my peace. And now, I may add, my character, too, is gone."

"Rubbish! What is disgrace nowadays to a man?" Cherry retorted with supreme contempt. "You ran off with a girl! It'll never hurt you. It'd make you more attractive . . . after I divorce you!"

"Divorce me?" Heftral echoed feebly.

"Certainly. You'll have to marry me, at least, to make this stunt of yours halfway decent. Then I'll get a divorce."

"But if the Black Dick bluff should go over?" he asked with a ray of hope.

"OK for the Sarlands," replied Cherry. "But I was thinking of the cowboys and the Linns, after the Sarlands go. We can't fool those sharp-eyed Westerners. However, they may hang you. And I suppose that would save my reputation, if not the notoriety."

"Hang me! I wish to God they'd come and do it," returned Heftral. "I'm surely at the end of a rope right now."

"No such luck," sighed Cherry. "You may come out of it scotfree. The woman pays."

"I . . . I'm most desperately sorry," Heftral said, wringing his hands. "I'd like to have . . . somebody . . . here to choke. But it can't be so bad. We'll fool or muzzle these Sarlands. As for the Westerners . . . well, they're not so free at gossip and Arizona is a long way from New York. You will. . . ."

"Stephen, don't jolly yourself," interposed Cherry. "You've ruined me irretrievably."

Cherry wished to drive this point home. Truthfully she did not consider he had done anything of the kind, although this escapade had the closest call to ugliness of any Cherry had ever experienced. She might be clear enough to get around it. For the present, however, she worked to make it appear very black and hopeless to Heftral. She appeared to be having fair success, for he swore under his breath, and, sitting down, he covered his face with his hands.

"You're a fine brave kidnaper and desperado," said Cherry. "Don't let the Sarlands see you look like that."

He took no heed of her banter. "I've ruined you . . . and . . . and what am I? When Elliott's word reaches headquarters, I'll be done for."

"Well, suppose you are fired. You can go on your own. Wouldn't it be better for you to discover *Beckyshibeta now* than when you were employed by the government?"

"You talk like a child," he replied wearily.

"Why?" Cherry inquired in lofty surprise. "I think I'm pretty gracious, considering."

"What do I care about *Beckyshibeta*?" he burst out with sullen passion. "When you step out of my life, there will be nothing left."

This was sweet incense to Cherry. Almost it made her softer and yield to the clamoring voice within.

"That is sad . . . if true," she returned with proper pity and constraint. "But you have only yourself to blame."

"Bah!"

"I respected you once . . . liked you," went on Cherry in merciless sweetness. "Now you have made me . . . hate you."

"I could expect nothing else," he said, lifting his head with dignity. "I am not asking your pity . . . or even your forgiveness."

"Oh, as to that, of course I could never forgive. One thing you've done, an angel herself could not forgive . . . though I don't quite fit into that category."

"Not quite," he responded dryly, and stood up, hard and stern. "But what's to be done? We're up against these confounded friends of yours."

"It'll be best to keep them here," replied Cherry. "Until something turns up. Carry on the Black Dick bluff. Let's see what an actor you can be."

"I'm no actor. I couldn't deceive a child."

"You deceived me," protested Cherry. "I imagined you gentle, kind . . . the very opposite to what you are. Be natural now. Be a brute to me, like you were. I'll play up to it. And make these Sarlands pay for butting in on our . . . what shall I call it? . . . our cañon paradise. Be a monster to Missus Sarland, and scare the everlasting daylights out of that fortune-hunting young sheik."

"That last will be easy," Heftral replied grimly.

Chapter Eleven

Heftral's preoccupation with himself interfered with his acting a part. But that very grim aloofness made him the more convincing and mysterious to the Easterners.

Chauncey was a picture of astonishment when he espied Cherry staggering into camp under a load of firewood.

"Don't you do it, Cherry," he said. "I'll get the wood." And leaving his mother, who importuned him to stay, he started off with Cherry.

"Hyar, girl, don't go traipsing out of my sight with that jackass," growled Heftral in so natural a tone that Cherry knew he was not masquerading.

Then while Chauncey went off alone, Cherry approached Mrs. Sarland.

"I've money and jewelry on my person," stated that lady nervously. "Isn't that ruffian liable to steal them?"

"Sure. He'll search you presently," affirmed Cherry.

"Search me!" gasped Mrs. Sarland.

"I should smile," replied Cherry cheerfully.

"Has he searched you?"

"Not yet. But anyone could see I couldn't hide anything. I've so little on."

"If he does I'll . . . I'll expire in my tracks," Mrs. Sarland declared, and she looked it.

Heftral yelled for Cherry to come back to the fire.

"Does he mean me, too?" asked Mrs. Sarland.

"You'll know when he means you. And for heaven's sake, obey him quick. He's an awful brute. Nothing for him to give you a good sound cuff."

"The unspeakable monster! Of all acts . . . to strike a lady. He should be flayed alive. . . . He strikes you, then?"

"Oh, often. I've learned to mind him promptly, and to keep my eye on him when he isn't occupied."

"What a horrible situation!" exclaimed Mrs. Sarland. "I see him eyeing me now. My crimes have found me out!"

"Girl, come hyar!" yelled Stephen loudly.

Cherry hurried back to Heftral, who continued, still in a loud voice: "What're you plotting with that old dame?"

"I was only sympathizing with her," replied Cherry.

Chauncey appeared, carrying a few sticks of firewood, and in a manner to avoid soiling his moleskin riding breeches.

Heftral noted this and glared. "Huh! 'Fraid of dirtying your pants," he snorted, and he snatched up a blackened frying pan and wiped it brusquely on Chauncey's breeches.

That, for the present, however, appeared to be the limit of Heftral's duplicity. He forgot again and lapsed into silence. Cherry helped him get supper. She was having the time of her life, with only one trouble, and that was to hide this fact. She found it no easy matter to look dejected and frightened when she felt actually the opposite. She certainly could stand this situation for a while. It would only grow more absorbingly funny and thrilling as time wore on. The Sarlands were completely taken in. They were scared out of their wits. Cherry realized that for the time being her reputation had been saved. But what if the cowboys came? Or anybody who really knew Heftral? Cherry groaned at the very idea. She was somewhat dubious about the reaction of the cowboys, especially Wess, to this kidnaping stunt of Heftral's. But so long as they did not resort to violence, she imagined their advent would heighten the interest. Cowboys, however, were an unknown quantity to her. It was quite possible that even she could not stop them in dealing what they might believe was summary justice to an offender of the desert creed.

"Come and get it," called Heftral most unwelcomingly.

"Get . . . what?" asked Mrs. Sarland, startled. The suggestion in those words and tone did not strike her happily.

"Grub . . . you tenderfoot!"

Heftral's mood had not hindered his capacities as a good cook, a fact to which the Sarlands, once set down to the meal, amply attested. For Cherry, aside from satisfying honest hunger, the meal was otherwise a considerable success. Conversation was lacking until toward the end of supper, Heftral told Mrs. Sarland she would probably starve to death and have her bones picked by coyotes.

"I opened your pack," he added by way of explanation. "You must have been going on a day's picnic."

"That Indian ate most of ours," ventured Chauncey.

"We can always get sheep," Heftral said to himself.

After supper he ordered the Sarlands to make their beds at the foot of the rock slope. Chauncey asked and obtained permission to cut some cedar brush to lay under their blankets. Heftral gathered firewood, while Cherry rested aside, dreaming and watching. When the shadows of the cañon twilight stole down, accentuating the loneliness, Heftral stalked away.

"What a strange desperado!" exclaimed Mrs. Sarland. "I think he must have been someone very different once. That fellow has breeding. A woman can always tell."

"Black Dick is the most gentlemanly outlaw in these parts," replied Cherry. "Despite his habit of cuffing," she added hastily.

"Cherry, I apologize for all the nasty remarks I made," said Chauncey. "If we get out of this alive . . . why, everything can be as it was before."

"Ah-huh," returned Cherry dreamily. Nothing could ever be the same again. The future and the world had been transfigured prodigiously. But she wanted the present to last, even if she were compelled to stand for more love-making from Chauncey Sarland. The young man, however, was still a little too perturbed over Black Dick to grow sentimental.

"Where does he sleep?" Mrs. Sarland asked anxiously.

"Black Dick? Oh, when he sleeps at all, it's right here by the fire. But he's an owl."

"Where's your bed?" asked Chauncey.

"Mine is high up on this ledge behind," replied Cherry.

"Couldn't you let Chauncey fetch it down by ours?" inquired the mother.

"Black Dick might not like that."

A bright campfire dispelled the gloom under the cliff if not that in the minds of the captives. Cherry, at last, stole away to be alone. Her heart was full—full of what she knew not. Yet some of it was mischief and a great overwhelming lot was a deep rich emotion that seemed strange and stingingly sweet. It threatened to take charge of her wholly; therefore, rebelliously, finding it real and true, not to be denied, she compromised by putting off resignation until later. Very difficult was it to crush down this feeling, to resist the most amazingly kindly feelings toward the Sarlands, to scorn forgiving her poor old dad, who had erred only in his love for her, and to fight off generally an avalanche of softness.

What could be expected to happen?—that was the question. Heftral had settled down to a waiting game, and he would stick there if they all starved. After all, he had been tempted into this thing; there were excuses for him, though, of course, no excuse whatever for the atrocious punishment he had meted out to her. The mask of night hid Cherry's blush, but she felt its heat. Contemplation of that would not stay before her consciousness.

Indians might drop in upon them, or tourists, or sheepmen, or possibly roving riders of doubtful character. The possibility of any or all of these occurrences was remote, but anything could happen. The cowboys would surely come. Cherry wanted that, yet she feared it. There was no hope of Heftral keeping up his deception for any considerable length of time. So Cherry was in a quandary. She desired the Sarlands to have a right good scare and leave Arizona under the impression they now entertained. She wanted dire and multiple punishments to fall upon Heftral's head. If it pleased her to assuage them later, that was aside from the question. If he could be reduced to abject abasement, to want really to be hanged, as he said, to drink the very bitterest cup of repentance, then would be the time for her denouement. For although he had not the slightest inkling, even the remotest hope, of the gratification of his two driving passions, Cherry knew. Cherry herself had done the discovering of *Beckyshibeta* and of the true state of her heart, but that did not make them any the less his. What a profound thought! Cherry trembled with it. There was a bigness about these discoveries that began to divorce her from the old Cherry Winters. She would, she must have her revenge; she fought this subtle changing, as it seemed, of her very nature. She still hated, but the trouble was she could not be sure of what. Cherry sighed. Oh, what a fall this would be! Cherry Winters, on a pedestal of modern thought, freedom, independence, equality—crash!

Nevertheless, despite everything, Cherry sought her bed, happy. For a while she sat on the ledge and gazed down into the circle of campfire light. Mrs. Sarland and her son huddled there, keeping the blaze bright, whispering, gazing furtively out into the black shadows, obviously afraid to seek their beds. Presently Heftral strode out of the gloom. Cherry tingled at sight of him. She marveled at herself—that any man could make her feel as she did. Pretty soon she must inquire into this state of mind that could revel in the presence of any male creature.

"Madam, the hour grows late," Heftral declared harshly, to the cowering woman. "Must I put you to bed?"

Whereupon Mrs. Sarland, exclaiming incoherently, made hasty retreat to her bed, which was under the ledge out of Cherry's sight.

"Young fellar, you sit up and keep watch," continued Heftral as he unrolled his camp bed near the fire. "And remember, no shenanigans. I always sleep with one eye open."

When Cherry took a last look, Heftral lay prone in the fire light, assuredly asleep, and Chauncey was nailed to the martyrdom of night watch.

The shadows flickered above Cherry on the stone wall, played and danced and limned stories there. If she could have chosen, she would rather have been here in this bed than anywhere else in the world. But all the strangeness and sweetness of the present at *Beckyshibeta* could not suffice to keep her awake.

Cherry's slumbers were disrupted by a loud voice. Heftral was calling his captives to breakfast. Cherry sat up and made herself as presentable as possible. The face that smiled at her from the little mirror did not require any paint or powder. It was acquiring a beautiful golden tan. Her eyes danced with delight.

She went down to breakfast. Heftral did not glance up, at least while she was close. She was glad for he easily could have penetrated her thin disguise. Chauncey was heavy-eyed and somber, and Mrs. Sarland was a wreck.

"Good heavens, you look like you've slept," was Mrs. Sarland's reply to Cherry's greeting.

"I sure have," Cherry returned, and forthwith went at her breakfast with a will.

"Lord preserve me from another such night," Mrs. Sarland prayed fervently. "I lay on the rocks . . . turned from side to side. My body is full of holes, I know. Mosquitoes devoured me. Some kind of animals crawled over me. I nearly froze to death. And I never closed an eye."

"That's too bad," replied Cherry. "But you'll get used to it after a while. Won't she, Mister Black Dick?"

"Wise men say a human being can get used to any kind of suffering, but I don't believe it myself," the supposed outlaw astonishingly replied, with his somber accusing eyes piercing Cherry in a fleet look.

"Mister Black Dick, you were a better man once?" Mrs. Sarland ventured almost with sympathy.

"Yes. Much better. I was ruined by a woman," he replied.

This startling revelation enjoined silence for a while, which was broken by the sound of hoofs cracking the rocks.

"Indians coming down the cañon," said Heftral, who had arisen.

"Oh, gracious! Are they hostile?" cried Mrs. Sarland.

"Well, about half friendly Navajos," returned Heftral.

Three picturesque riders rode from the cedars into camp. One of them, particularly, caught Cherry's eye, as he dismounted in a sinuous action. He was tall with a ponderous head that made him appear topheavy. He wore brown moccasins, corduroy trousers, a leather belt with a large silver buckle and shields, and a maroon-colored velveteen shirt. His huge sombrero with ornamented band hid his features, but Cherry could discern that his face was red.

"Better eat while the eating is good," warned Heftral.

Then he spoke to the Indians in Navajo. Their actions then signified that he had asked them to partake of the meal. Cherry was glad she had about finished hers. The meat, the biscuits, the potatoes disappeared as if by magic. Mrs. Sarland, who had filled her plate, but had scarcely tasted anything, appeared electrified to see her portion of breakfast disappear with the rest. To do the Indians justice, however, she was not holding the plate at the moment. She had set it on a rock by the campfire.

"Ugh," grunted the big Indian after each bite.

Heftral had made fair-size biscuits, but one bite sufficed for each.

"That wretch appropriated all my breakfast," declared Mrs. Sarland, astounded and angry. Evidently she took it for granted that these Navajos could neither speak nor understand English.

"Of all the hogs." ejaculated young Sarland. "Mother, that Indian made away with nine biscuits. I counted them."

"Mister Dick said they were half friendly," complained Mrs. Sarland. "I declare I don't see it."

Heftral contrived in an aside to whisper to Cherry: "That big Indian is smart. Keep your mouth shut and for that matter stay right here."

"Don't worry, Stephen," whispered Cherry. "I'll stay in camp. What's his name?"

"The cowboys call him Ham Face."

Presently Cherry had an opportunity to get a good look at him. The sobriquet was felicitous. He certainly had a face that resembled a ham. But it was also a record for desert life. Cherry could not decide whether he was young or old. He had great black eyes, piercing and bold, yet somehow melancholy. There were sloping lines of strength and he had a thoughtful brow. Seating himself before Mrs. Sarland, he spoke to her in Navajo.

"What'd he say?" she asked, half fascinated and half frightened.

"Missus Sarland, I regret I do not translate Navajo well," replied Heftral. "But he wanted to know something or other about why you wore men's pants."

Cherry did not believe a word of that. She could tell when Stephen was lying.

"The impudent savage!" ejaculated the woman indignantly.

Ham Face addressed her again, gravely, with a face like a mask.

"He wants to know if you are any man's squaw," explained Heftral.

"Mother, you've made a conquest," young Sarland laughed.

That affronted his mother who got up from beside the Navajo and left the campfire. Ham Face followed her, much fascinated evidently, by her general appearance. It was to be admitted, Cherry thought, that Mrs. Sarland in tailored riding breeches, much too small for her portly figure, was nothing, if not a spectacle. When she became aware she was being followed, she grew greatly perturbed, and hastened this way and that, though not far from the others. Ham Face pursued her.

"What's the fool traipsing after me for?" she cried.

Finally in sheer fright she came back to the seat beside her son, and sat there fuming, tapping the ground with her boot. Ham Face continued to walk around her and study her with grave eyes.

"Talk about the noble red men!" she exclaimed. "They're abominably rude. . . . Why don't they go away?"

The three Navajos appeared to be in no hurry. Ham Face kept devoting himself to Mrs. Sarland, while the other two smoked cigarettes and talked in low tones to Heftral. Cherry had taken refuge behind the packs, from which only her head protruded. Chauncey was interested despite his alarm. At length Ham Face's attention to Mrs. Sarland became so marked that the nervous high-strung woman burst into a tirade that might have been directed at the whole Indian race.

Ham Face imperturbably lighted a cigarette and blew a puff of smoke upward. "Pardon me, Madam, if I seem to stare," he remarked in English as fluent as her own. "But you are the most peculiar-looking old lady I've seen. I'd like to introduce you to my squaws. When I was in New York and Paris, during the war, I met some modern up-to-date women, but you've got them beaten by a mile!"

Mrs. Sarland's jaw dropped, her eyes popped, and with a gasp she collapsed. Cherry, standing behind the packs, stuffed her handkerchief in her mouth to keep from shouting in glee. Ham Face was assuredly one of the educated Navajos to whom the cowboys had referred.

After that he ceased annoying Mrs. Sarland, but presently, after an enigmatical look at Cherry, he joined Heftral and his two comrades near the horses. They conversed a little longer. Then the Indians mounted and rode away. Ham Face turned to wave a hand at Mrs. Sarland.

"*Adiós,* little Eva!" he called.

When they disappeared, Mrs. Sarland came out of her trance.

"That long-haired dirty ragged savage!" she raged. "To think he understood every word I uttered, and then talked just like a white man. . . . He added insult to injury. Oh, this hideous Arizona with its lying traders, cowboys, Indians, outlaws, and pitfalls! Oh, my son, my son, get me out of this mess."

"Mother, I've a feeling the worst is yet to come," replied her young hopeful.

Cherry got up from where she had sprawled, and tried to catch Heftral's eye. But his face was averted and he stood motionlessly in a strained attitude of one listening.

"What is it?" whispered Cherry.

"I thought I heard a horse," he replied. "Not the Indians. It came from down the cañon."

"Hands up!" rasped out a hard voice from behind them.

Cherry stood paralyzed. She saw Heftral extend his arms high, and then slowly turn. His ruddy tan fled. "My God . . . it's really Black Dick himself," he breathed huskily.

Cherry's heart skipped beating and then leaped. Turning, she saw two men in rough rider's garb. The foremost was heavy and broad, with what seemed a black blotch for a face. He held a gun that was pointed at Heftral.

"Howdy, Professor," he said. "Jest stand steady-like while Snitch gets your gun."

The second man, a little red-faced, red-headed, bowlegged person, with a greasy, blue leather shirt, appropriated Heftral's weapon, and then very deftly his wallet.

"Hum. Looks flatter'n a pancake to me," said the robber, eying the latter with disdain. "Wal, mebbe these hyar tenderfeet will be better heeled."

Mrs. Sarland and Chauncey stood, rigid, with hands high and startled expressions.

"Reckon Willie White Pants ought to have a lot of money, an' if he hain't, Missus Hatchet Face will."

A swift search of Chauncey brought to light a few bills of small denomination and some change.

"Wal, if he ain't a two-bit sport!" exclaimed the leader in disgust. "All them fine togs an' no yellow coin. Say, lady, have you any money an' vallables?"

"Not h-h-here," stammered Mrs. Sarland. It was plain that not only was she lying but very frightened.

" 'Scuse us, lady, fer gettin' so familiar when we ain't even been introduced. I'm Black Dick, from the border, an' this hyar pard of mine is Snitch Jones."

"Oh, my! There are *two* Black Dicks," groaned Mrs. Sarland.

"Wal, there's only one real Black Dick an' I'm the gent," the robber returned with lofty humor.

"He calls himself Black Dick," burst out the woman, dropping a weak hand to point it at Heftral.

"Y-yes . . . so . . . he does," Chauncey corroborated impressively.

"The hell you say. Wal, now, I call that complimentary. But, folks, he was only joshin' you. Mabbe havin' fun with my rep."

"You . . . you mean he isn't Black Dick and you are?" faltered Mrs. Sarland.

"Precisely an' exactly, lady," Black Dick returned amiably.

"Who is he, then?"

"Wal, I ain't sure, but I think he's Stephen Heftral. The cow-men hyar aboot call him Profess or Bone Digger."

The guilty archaeologist dropped his hands with a laugh and sat down abruptly. Cherry realized that the cat was out of the bag. Chauncey forgot to be scared and bent glances of reproach upon Cherry and fury upon Heftral.

"Impostor! Liar!" Mrs. Sarland burst out.

"Wal, I'll be dog-gone!" Black Dick ejaculated with mild interest. "Snitch, somethin's up hyar, an' I've a hunch it's amoozin'. But we mustn't forget to collect all vallables fust."

"Fork over, mum," Snitch said, thus admonished, his eager hands extended,

"I . . . I tell you I've nothing," Mrs. Sarland replied weakly.

"Search her, Snitch," ordered Black Dick sternly. "Hey, lady . . . keep them hands up."

Whereupon the little red-headed ruffian went at Mrs. Sarland with an alacrity and verve that made Cherry nearly choke, while at the same time she felt misgivings as to what might happen to her.

"Aha! Hyar's a lump of somethin' that feels heavy an' sounds moosical," announced Snitch, slapping at Mrs. Sarland's hip pocket.

"You thieving, lecherous . . . scoundrel!" Mrs. Sarland screeched.

It must have positively hurt her to see that fat jingling bag brought to light. Snitch burst it open. Greenbacks, gold coins, jewelry!

"Whoopee!" yelled the little robber. "It's a haul, boss. This hyar lady shore didn't bulge all over fer nothin'."

"Business is lookin' up," remarked Black Dick with satisfaction. "Now, Snitch, hand all that over to me, an' have a look at this gurl. Looks to me she'd have a million . . . if you jedge by eyes. . . . Ain't she a looker?"

As Snitch approached Cherry, grinning, eager, full of the devil as well as greed, she suddenly lost half of that emotion under which she had been laboring. This was not so funny.

"Stephen!" she cried. "Don't let him touch me."

"Be sensible, child. They've held us up," admonished Heftral.

Cherry slipped off her diamond ring and stretched it out at the length of her arm and let it drop in Snitch's palm. "That's all I've got. Honest," she said earnestly, in the stress of wanting to escape those rude hands.

"Little gurl, you don't look like a prevaricateer, but we jest can't trust you," Black Dick stated soothingly.

"Peaches, if you run it'll be the wuss for you," Snitch added, reaching for her.

His touch, following the devilish little gleam in his eye, inflamed Cherry. With one wrench she tore free and struck at Snitch with all her might. A quick duck of head just saved him.

"Whew!" he ejaculated, astounded and checked.

"Wow!" added Black Dick in gleeful admiration. "She strikes like a sidewinder, Snitch. If that one had landed you've hev knowed it. . . . Wal, now, what a fiery wench!"

Cherry blazed at the leering astonished robber. "You damn' little beast! If you touch me again, I'll knock off your red head!"

Black Dick guffawed uproariously, while Snitch, though he joined in the mirth, took her seriously.

"Who'd 'a' thunk it, boss?" he said. "Look at that tight little fist an' the way she swings it."

"Wal, I reckon I'm noticin'," the leader said, sheathing his gun and approaching. "We gotta be gennelmen, you know, Snitch. See hyar, mighty little gurl, are you tellin' us true? You hain't nothin' on you but this ring?"

"That's all," returned Cherry, breathing hard.

"Wal, turn round fer inspection," he ordered. Cherry did as she was bidden.

"Do it again, an' not so damn' fast. This ain't no merry-go-round."

Whereupon Cherry, realizing that she was to escape indignity, careened for their edification like a dress model in the Grande Maison de Blanc.

"Peaches, you ain't got a whole lot of anythin' on," Snitch remarked fervidly.

Black Dick surveyed her with the appraising eyes of a connoisseur.

"Wal, sweetie, I reckon if you had a dime hid on you, I could see it," he concluded with finality.

Chapter Twelve

"Say, you're gettin' too big a kid fer sech short dresses," Black Dick observed disapprovingly to Cherry.

"We were caught in the rain and my clothes shrunk," explained Cherry.

"Reckon you're about sixteen years old, hain't you?"

"Oh, I'm a little more than that." Cherry dimpled, very much pleased.

"How much?"

"Several years."

"*Humph!* No one would take you fer a grown girl. I'm afeared your mother hain't brought you up right . . . lettin' you run around with your fat knees all bare."

"Fat? They're not fat," retorted Cherry, promptly insulted.

"Excuse me. Wal, they're bare. You can't deny that. An' after I give your ma a lecture, I'll give you one," concluded Black Dick. "Snitch," he said to his lieutenant, "you go diggin' around an' see if thar's anythin' more wuth takin'."

Thereupon he confronted the dejected and crushed Mrs. Sarland. "Look ahyar, lady," he began, "your gurl says she's eighteen years old. An' I'm tellin' you she hain't been brought up decent. Wearin' sech clothes out hyar in the desert. Why, it ain't respectable. An' it ain't safe, neither. You might meet up with some *hombres* thet was not gennelmen like me an' Snitch."

Mrs. Sarland was spurred out of her apathy into a wrathful astonishment that rendered her mute.

Black Dick evidently saw that he had made a profound impression. "I took her fer a kid, like them I see in town, wearin' white cotton socks thet leave their legs bare," he said. "An' hyar she's of age. There ought to be somethin' done about it. You ought to be ashamed of yourself to let your dautter run around like thet."

"My daughter?" burst out Mrs. Sarland furiously. "That flapper! Not much! She's no kin of mine."

"Excoose me, lady. I had a hunch she was sister to this dude you've got with you," Black Dick returned coolly. "Come to think aboot it I might have knowed from her looks."

Snitch approached at this moment, carrying sundry articles he had taken from Mrs. Sarland's saddle. One of them was a light handbag, which Black Dick promptly turned inside out. It contained gloves, handkerchief, powder puff, cosmetics and like articles, and also a magazine with a highly colored front page. The robber kept this and returned the other things.

"Snitch, you poke around some more," he said laconically, and turned to Cherry. She, from her perch on the packs, had expected this and prepared herself with sad face and tearful eyes.

"Wot's your name?" he asked.

"Cherry."

"Kind of suits you somehow. . . . Wot you cryin' aboot?"

"I'm very scared and unhappy."

"Scared? Of me?"

"Oh no. I'm not afraid of you. I think you're a *real* man. But these people have kidnaped me . . . to get money out of my father."

"Ah-huh. Wot'd this fellar Heftral pretend he was me fer?" Black Dick asked, growing more and more curious.

"I suppose to intimidate me. But he wasn't a bit like you."

"So thet old bird is a kidnaper?" mused Black Dick darkly.

"An' Heftral's been roped in the deal. Wal, this is funny. And, say, Miss Cherry's not a flapper?"

"A flapper is a young chicken just trying its wings," Cherry said.

"Shore. I ain't so dumb as I look. But the old lady there called you a flapper, an' the way she said it struck me more'n that."

"Indeed it is," Cherry responded feelingly. "Flapper is a name given us young girls by nasty, jealous people. They say a flapper is not good . . . that she swears, flirts, drinks, smokes . . . and worse. That she's to blame for the indecent style of clothes these days . . . which is a lie . . . that she won't obey her parents or go to church or be satisfied with one husband . . . or . . . or anything."

"Wal, I'll be dog-goned," Black Dick said with sympathy and disdain. Cherry was tremendously delighted to observe that Heftral was listening. "Shore are a lot of mean people. Now I'm only an old desert pack rat, snoopin' round when I get broke, but I could see you was a nice girl. I was jest throwed off a little by your dress bein' so short."

"Thank you, Mister Black Dick," said Cherry, thinking that never had she received more sincere approval.

"Wal, we'll see wot can be did with this old hen," said the robber. Then he happened to notice Heftral sitting there as if he had not a friend in the world.

"Say, Heftral, my Navvy friends tipped me off aboot these pickin's. And what were you up to? Don't you reckon it's dangerous pretendin' to be me? There are men who'd shoot at you fer it."

"I never thought of that at the time," Heftral returned, lowering his voice. "The honest truth is I was just in fun. And I'm not so sure it was all my idea."

Then they got their heads together and conversed in such

low tones that Cherry could not hear any more.

"Boss, there ain't any more stuff worth hevin', onless it's the grub," announced Snitch, coming up. "Some orful fancy eats."

"Well, I've a grand idee," said Black Dick, slapping his knee, and he winked one of his great bold black eyes at Cherry. "We're goin' to have aristocracy cook for us."

Whereupon he approached Mrs. Sarland with a slow rolling step, his sombrero cocked on one side of his head, his right thumb in the armhole of his vest, and his left hand holding onto the magazine.

"Lady," said Dick grandly, "you're goin' to be honored by cookin' a meal fer Black Dick. An' if you don't do your best, I'll feel it my boundin' duty to tote you off an' larn you how."

Mrs. Sarland fell back with horror in her face.

"I like my wimmen with spunk," went on the desperado. "Could you larn to cuss, an' toss off a drink, an' kick me in the shins?"

"Merciful heavens . . . no!"

"Wal, then, you cook an' Whitepants hyar can be cookee. Rustle up some firewood. . . . An' now, sister, waddle along. An' mebbe I'll let you off."

"Beast!" Mrs. Sarland screamed, and she ran toward the campfire.

"Cook dinner then, you two!" yelled Dick. "An' don't be all day aboot it."

Cherry had observed that these men, despite the earlier action of robbing the party, and their later antics, took occasion now and then to gaze up and down the cañon. The younger one, Snitch, was particularly keen. These outlaws expected someone to come along or else were just habitually cautious and watchful.

Black Dick and Snitch sat down close together, with the magazine on the former's knees. They had the air of guilty gleeful schoolboys about to partake in a thrilling and forbidden act. They made a picture Cherry would never forget, and reminded her of the mischievous cowboys. All these natives of Arizona had some inimitable Western quality, the keynote of which was fun.

Dick's huge dirty hands turned the pages, until suddenly they froze, then the bent heads grew absorbed.

"Jerusalem!" ejaculated Dick.

"Ain't she a looker!" exclaimed his comrade raptly.

They turned a page and giggled. Then Black Dick looked up, swept the immediate horizon, and, happening to see Cherry, he waved a hand, as if to tell her to go away far back somewhere and leave them to their joy. Dick turned another page, and they whispered argumentatively. Another page brought a loud gasp from Snitch and something that sounded very much like an oath from Black Dick. Then they were as petrified.

"My Gord!" finally burst out Dick. "Snitch, do you see wot I see?"

"I'm lookin' at thet lady in the Garden of Eden," Snitch replied, breathing heavily.

"She hain't got a damn' thing on," Dick said in consternation. "Say, this must be gettin' to be an orful world."

"Wonder who tooked thet picture," returned Snitch. "It had to be tooked by a fotoggrapher."

"It says so . . . an' a man at thet. Shore I wouldn't been him fer a million dollars."

"I'd tooked thet picture fer nuthin'," said Snitch.

Black Dick continued turning the pages, very slowly, as if he expected one of them to explode and blow them to bits.

"Wal, hyar's somebody with clothes on . . . sech as they are," he observed presently.

"Actress. Not so bad, huh? You'd get a hunch there ain't any men in New Yoork."

"Men don't cut much ice nowheres," Dick said shrewdly. "When Eve got thick with thet big snake, they fixed it so men did all the work, or become tramps like us, or went to jail."

"Dick, it ain't so long ago when the pictures we seen . . . most on them cigarette cairds . . . was wimmen in tights," Snitch said reminiscently.

"Shore, but it's longer'n you think. You can bet there ain't nothin' like that these days. The world is goin' to hell."

"Hold on," interposed Snitch, halting Dick's too impetuous hand. "Heah's a nice picture."

"Nice? Snitch, you was brought up iggnorant. Thet ain't nice. Can't you see it's two girls in a room? They're half undressed an' smokin' cigarettes. Turrible fetchin', but shore not nice."

"Read what it says."

Black Dick took time to go over the page cautiously before he committed himself. Finally, tracing with a big finger, he began haltingly. "Clara (between dances). 'Mabel . . . why . . . did . . . you . . . stop . . . wearing . . . corsets?'

"Mabel. 'I . . . had . . . a couple . . . of complaints.' "

Black Dick looked up at Snitch, and Snitch returned the glance, then went back to the page. "What you make of that?"

"Complaints? Somebody didn't like them corsets of Mabel's."

"Wal, supposin' he didn't?"

Switch jerked up, scintillating with sudden brilliance. "Don't you savvy? It says 'between dances.' They was a dance. Har! Har! Har!"

"Wal, the durned hussy," Dick exclaimed, exasperated. "Switch, this hyar all ain't so damned funny. Thet's the furst readin' I've did since the war. Wal, time changes everythin'. . . . But, Snitch, we ain't so bad off. Shore, we're often hungry an' oftener broke waitin' fer a chanct like this, an' we're dirty an' unshaved, with a few sheriffs lookin' fer us . . . but I'm damned if I'd change places with any of them people . . . even thet photoggrapher. Would you?"

"Nary time, Dick. Give me a hoss an' the open country," replied Snitch, rising to take a look up and down the cañon. Black Dick's ox eyes rolled and set under a rugged frown. Evidently in the magazine he had been confronted with a mysterious and perplexing world.

Cherry decided about this time that this desert rat several sheriffs were looking for was not half a bad fellow.

Presently Mrs. Sarland called them to the meal she had been forced to prepare. She was very red and there was a black smudge on her nose, but she faced them with confidence. Snitch let out a whoop and alighted on the ground with his legs tucked under him—a marvelous performance considering the long spurs. Black Dick surveyed the white tablecloth spread upon the tarpaulin and the varied assortment of cooked and uncooked food.

"Wal, if I ain't dreamin' now, I'll have a nightmare soon," he said, and squatted down. Snitch had already begun to eat. Dick, observing that he had not unfolded his napkin, took it up and handed it to him.

"Wot's . . . thet?" Snitch asked with his mouth full.

"You ignorramus. Sometimes I wonder if your mother wasn't a cow. . . ."

"Wal, I never had indigestion or colic, but I'm goin' through hyar if it kills me."

Cherry had seen hungry cowboys eat, to her amazement and delight, but they could not hold a candle to these outlawed riders of the range. Their gastronomic feats were bewildering, even alarming to see. Not a shadow of doubt was there that Mrs. Sarland had served concoctions cunningly devised and mixed to make these men ill, if not poison them outright. Sandwiches, cakes, sardines, cheese, olives, pickles, jam, crackers, disappeared alike with hot biscuits, ham, potatoes, and baked beans. When they had absolutely cleaned the platter, Black Dick arose and quaintly doffed his sombrero to Mrs. Sarland.

"Madam, you may be a disreputable person, but you shore can hand out the grub," he said.

Snitch had arisen, also, but his attention was on the far break of the cañon, where clouds of dust appeared to be rising. "Look at that, pard," he said.

"Ah-huh. Get up high somewheres, so you can see," returned Dick, and strode toward the horses that had strayed to the cedars. When he led them back, Snitch had come down from the ledge.

"Bunch of cowpunchers ridin' up the cañon," he announced.

"Wal, we seen 'em furst," his comrade said, mounting. Then he surveyed the expectant group before him. "Madam, I reckon I'll never survive thet dinner you spread. Heftral, if you ain't in fer a necktie party, I don't know cowpunchers. Miss Cherry, so long an' good luck to you. Chauncey, if we ever meet again, I'm gonna shoot at them white pants."

He rode away. Snitch, swinging to the saddle, flashed his red face in a devilish grin at Cherry.

"Good bye, Peaches!" he called meaningly. "I'd shore love to see more of you."

Spurring his horse, he soon caught up with Black Dick. Together they rode into the cedars and disappeared up the cañon.

"Thank God, they're gone!" Mrs. Sarland cried, sinking in a heap. "Gone with every dollar . . . every diamond I possessed! Chauncey Sarland, you will rue this day."

Cherry had been realizing the return of strong feeling. It did not easily gain possession of her at once. There was a contest in her mind, which went down before memory. The cowboys were coming. And that recalled the bitter shame and humiliation Heftral had heaped upon her. She positively writhed at recollection of the spanking he had administered. Something sharp and stinging had attached itself to that memory. The farther away from it she got, the more bitter and mocking it returned. How impossible to forgive or forget! The anger within her was like a hot knot of nerves suddenly exposed. She hated him, and the emotions that had developed since were as if they had never been.

"Mister Heftral, the cowboys are coming," she said significantly, turning to him.

"So I heard," he replied curtly. He looked hard and he was slightly pale. Perhaps he appreciated more than she what he was in for. Cherry was disappointed that he did not appeal to her. But she would only have mocked him and perhaps he knew that.

The dust clouds approached, rolling up out of the cedars. Crack of iron-shod hoof on rock, the crash of brush, and rolling of stones were certainly musical sounds to Cherry. There was something else, too, but what she could not divine. She knew her heart beat fast. When Wess rode out of the cedars, at the head of the cowboys, it gave a spasmodic leap and then seemed to stand still. How strange a thought accompanied that. She wished they had not come. They did not appear to be a rollicking troupe of gay cowboys; they were grim men. It was very unusual for these cowboys to be silent.

Wess halted his horse some little distance off, and his companions closed in behind. His hawk eyes had taken in the Sarlands. Cherry noted what a start this gave him. She heard them speaking low. Then Wess dismounted, gun in hand. That gave Cherry a shock. This lout of a cowboy, who she could twist around her little finger, seemed another and a vastly different person. They all slid off their horses.

"Reckon Heftral's got a gun, but he won't throw it," said Wess. "Wait till I . . . see who these people are."

He strode over to confront Mrs. Sarland and Chauncey.

"Who are you people?" he asked bluntly.

"I am Missus Percival Sarland, of New York, and this is my son Chauncey," she replied with dignity.

"How did you get heah?"

"We employed an Indian guide."

"How long have you been heah?"

"It seems a long time, but in fact it is only a couple of days."

"What'd you come for?"

"We *used* to be friends of Miss Winters," returned Mrs. Sarland significantly. "We heard at the post she was out here, so we came . . . to my bitter regret and shame."

"Who else has been here?"

"Two miserable thieving wretches," burst out Mrs. Sarland. "Black Dick and his man. They robbed us."

"Reckon they saw us an' made off *pronto*?" went on Wess, his keen eyes on the ground.

"They just left . . . with all I had," wailed Mrs. Sarland.

"You're lucky to get off so easy," Wess said curtly. "You found Miss Winters an' Heftral alone?"

"Very much alone," the woman replied scornfully. "He had kidnaped her."

"That's what *she* says," interposed Chauncey with sarcasm.

"Ah-huh. I savvy," Wess replied fiercely. "You're intimatin' Miss Winters might have come willin'?"

Chauncey was about to reply, when one of the cowboys, whose back was turned and who Cherry could not recognize, slapped him so hard that he fell off the rock backward.

"Wal, you better keep your mouth shet about it," Wess said with a wide sweep of arm shoving the belligerent cowboy back. "Thet shore won't save Heftral."

"Oh, this awful West!" screamed Mrs. Sarland. "You're all alike. Cowboys . . . robbers . . . traders . . . Indians . . .

scientists! You're a mob of deceiving bloody villains."

"Madam, I reckon it ain't goin' to be pleasant around heah. You an' your dandy Jim better leave *pronto.*"

"Leave! Where and how? That man drove our guide away. We can't saddle and pack horses, and much less find our way out of this hellish hole."

"Take yourself off then, out of sight," he continued harshly, and turned to come toward Heftral and Cherry, his gun low, but unmistakably menacing. Lorenzo, Mojave, Zoroaster, and Tay-Tay came striding after him. The musical jingling of their spurs did not harmonize with their demeanor.

Wess fixed Cherry with a cold penetrating stare. She realized that for him, as a glorious entity—a girl to worship—she had ceased to exist. This job of Heftral's had ruined her with Wess beyond redemption. Cherry was afraid to look in the faces of the others, for fear she would see the same condemnation. It was a sickening conception. It added fuel to the fire of her roused wrath at the perpetrator of this situation.

"You beat it," Wess ordered with a slight motion of his gun, signifying that Cherry was to get out.

"What for?" she asked sharply.

"This heah ain't no place for a . . . a woman," he replied. He was going to say lady. Cherry saw the word forming on his lips, but he changed it. She was no longer an object of respect, even to these crude cowboys. Her spirit flamed at them, at herself, at Heftral.

"After what I've gone through, I can stand anything. I'll stay," she said heatedly.

He gave her a strange glance. What eyes he had—like hot blades! No man had ever dared to look at her with such unveiled disillusion.

"Heftral, stand up an' stick out your hands," ordered Wess.

The archaeologist looked up, disclosing a dark set face and

eyes that matched the cowboy's. "You go to hell," he replied coolly.

"Fellars, jerk him up off thet pack an' tie his hands behind him."

This order was carried out nearly as quickly as it was said. Heftral was a bound man. The sight seemed to add a raw fierce something to Cherry's mood. She was answering here to unfamiliar feelings.

"Thanks," returned Wess, "but I ain't aimin' to go where you belong. . . . We don't care pertickler to heah your musical voice, either, but if you're any kind of man, you'll say whether you kidnaped Miss Winters or not."

"Certainly I did, you knuckle-headed cowpuncher," retorted Heftral.

"You heah thet, boys?" Wess called imperiously.

"We shore heerd him!" yelled the others as one man.

Cherry's augmenting excitation almost precluded her usual observations and calculations. Her own position had been so unreal that it was hard to judge anything else without bias or doubt. These cowboys, particularly Wess, were most singularly unlike any men Cherry had come to know. Was it that she had been struck by a rawness and hardness in them—traits that had not been brought out before—or were they just a little too . . . too something to be absolutely genuine? But despite these thoughts, she began to feel hot and cold by turns.

"Fetch a lasso," ordered Wess, dragging Heftral forward. "An' look fer a cedar high enough to hang this guy."

They moved off in a body toward the cedars, leaving Cherry almost paralyzed. She saw them stop under one of the first trees. They were talking in low tones. Evidently Heftral spoke. The cowboys guffawed in ridicule. Then Mrs. Sarland and Chauncey hurried up to Cherry.

"What are they going to do?" Mrs. Sarland panted.

"Hang him," whispered Cherry in awe.

"Serve him quite right," declared the woman, nodding in great satisfaction. "If only they had that dirty Black Dick, too."

Cherry broke from her trance and ran the short distance to the group. She heard the Sarlands following. Cherry would have been at her wit's end without the fright that had inhibited her. Certainly she would have to do something. If she gave way to a growing idea that the situation was beyond her—what might not happen? She gathered there had been an argument between Wess and the cowboys, for she heard sharp words on each side, and then suddenly at her approach they were silent. Heftral appeared less upset than any of them. The look of Wess gave Cherry an icy chill. She had not been much frightened at Black Dick. But this lean-faced cowboy! All in a flash her hatred of Heftral and her unworthy passion for revenge were as if they had never been. She seemed as vacillating as a wind-vane.

"Wess . . . wh-what are you going to do to him?" she asked, struggling to control her voice.

"We're goin' to make it the last time this fake scientist kidnaps a girl," replied Wess.

"But . . . that rope! You can't really hang a man for so little. Why, you'd hang, too, if you did such a thing. There'd be an investigation."

"Real kind of you, miss, to worry aboot us," Wess returned ironically. "Duty and the law are one and the same in Arizona. By hangin' this fellar, we save the government expenses of keepin' him in jail."

"But he didn't do anything so . . . so very terrible," Cherry went on, still struggling.

"Look heah, young woman," Wess said, sharp and dark. "Heftral kidnaped you, didn't he?"

"Yes," admitted Cherry.

"Wal, thet's aplenty. But it shore wasn't *all* . . . now, was it?"

questioned the cowboy, his piercing suspicious eyes on hers. Wess was not to be deceived. His jealousy probed the secret and his naturally primitive mind made deductions.

Cherry blushed a burning scarlet. It was a hateful thing to feel before those keen-eyed boys who had revered her. It had as much to do with an upflashing of furious shame as the recollection of Heftral's one unforgivable indignity.

"Fellars, look at her face. Red as a beet!" ejaculated Wess passionately.

"Aw, Wess, cut it," burst out Mojave.

"Ain't you overdoin' it, Wess?" Zoroaster asked darkly.

"Y-y-y-you . . . ," Tay-Tay stuttered in unmistakable protest. But he never achieved coherent speech.

"Damn you all! Shut up!" Wess hissed in a deadly wrath. If his comrades meant to intercede on Cherry's behalf, at least to save her from insult, he certainly intimidated them for the time being.

"Miss Winters, you can't say honest that Heftral didn't mistreat you," asserted rather than asked Wess. He was a hard man to face and Cherry, strangely agitated, yet still not roused, was not equal to it. Besides, his words were like stinging salt in a raw wound.

"No matter what he did . . . you can't hang him," burst out Cherry.

Wess turned a purple. The other cowboys subtly changed.

"Wal, for gawd's sake!" bawled out Wess. "Ain't thet jest like a woman?"

"An' he stole my hoss, too," Mojave added darkly.

"But, Mojave, my father would buy you a hundred horses," Cherry spoke up eagerly.

"Say, miss, what's your father got to do with this?" demanded Wess. "He didn't steal the hoss. Heftral did. An' thet's as bad as stealin' you. 'Course Arizona has quit hangin' hoss thieves. But when you put the two together, why it's shore a hangin' case. Miss Winters, your friend Heftral ain't only a villain. He's a coward."

"I'm beginning to think a lot of things about you," retorted Cherry hotly. "And one of them is . . . you're a liar."

Wess flinched as if he had been lashed with a whip. His eyes burned and his face became like flint. "Wal, I ain't no kidnaper of girls . . . whether they're innocent or not," he said coarsely.

Heftral turned half around to look at the circle of cowboys behind him. "Fellows, I'll be perfectly willing to be hanged if you'll grant me one request."

"You talk to me," ground out Wess. "I'm boss of this rodeo. What you want?"

"I'd like my hands untied so I can beat your dirty loud mouth shut," replied Heftral ringingly.

Wess completely lost control of himself, and, lunging out, he struck Heftral a sounding blow, knocking him flat.

"Oh, you dirty coward!" cried Cherry. "To strike a man whose hands are tied!"

Mrs. Sarland screamed: "They're all outlaws, blacklegs, murderers!"

It was Tay-Tay who assisted Heftral to rise to his feet. Blood was flowing from his mouth.

"Mebbe thet'll keep your mug shet," declared Wess. He was proof against the withering scorn in Heftral's look.

"Say, Wess, this ain't gettin' us anywheres," interposed Mojave. "Mebbe we're far enough."

"Move along, Heftral," Wess ordered, shoving his gun into Heftral's side. He forced the archaeologist to walk on to a point under a high-branched cedar. "Somebody throw a rope over thet limb."

But nobody complied with this order. Again Cherry intuitively guessed that this situation had not been what it looked on the face. The cowboys were a divided group. Wess was deadly, implacable. No doubting his real intention! Cherry had sensed his jealousy and now realized his brutality. But another sharp scrutiny of the other faces convinced Cherry that with them it had been a well-acted jest, which Wess was trying to drive to earnest. But he would never succeed. Cherry racked her brain for some expedient to circumvent him.

Wess snatched the lasso from Mojave and threw the noose end over the branch, pulled it down, and with the skillful dexterity of a cowboy tossed the loop over Heftral's head.

"Thar's your necktie, Mister Kidnaper," he said with fiendish satisfaction.

Mojave seemed to pull himself together. Cherry caught his quick significant glance at Lorenzo, and she took her cue from that.

"Wal, I'm pullin' the rope," announced Mojave, stepping forward.

"Nothin' doin'. . . . I'm the little *hombre* who hangs this gent. It's my rope," replied Zoroaster.

"I weel pull the rope," Lorenzo said impressively.

"W-w-w-wh-where do I come in?" stammered Tay-Tay, evidently offended.

Cherry was now almost certain of her ground, except for the silent Wess. "Gentlemen, let me decide which of you shall have the honor of being the first to crack Heftral's neck," Cherry interrupted, with entire change of front.

They gaped at her, nonplussed. Wess's tense face relaxed to a slight sardonic grin. Cherry feared him. The majority would rule here. Besides, she had an idea.

"Let me decide, please," she continued.

"F-f-f-fair enough," said Tay-Tay.

"Pick me, Miss Cherry. I'm the strongest," entreated Mojave, who seemed to be returning to his natural self.

The others, excepting Wess, loudly acclaimed their especial fittingness for the job.

"I can't show any favoritism among you boys," went on Cherry. "Lay down your guns. Then blindfold me. I'll pick one of them up and whoever owns that gun shall have the first pull."

"Fine idee," declared Mojave, and then deposited his gun at Cherry's feet. One by one the others gravely complied, until it came to Wess. He held the lasso in one hand and his gun in the other. Cherry feared he would block her daring scheme, which was to get possession of all the guns and hold up the cowboys.

"Chauncey!" gasped Mrs. Sarland. "She's a barbarian! A fit consort for the likes of them! To think I ever allowed you to anticipate marrying such an impossible creature!"

"That'll be aboot all from you, madam," Wess retorted threateningly.

"Come, Wess, your gun!" Cherry called in a nervous hurry. "Who'll lend me a scarf?"

"You're smart, but you can't fool me," rejoined Wess darkly. "I don't lay down my gun fer no woman. I'm onto you, miss. . . . Now you easy-mark cowpunchers, jest step back. Stop! Never mind pickin' up them guns."

Slowly the cowboys edged back, and Cherry with them. At that moment Wess was infinitely more calculated to inspire fear than had been Black Dick. Wess had this game beaten and knew it. He exchanged rope and gun from one hand to the other. With a quick pull he tightened the noose hard around Heftral's neck, straining his body, lifting him a little.

"Reckon it's a doubtful honor, but I'll have it myself," he said, his cold eyes on Cherry.

"My God! Wess, you don't mean to go on with it?" cried Cherry, finding her voice.

"I shore do. I've got the goods on Heftral. You accused him, an' he confessed. Everybody present heard you both. An' there ain't a court in Arizona that'd hold me fer a day."

He was triumphant and malignant. Fierce jealousy had brought out the evil in him. Cherry had a terrible realization of her guilt—for she had flirted with this hot-headed cowboy. She had looked upon him with caressing eyes; she had listened to his sentimental talk and let him hold her hand. What an idiot she had been! Vain as a peacock, detestably bent on conquest—heartless, wrong. Wess resembled a devil and he certainly had overwhelming odds in his favor. Cherry seemed to be sinking in stupefied terror. Almost blindly she stepped out.

"Wess, for God's sake . . . don't . . . don't add murder to this . . . this thing," she implored.

"So! You're intercedin' fer a man you swore treated you out-rag-eous?" sneered Wess.

"Yes. I beg of you. Don't let your . . . your . . . whatever actuates you . . . go any further. Cool down. Think!"

"I've been thinkin' all right," he rejoined with brooding intimation.

"Heftral did not kidnap me," spoke up Cherry, gathering strength. "I came with him willingly."

"What's thet?" snarled Wess, almost crouching.

Heftral responded with his first show of perturbation. "Wess, don't you believe a word she says. She's trying to clear me by implicating herself."

"Wal, she's a liar all right, but mebbe this is straight," Wess said somberly. "Say, gurl, if you come willin' . . . what was it fer?"

"One reason was I wanted to get a kick out of it," replied Cherry coolly. "I was sort of blasé. Tired of ordinary life. I wanted something new, different."

"Ah-huh. An' how aboot this heah out-rag-eous treatment?" Wess asked gruffly.

To have saved Heftral's life Cherry could not have stayed the coursing flame of red that burned from neck to face. But her spirit flamed likewise.

"I disobeyed him," she confessed bravely. "He . . . he chastised me. . . . I deserved it."

"Haw! Haw!" Wess guffawed loudly, mirthlessly. That laugh contained bitter doubt, scorn, hate.

"Wess, I'm afeared I hear hosses," interrupted Mojave sharply.

"So, you come willin', huh?" he questioned with terrible eyes on Cherry. "Liked to be treated out-rag-eous, huh? Wanted a new different kick, huh? Wal, now watch your *lover* kick!"

Wess was a bully and a brute. But he did not know the fiber of the girl he had so grossly insulted. That was all Cherry required to find herself. As Wess bent down to stretch the lasso over his hip, dragging Heftral to the tip of his toes, she sprang forward. She grasped the tightening rope above Heftral's head and pulled it loose. Then she confronted Wess.

"Stop, you madman!" she cried imperiously. "Don't you dare. . . . If you do I'll *kill* you!"

"Wal, fer gawd's sake!" ejaculated Wess, surprised into his usual expression, and he momentarily slackened the lasso.

Quick as a flash Cherry seized the noose and flipped it from Heftral's neck. "Listen, cowboy!" she said. "What business is it of yours? If Heftral and I wanted to come out here to *Beckyshibeta* and lie about it that was *our* business. But it's gone too far for jokes now." Cherry backed up against Heftral and took his arm.

"Shore it's gone too far!" Wess returned furiously, recovering from his amaze. "An' you haven't give me one reason why he shouldn't hang."

"Very well, I'll try another," Cherry said with calm proud exterior, while inwardly she was in a state of exaltation. "I love him. Can you understand that? I *love* him."

For a long moment all her hearers seemed petrified. Wess

looked shocked into incredulous defeat. Then he choked out: "You white-faced hussy!"

"Shet up!" Mojave yelled sternly. "Heah comes Linn an' some Indians. Mister Winters, too. All ridin' like hell. Cool down, Wess, or you'll get yours."

Chapter Thirteen

The instant Cherry had a close scrutiny of her father's face, which was when he reined his horse before the group, she knew his gay greeting and nonchalant survey of them had no depth. He had always been a capital actor, but he could not deceive his daughter.

"Hello, Cherry!" he had called out, before reaching them. "How are you? Little white, aren't you, for a modern Amazon?"

Cherry's emotion, whatever its great extent, suffered a swift transition to fury. Nevertheless she had wit enough to remember that this was no time to play against her father. Her cue was to be miserable and happy at one and the same time. At that she need only be natural.

"Howdy, Stephen," Winters said genially, sitting his horse at ease and gazing down upon the center of this motionless group. "Bet you're glad I arrived. Sorry we are rather late. But that darned storm turned us back."

Cherry removed herself from such close proximity to Heftral. What had she said and done? She did not regret it, but the lofty spirit that had prompted it was failing. Heftral stood there, pale, with gleaming eyes and bloody lips, his hands still bound behind him. The noose that Cherry had thrown off dangled not far above his head. The cowboys stood on uneasy feet. Wess still held his gun, and it was manifest that a dim realization of his part in this farce had dawned upon him. He was sweating now.

The guns of the other cowboys lay where they had deposited them.

Winters surveyed this scene with the air of a Westerner of long experience. He was very cool. Then he espied the Sarlands, and doffed his sombrero.

"Good day, Missus Sarland. Hello, Chauncey. I hope you have had a nice little visit with Cherry and her fiancé."

If anything could have struck fire from Mrs. Sarland that speech might have done so, but she was beyond words. But Chauncey, now that danger had passed, showed an ugly temper.

"We've had a rotten visit, if you want to know," he howled. "We've been deceived, insulted, beaten, and robbed."

"Robbed! Oh, not quite that, I'm sure," replied Winters, laughing. "No doubt Heftral's a desperate character, but I can't believe he'd steal."

"We were held up and robbed by Black Dick and his partner," Chauncey continued hotly.

"All my diamonds . . . and money . . . gone!" wailed Mrs. Sarland.

"Indeed. That's too bad. It's something of a shock," returned Winters solicitously. "But I'll make your losses good. You see, I didn't calculate on a real desperado." Here he laughed. "It's all a little joke of mine. I wanted Cherry to have a scare. So I persuaded Heftral to run off with her. My plan was to send the cowboys the very same day. But they didn't get back, and, when they did, the washes were flooded by the storm."

"Somebody untie my hands!" called out Heftral, cutting and grim. "I'll show you what kind of a joke it was."

Mojave was the cowboy who complied with the request, and it was plain he was nervous. He whispered something to Heftral. But it did not prevent Heftral, the instant he was free, from making long strides to confront Wess.

"You're a skunk," Heftral said deliberately. "I always had you figured as a bully and a conceited ass of a cowboy . . . mushy over every girl who ever came out here. But not till today did I know you to be a dirty foul-mouthed scoundrel. You. . . ."

"Hold on, Heftral," Winters interrupted, aghast. "I told you I was to blame. Wess was only following my instructions."

"Heftral, we'll shore make allowance for your feelin's," added Linn conciliatingly. "But you're usin' strong language . . . too strong for a little joke."

"Joke, hell!" flashed Heftral. "This locoed cowboy meant to hang me!"

"Good God! Why, boy, you're quite out of your head," expostulated Winters.

Linn began to see something serious in the situation. And he took his hint more from Wess's face than Heftral's words. Slipping out of his saddle, he strode quickly to get between the men.

Heftral gave him a shove that almost upset him. "Don't you butt in. You're a little late to save me the rottenest deal any man ever got. And you're a lot too late to save this cowpuncher of yours from the damnedest kind of a beating."

"Man! Look out for thet gun!" warned Linn shrilly.

"I don't care for his gun," replied Heftral. "He wouldn't shoot a rabbit."

"Wal, I'd shoot a coyote damn' quick . . . or a gurl-chasin' scientist," Wess replied, laughing coarsely.

"Drop thet gun!" ordered Linn. "Can't you see Heftral is unarmed?"

"I'm takin' no more orders from you," the cowboy said sullenly.

"You bet your life you're not!" shouted the trader angrily. "But you throw thet gun on Heftral an' you'll have me to deal with."

Suddenly Heftral, in a pantherish spring, leaped upon Wess,

and caught his arm just as he was lifting it with the gun. Heftral threw all his weight upon that gun arm, forced it down. Wess struggled and, cursing, yelled: "Leggo, or I'll plug you!"

Heftral bent swiftly to fasten his teeth in the dangerous hand. The cowboy let out a howl of pain and fury.

Bang! Bang!

Cherry screamed and hid her eyes in horror. She heard the thud of feet and wrestling of bodies, then hoarse calls from the onlookers. Her heart seemed to burst. This awful farce was going to end in a tragedy. Heftral! Terror forced her to open her eyes. Wess had dropped the gun. The hand Heftral gripped was red with blood. On the instant Heftral gave the gun a kick. It flew to the feet of Mojave, who bent and snatched it up. Then Heftral, releasing Wess, struck him full in the face with a blow that sounded like a mallet. Wess went down with a sodden thump.

Nobody wasted any more words. The spectators were too intense for speech, and the contestants too mad with rage. Heftral seemed a man who once in his life had let go. Wess, as he bounded up like a cat, looked a demon.

He rushed at Heftral and the fight began. Cherry could not watch it, though now she had fascination added to her horror. But there was enough gentleness left in her to make her shrink instinctively. She stood there with hands pressed over her eyes. Though blinded she still heard. And the smash of fists, the scrape of boots, wrestling tussles of hard bodies in contact, the pants and whistles of furious breathing—these were worse to hear than to see. How must the battle go? Heftral, the gentleman, the mild-mannered archaeologist, would surely be worsted by a younger man and one inured to all the roughness of the desert. Crash! One of the fighters had been knocked into the cedar brush. He burst up again, bawling awful curses. Wess! What a hot tingling thrill Cherry had! It seemed to change her very nature. She wanted more than anything ever before in her life for Heftral to beat down the vile-mouthed cowboy. She had divined the cause of Heftral's white anger. It was because of Wess's bald insinuations. Heftral was fighting for her, to whip the cur before those onlookers who had heard. So it was impossible for Cherry to keep her eyes covered any longer.

She found she stood alone. The fighters had worked away up the bench. Even the Sarlands had followed the men. Cherry ran. She saw Heftral first, face turned toward her. He was all bloody and dirty. Then Wess's visage swept around into sight. He was horribly battered, his face resembling a bloody beefsteak. He lunged wildly. He had no science. Heftral was agile, swift, and when he struck out, he landed. Wess plunged down at Heftral's legs, caught them, and dragged him down. They clinched furiously, and rolled over and over, now one on top, then the other. Wess kicked viciously. It was clear that he was trying to dig his spurs into Heftral's legs. The cowboys yelled their derision of this further evidence of Wess's cowardly tactics. He must have imagined that a rough-and-tumble fight would give him the advantage. But it soon became clear that he was as badly off as in a fair stand-up fight. Heftral was out to give the cowboy a terrific beating, and it looked as if it would end that way.

Once, when in their rolling over Wess landed on top, he snatched up a dead branch, quite weighty, and brought it down hard upon Heftral's head, where it cracked into many bits.

"You scurvy dog!" yelled Mojave, who was now plainly Heftral's champion. "If you knock him out that way, you'll have me on you."

But if Wess heard, he paid no heed. He snatched up a rock and swung that.

"Drop it or I'll shoot your arm off!" shouted Linn, whipping out a gun.

The maddened cowboy tried to smash Heftral's head. Missed him! Linn meant to shoot, but obviously feared he would either kill Wess or hit Heftral. Then he grasped his gun by the barrel, meaning to hit Wess with it. The cowboy struck again with the rock. Heftral dodged, but was slightly hit.

"For God's sake, Linn, stop him! He means murder!" Winters called, frightened.

"Oh, Stephen . . . don't let him kill you!" screamed Cherry wildly.

Mojave leaped close to do something, no one could guess what. Mrs. Sarland collapsed in a faint. Heftral might not have been doing his utmost before, because his fury and strength became marvelous. With one powerful blow he knocked the stone flying out of Wess's hand. Another broke Wess's hold on his throat. Then he heaved mightily. He tossed Wess clear of him, and was on his feet as quickly as the cowboy. He rushed Wess. A blow stopped the cowboy. The next staggered him. Heftral swung his left—biff! Then his right—smash! Wess, who was falling at the first blow, shot down with the second as if it had been from a catapult. He fell headlong, and slid over the brink of the bench, to crash into the brush below.

Heftral glared a moment at the puff of dust that the cowboy had raised, then, striding to his pack, he picked up his towel and went off down the slope toward the creek.

Cherry was so tottering and weak that she sat down on a rock. Linn sheathed his gun.

"Wal, that was good," he declared in great relief. "I hope he broke his neck. Some of you boys go down and see. . . . Winters, Missus Sarland has fainted. No wonder. Thet came near bein' a real scrap. Young man, fetch some water, an' we'll bring your mother to."

Cherry sat dizzily conscious of the subsiding of the terrible emotions that had swayed her. Very slowly she recovered. Mrs.

Sarland was revived and lifted to a seat. Linn appeared very kindly and solicitous. Cherry's father wore a haggard look of remorse displacing fear. Chauncey, who hovered over his mother, showed the pallor of a girl, and hands that shook. Mojave was the only cowboy left on the bench.

"What in the hell happened?" Linn questioned sternly.

"Boss, I swear it was as much of a surprise to us as to you," Mojave began most earnestly. "The boys will back me up in that. . . . You know Mister Winters was awful keen on makin' this fake hangin' look like the real thing. We had our orders to do some tall actin' . . . like them motion-picture fellars. You can bet we had a lot of fun plannin' this. Talkin' it over. We must've *looked* terrible mad, as if we meant bizness. Wal, Wess acted so powerful good thet we all was plumb jealous. Even when he began to say nasty things we thought he was only oversteppin' a little. When he insulted Miss Cherry . . . then I was flabbergasted. Same with the other boys. Once I opened my trap, but Wess shet me up *pronto.* Still it was all so sudden I jest couldn't see through Wess until he called Miss Cherry a white-faced hussy."

"Ah-huh. Aboot time you seen through him, I'll say. Wal?" growled the trader.

"Then it all come in a flash," went on Mojave, breathing hard. "We was obeyin' orders . . . havin' an awful big kick out of it. But Wess wasn't actin'. He meant to hang Heftral. No doubt of thet, sir. He had it all figgered out an' knowed the facts would clear him in any court."

"But the damn' locoed idjet!" burst out Linn. "To hang Heftral in earnest! What on earth for?"

"Wal, I ain't shore. But I believe Wess thought Miss Cherry was his gurl," Mojave replied manfully, though it was evident he hated to be frank. "He shore talked like it. An' when he seen . . . wal, that he was what you called him, boss, why he went plumb out of his haid with jealousy."

"Ah-huh. Wal, I'm damned!" ejaculated Linn.

Winters had listened to all this conversation and now he turned to his daughter. "Cherry, you let that cowboy make love to you," he said. He did not ask; he affirmed.

"Dad, I did," replied Cherry bravely. It was confession that was accusation. "To my regret and shame . . . I did. I let him talk a lot of nonsense. Even let him hold my hand."

Winters evidently thought better of any severe arraignment of his daughter at that moment. The look on her face, the strain and content of her words told him much.

"Well, to allow your hand to be held is no crime," he said gravely. "But in this case it nearly led to murder. I hope it will be a lesson to you."

Cherry dropped her face into her hands and hid it. She actually shivered at his kindly reply, but burned inwardly with something that seemed to sear. Lesson! What lesson had she not had? She would be days accounting for them and their clarifying and transforming power. Now there was only one man in all the world whom she would allow to hold her hand. And would he want to?

Zoroaster and the other cowboys came back from below. "Wess's not crippled, sir," he reported. "Bad bunged up, but nothin' serious."

"Able to ride?" asked Linn tersely.

"I reckon so, if someone shows him where to go. Both eyes are swelled shet."

"Wal, let's see. The Indians can look after us. You boys take him back to the post. Tell Missus Linn to pay him off an' let him go. Clear out now. . . . An' say, boys, if you want to stay with me, keep mum aboot this deal. Not one little word. Savvy?"

They promised soberly, and, picking up their guns, they led their horses down through the cedars out of sight.

"Reckon we might as well stay heah fer a day or two, hadn't we?" inquired Linn of Winters. "The Indians will look after our horses, an' pack firewood. I can cook."

"Surely. I want to see this *Beckyshibeta.* Besides . . . ," replied Winters, who, happening to glance at Cherry, did not complete what had been on his mind to say. Then seeing Heftral returning, he advanced to meet him. He certainly got a cold shoulder from that individual. Standing blankly a moment, he threw up his hands, then stalked off tragically. Cherry had seen this little by-play. So had Linn, who was not above chuckling. This and Heftral's reception of her father did much to spur Cherry back to some semblance of a sane young woman.

"Wal, lass, it was an awful mess, wasn't it?" the trader said sympathetically as he seated himself beside Cherry.

"Mess is the word, Mister Linn," replied Cherry, finding her voice somewhat strained.

"Your father had good intentions," went on Linn. "But jumpin' horn toads! What a damn' fool idee. He never told me till it was all done, an' the cowboys on your trail. Shore I could have held them back, or come along. I thought somethin' was kinda queer. Sort of in the air. But, Lord, how could I guess it?"

"Don't apologize, and please don't be sorry for me," murmured Cherry.

"Aw now. . . ."

"What this . . . this mess has done to me I don't realize yet," Cherry interrupted. "But today has been terrible. . . . When I . . . I get my nerve back, I'll be all right. I don't blame Dad. He meant well. He wanted to give me a . . . a wholesome scare. I'll say he succeeded beyond his wildest hopes. . . . Still, it was my fault, Mister Linn. I can't crawl out. I must have driven poor Dad crazy. And that miserable cowboy, Wess. I don't know what to say. I . . . I wanted Heftral to kill him. Think of that!"

"Wal, I'd have shot Wess myself if I hadn't been leery of hittin' Heftral," said Linn. "Don't you waste too much pity on Wess. He's plain no good. I know a lot of things aboot Wess. He was a good man with hosses an' cattle. An' not a hard drinker. I've gotta say thet fer him. But Wess always was loony aboot girls. He wouldn't up an' marry one. No sir-ee! He always said he didn't want to be hawg-tied. . . . Wal, I reckon he had a genuine case over you."

"As far as Wess is concerned . . . and that terrible fight . . . I am solely to blame," confessed Cherry, almost choking. "It makes me deathly sick. Mister Linn, I . . . I made a fool of. . . ."

"Never mind, lass," interposed the trader, putting a rough, kind hand on hers. "I heard what you said to your Dad. You're game, as we say in the West, an' takin' your medicine. You jest didn't savvy cowboys, much less a dangerous *hombre* like Wess. We're lucky it didn't turn out bad. Heftral shore was chain-lightnin' when he woke up, wasn't he? Wal, I reckon, after all, the most dangerous men are the quiet, deep ones. I'll never get over the surprise he gave me, though. . . . Now, you pull yourself together. Reckon I'd better look up your Dad."

With that Linn arose, and, giving the Indians some instructions, he strode off in the direction Winters had taken. Cherry felt that she had pulled herself together, in a sense, though she was far too wise to trust herself yet. Still, she had to go about facing things, and she chose the hardest first. She went up to Heftral. He had changed his stained, torn shirt for a clean one, and washed the blood from his cut and bruised face. And he did not appear such an ugly sight as she had anticipated.

"Stephen, it was . . . fine . . . wonderful for you to fight that way for me. You . . . I . . . I can't find words."

"What I did is nothing compared to the way you stood up before them and lied for me," he said with deep feeling.

Cherry had forgotten about that. All in a second she felt unaccountably tender and realized she was on most treacherous ground. She had not lied, and she longed to tell him so. She longed to tell him more than that. Her mental aberration actually extended to the point of a yearning to kiss those cruel disfigurations he had sustained in defense of her. The end of the old Cherry Winters had about arrived. Yet she clung to her desperately.

"Don't look so distressed," he went on. "They all know you lied to save me and they'll think more of you for it."

"I don't care what they think," returned Cherry. "I'm pretty much upset. I just wanted to tell you how I felt . . . about your fighting for me . . . and to ask you . . . please not to quarrel with Dad."

"Sorry I can't promise. It's certainly coming to that gentleman," Heftral said grimly.

Cherry was not equal to any more just then, and when she slowly ascended the little rock slope to her retreat, she realized how unstrung she was. Once there she lay down on her bed and did not care what happened. She did not quite sleep, but she rested for a couple of hours. Still she did not feel up to the exigencies of this hectic situation. Curiosity, however, was an entering wedge into the chaos of her mind. She sat up and tried to make herself more presentable—thinking, with a wan smile as she saw the havoc in her face, that this was a favorable sign of returning reason.

The Indians appeared to be busy around the campfire, cleaning the mess left by Black Dick and his partner. Never would she forget them. And pretty soon she would find herself in the unique and embarrassing state of inquiring into their wholesome effect upon her. The Sarlands were fixing up some kind of a shelter in the cedars, and evidently were quite interested. Cherry reflected that an adjustment to their material loss might make considerable difference in their reaction. Heftral and Linn were nowhere to be seen. But presently Cherry espied her father. He had been so near, under the wall in the shade, that she had overlooked him. Hatless, coatless, vestless, collar open at the neck, dejected, he certainly presented a most unusual counterpart of himself. For an instant Cherry had a wild start. What if Heftral had chastised him, too? But no, that was improbable. Nevertheless something had happened to Mr. Winters, and sight of him this way revived Cherry's spirit and the duplicity she must continue if she were to bring this issue to a complete rout of him and Heftral. Could she carry on? She would or die in the attempt! These two detractors had not by a great deal been punished enough to satisfy her. Especially Heftral. So after thinking it over for a little longer, Cherry went down to her father.

"Well, Dad, you appear to be having a most enjoyable time," she said.

"Ah! Hello, Cherry. Yes, I'm having a grand time. Ha! Ha!" he replied.

It was worse than Cherry had imagined. She began to soften a little, though she never would let it show. "How do you like *Beckyshibeta*?" she asked.

"Becky-hell and blazes!"

"What's happened, Dad?" she went on quietly.

"Nothing. I've had the most uncomfortable hour of my life," he rejoined miserably. She saw that unburdening himself would be well, so she encouraged him.

"I didn't know that man Heftral at all," he exploded.

"Neither did I," replied Cherry musingly.

"Cherry, that confounded Westerner came up to me with fire in his eye. And he said . . . 'Damn you, Winters. I ought to punch you good.' I thought he was going to do it, too. So I made some feeble reply about how sorry I was to place him in such a fix. 'Fix? Hell!' he yelled at me. 'I'm not thinking of myself. It's the fix you've got *her* in. It's not I who'll have ruined her reputation. It's *you*! You made a fool of me. But you've *hurt* her. Those Sarlands will be nasty. Your own daughter. You made me believe she was a wild girl, going straight to the devil.' I yelled back at him that you *were*. Then he shut me up all right. I knew I was going to get something. He was red as a lobster. He shook that big fist under my very nose. He called me a blankety-blank liar! Then he swore at me. He cussed me. Such profanity I never heard. He must have collected it from every cowboy in the West. He never stopped until he was out of breath. Then he went off somewhere with Linn."

Cherry was certainly experiencing drains upon her feelings and willpower that she had not bargained for. And the fear that she might betray herself made her flippant.

"Is that all?" she inquired.

"All? Good God! What would you want? Have him beat me up like he did that cowboy?"

"I thought perhaps he might."

"You'd have been an orphan all right, if he had. . . . Cherry, you don't mean you're dead sore at me?"

"You are an unnatural parent," returned Cherry, beginning to revel.

"Why, I thought I'd been the easiest dad any girl ever had," he protested, not without pain. "Our friends always took me to task for giving you freedom . . . everything you wanted."

"Yes. But never the love I was so hungry for," Cherry said cruelly.

"Cherry!" he exclaimed, amazed and shocked. "I always worshiped you . . . and spoiled you. This miserable trick I played on you . . . that's turned out so badly . . . why it was a proof of . . . of. . . ."

"Not of faith, Father," she interrupted coldly.

"Faith! Of course it was faith. I swore to myself that our rotten life in the East had not yet ruined you."

"Please do not argue with me," she returned sweetly. "The thing's done. *You* have ruined me, that's certain. And I'll never, never forgive you."

This so crushed him that she had to leave before she must yield to an irresistible softness. And by way of a counter-irritant she went over to talk to the Sarlands. They were cold as Greenland's icy mountains. But presently her sad face, and the struggle she apparently was making to keep up, quite warmed Mrs. Sarland. Her son, however, came around slowly. Finally he broke out in a tirade against Heftral and her father.

"Yes, I know, Chauncey, they're all you say and more. But that doesn't help me. I was perfectly innocent. You know what kind of a girl I am."

"You bet I do. But, Cherry, that about coming here willingly? Then you stood up so . . . so wonderfully and said you loved him!"

"You dumbbell. I was trying to save his life," protested Cherry.

"It was great of you, old girl, believe me," Chauncey replied fervently. "And I believe you did."

Cherry decided that would be about all for an entering wedge. The Sarlands would be hard to handle. Under her direct influence they would respond, but, once away from it, they would be likely to gossip, unless she could make them loyal to her. On the face of it that seemed an impossible task. And she was silly to hope for it, selfish to ask for it. She began to stroll around, hoping to get a peep at Heftral, conscious of a sneaking delight. She saw Linn returning to camp, but the archaeologist had vanished. Could it be possible that the man was again digging for *Beckyshibeta*? If so, she would have to hand him a laurel wreath. She could not, however, venture to find out, and had to content herself with waiting.

Out of sight of camp Cherry found a lofty perch in the sun and there she succumbed to the glory and dream of this cañon country. There was no sense or use in trying to resist its charm. But it was a way with Cherry to try to understand what got the best of her. This place had taken hold of her heart. It would have done so even if that rather unknown organ had not shown astonishingly weak points.

What was the spell of this deep fissure in the rocks? She dreamily attended to her senses. It had such a strange sweet dry fragrance, with sage predominating, but with other perfumes almost as clean and insidious. It was as colorful as a rainbow. It changed with the movements of the sun, never very long the same. It had mystic veils of light, rose and pink at dawn, amber and gold at this hour of high noon, and in the afternoon with shadows lengthening, deepening into lilac, purple, black. Then the immensity of the cliffs, the lofty rims, the far higher domes and mesas beyond, the hundreds of inaccessible and fascinating places where only squirrels and birds could rest—these added to the spell. Not a little, too, was the evidence of a wild people once having lived and fought and died here. Perhaps loved! Lastly Cherry was discovering the blessedness of solitude, the something leveling in loneliness, the elevating power of the naked sheer walls with their inscrutable meaning.

All of which led to a consciousness of the thing that had come to her. She called it *thing,* when she confessed to her soul that it was new, transforming, exalting love. And she dared not give in to that just yet. When she must, when she could no longer stand the old Cherry Winters, when pride and vanity, and a bevy of other faults must go by the board, then she would face the truth and its appalling problems. She had a tremendous consciousness that she would engulf all—this marvelous desert, her aging, worrying father, her friends—and Heftral. And it was going to hurt almost mortally.

★ ★ ★ ★ ★

Cherry returned to camp. Sight of Heftral thrilled yet shocked her. That hour alone in the cañon had transformed him in her mind. And the reality of him was confounding.

Evidently she had interrupted a conference, or at least an argument. She caught Heftral's slight gesture to enjoin silence.

"Wal, Heftral," Linn said. "I reckon Miss Cherry needn't be excluded."

"If I'm intruding," Cherry replied haughtily, turning to go.

Linn detained her. "We was jest talkin'," he said, "an' mebbe you might put a word in. Heftral has lost his job. Mister Elliott, haid of the New York Museum, is now at the post, waitin' for some of his men to come over from New Mexico. 'Pears he's been ag'in' Heftral's explorations out heah. Wants to find *Becky-shibeta* himself. After Heftral has dug up the desert. Wal, he took this unauthorized trip of Heftral's out heah as an excuse, an' fired him. Your father feels bad aboot bein' to blame, and he offered Heftral substantial means to go on with his explorations on his own hook. Heftral turned it down cold. . . . What do you think aboot it?"

"I? Oh, I think it very unfortunate and distressing that Mister Heftral should be discharged . . . and disgraced through father's idiotic scheme," replied Cherry. "Certainly Father could do no less than offer to repair the material loss. And just as certainly Mister Heftral could not accept it."

"Why not?" demanded Winters.

"Well, Dad, if you're so dense you can't see why . . . I am not going to enlighten you."

"Thank you, Miss Winters," said Heftral. "You understand, at least."

Winters might have exploded then, if he had had energy enough left to express himself as he looked. As it was, his first exclamation was unintelligible and scarcely mild. Then he added: "If you temperamental young fools weren't at loggerheads, I could still save the situation."

"Yes, you could," declared Heftral sarcastically. "Winters, my private opinion is that you might save your face if. . . ."

"See here, you hot-headed jackanapes!" interrupted Winters. "You've insulted me enough."

"I could still add injury to insult," Heftral retorted.

Here Linn stepped into the breach and tried his Western common sense and kindliness upon the troubled waters. Cherry had been thinking desperately. What astounded her now was that she simply could not stand Heftral's unhappiness. She, who had wanted to make him writhe and moan and curse himself with remorse!

"Mister Heftral, may I have a word with you alone?" she asked, very business-like. No one could have guessed there was a lump in her throat.

"Certainly," he said with freezing politeness, "if you consider it necessary."

He went aside with her, manifestly with misgivings. Cherry heard her father whisper to Linn: "Now what's she up to? There's no telling about a woman."

Cherry maintained an outward composure. She could rise to the moment and this one was big. "Will you make me a promise?" she asked.

"I couldn't very well be surprised at you. And if you'll pardon my bluntness . . . no, I won't," he replied.

Cherry was looking with a woman's penetrating intuitive eyes into his face, and what she read there made the ordeal worse, yet gave her a hint of the assurance she needed.

"Well then, *if* you make me a promise . . . will you keep it?" she continued steadily.

"Yes. If!"

"Do you recall the last time I was around where you were digging?"

"I'm not likely to forget it."

"I am going to tell you the honest truth."

"Miss Winters, are you capable of that?" he asked acidly.

"If you were big enough to fight for my honor, you can be big enough to give me the benefit of the doubt . . . when I particularly appeal to you. Will you?"

That struck him deeply. He lost his grim cold look of doubt and became merely wretched. "I'm not quite myself. But tell me what you want to."

"If I reveal something to you, will you promise never to tell it to anyone?" she asked hurriedly and low.

"I don't see any need of your revealing secrets to me," he replied.

"Will you promise?" she went on, appealing as well with her eyes.

"You can trust me," he said, surrendering in spite of himself.

"Thank you. The secret you have promised to keep is that *I* have found *Beckyshibeta* for you," she whispered. "Go at once far beyond that place where I crossed and risked my life . . . where I taunted you and you told me to go to the devil. . . . Go high up around the great cracked leaning rock. Find a stairway of little cut steps in the stone. Follow them. They will lead you to *Beckyshibeta.* Don't doubt. Don't laugh. But go!"

Cherry did not wait to see his incredulity or to hear whatever he might have to say. She hurried away, up to her ledge, the attaining of which was about all she could do. What had it not cost her to hide her joy at this priceless gift to him, and her own great secret? When she sank to her knees upon her bed, and looked back, Heftral had disappeared. Soon he would learn that her words had not been idle. The greatest ambition of his life attained! *Beckyshibeta!* How would he return to her?

Chapter Fourteen

Cherry had anticipated peace, satisfaction, relief from her whirling thoughts. But the exact reverse was the case. Suppose it had not been *Beckyshibeta* at all? What a horrible mistake! Her eloquence, her exaction of a sacred promise, her cool certainty had convinced Heftral. But she might have been wrong. How could she be sure about cliff dwellings?

So she was tortured. How to make amends to Heftral if she had blundered. Of course she could give him herself. It did not seem possible that she could rival *Beckyshibeta* in this mad scientist's valuation; nevertheless she might be some little consolation. That would be what she must do; that was what she had intended for long endless growing hours. Only it would have to be done at once, right there where this catastrophe had happened, instead of waiting until she felt utterly and forever avenged.

An hour passed, surely an hour Cherry would never want to live over. The camp was deserted. She had not heard anyone leave. And presently she felt that she could not lie there any longer, waiting in actionless suspense. She must move around, do something.

Cherry wandered in the opposite direction to the one she was sure the others had taken. She went around under the cliffs farther on that side than she had ever been. But for once the speaking walls had no power of solace. She was not ready to take earnest heed of her own spiritual case. It was Heftral of whom she was thinking. If she had actually discovered *Beckyshibeta,* she would presently be the most fortunate—the happiest of women. She did not try now to reason out why. It was something she most devoutly believed and prayed for.

She found a clump of sage and lingered in it, reveling in its fragrance and color. She gathered an armful of the sprigs, meaning to treasure them in a pillow, to have near her a memory—stirring sweetness of the desert. Then she sat down with the sage in her lap, and tried to plan clearly her procedure from this hour. But she could only dream, because everything was uncertain.

Time passed, however, and upon her return to camp she found all the others there, except Heftral. At first glance they appeared to be friendly enough. There must be some occasion for intimate talk. Then her father espied her and came running. Cherry breathed a deep full relief. Mr. Winters was not given to overexertion in ordinary movements or when he was gloomy.

"I've had the very devil of good luck," he announced as he reached her, and, quite forgetful of a former state of mind, he put his arm around her and squeezed her.

"You have? Well, that's fine," replied Cherry, yielding to him, as he pulled her to a seat on a rock.

"Heftral and I have made up," said Mr. Winters with great pleasure and satisfaction.

"Made up! Indeed? I did not imagine it possible that he would ever forgive you . . . either." Cherry added the *either* as an afterthought. It quite escaped Mr. Winters.

"Cherry, the lucky dog discovered the lost pueblo . . . *Beckyshibeta*!" exclaimed her father.

"Oh! How wonderful!" Cherry did not have to dissimulate. She must be very careful not to show how happy the information made her. After that sudden start of joy, of flashing heat on her face, of bursting blood, she managed to find herself again.

"It's true. And, well, I don't know when I've been so glad about anything."

"Tell me about it," said Cherry composedly, although she kept her face half averted.

"Linn was showing us the ruins," Winters went on, wiping his hot face. "We ran into Heftral. I declare I thought he was crazy. So did Linn. At first we did not take him at all seriously. He convinced us finally. He had discovered *Beckyshibeta* . . . the pueblo about which archaeologists have been raving for years. Quite by a strange lucky accident. He was radiant. I never saw a man so completely happy. He was so absurdly grateful to me for sending him out here. Why, the fellow embraced me. I was embarrassed, remembering how he treated me a few hours before. . . . Cherry, he had actually forgotten. I declare it upset me . . . I was so glad. I like Heftral, and when I queered myself with him, it hurt. He's one of the finest chaps I ever knew."

"I'm glad . . . for his sake and yours," rejoined Cherry. "This discovery must mean a great deal to him?"

"I didn't understand that until after he rushed off again," replied Winters. "Linn told me. It means fame and money to Heftral. In one word . . . success. Scientifically this is a very important discovery. *Beckyshibeta* is one of the greatest pueblos, says Linn. An ancient buried city. Then the best of it is that Heftral was not working for the museum people when he found the pueblo. He was all on his own. That upstart Elliott, you know, fired him. Linn says Elliott will about expire. Heftral will have the credit, and everything else that comes with it. The work of excavation will be under *his* control, instead of Elliott's. I'm just tickled over it."

"Excavation," mused Cherry. "He will undertake that? Won't it be expensive?"

"I'll back him. It's a big thing," Winters replied heartily.

"Do you think Mister Heftral would accept that?"

"Stephen has already accepted," went on her father happily. "He said he could raise any amount of money. The government would want to help. Patrons of scientific research would want to donate . . . to have their names connected with *Beckyshibeta*. But I beat them to it. And Stephen was delighted."

"Where is . . . he now?" asked Cherry with her glance downcast upon the bunch of sage. It would never have done for her to let anyone see her eyes then.

"He went back. Linn and I tried to follow him. But he crossed a terrible place. We'd have broken our necks. So we returned to camp."

It was night with silvery radiance streaming down over the dark cañon rims. The moon was rising. Cherry lay in her blankets, waiting to see the white disk slide up over the black ragged rock line above. She had not cared to trust meeting Heftral at the campfire and, pleading fatigue, had retired to her ledge, where her father brought her supper.

Heftral did not return until the others had finished their meal, and then he quite forgot to eat. His ragged appearance attested to hours of contact with the rough rocks, and his radiant face to the discovery that had made him a changed man. While he talked to Linn and Winters his glance went so often toward Cherry's perch that she feared she might be caught peeping. But she was in dark shadow there, and could safely revel in watching and listening. If she had ever seen three happy men, it was then.

The Sarlands had thawed considerably. They hovered around Heftral, fascinated, and warming to the man's enthusiasm. When at last they went off to their camp, Linn said: "Wal, Winters, can you dig up a drink?"

"No. I didn't bring any," Winters replied regretfully.

"How aboot you, Heftral?"

"I had some for possible snakebite, but it leaked out."

Linn turned over his saddle and procured a flask. "Heah, friends, we'll drink to *Beckyshibeta*!"

What a long time they were in getting ready for bed. At last Heftral was left alone. He sat for what seemed an endless hour, gazing into the ruddy dying fire. What was he thinking about? Fame and fortune, the goddesses of all men's ambitions, thought Cherry jealously. Certainly he did not appear to remember her.

The moon soared across the narrow opening between the rims of rock above; the dark shadow on one side of the cañon moved magically across to the other. An impenetrable silence enfolded the lonely place. Cherry had sat up peeping until her back ached. Several times she lay down again, only to rise up and peep once more. Heftral was a magnet. She laughed happily under her breath as she watched him. If he but knew!

Winters and Linn lay prone in their beds, deep in slumber. It touched Cherry to see the silver of her father's hair, bright in the moonlight.

Heftral glanced rather markedly and long at them. Then stepping noiselessly, he entered the zone of shadow and vanished. But soon the outline of his head and shoulders were silhouetted against the moonlight. Cherry gave a wild start and shrank back. He was climbing to her ledge.

The sudden burning of her face and beating of her heart accompanied a panic she could not quell. But she covered herself with the blankets and feigned sleep. To her own eyes it had been almost as bright as day up there. But Heftral, coming from the open moonlight, would find it dark. Yet if he stayed long enough. A child could read her heart in her face. She heard a slight rustling on the rock, and she began to tremble. Then ensued a long lapse in which her acute senses registered nothing. Next she felt his presence. He was there, gazing down upon her. How could she lie still? What was his intention? Then she divined that he would surely awaken her, and she sought to still her nerves. Something lightly brushed her hair. His hand or his lips? Another instant she knew, for she caught a slight sound of intense breathing very close to her face. He had kissed her hair. Cherry stiffened with the demand she made upon her sensibilities. If he dared to kiss her lips, her rigid arms would fly up around his neck. She knew it. She waited, surrendering in her heart, ready to end the fight royally.

But instead he touched her softly and whispered: "Cherry."

That saved her. She caught at her ebbing self-control, and her conscious-swift thought balanced her emotion.

"Cherry," he whispered. "Wake up. It is I . . . Stephen."

She opened her eyes, not needing to pretend a start. She saw him distinctly—his face pale, rapt. He kneeled beside her.

"Oh! Who? What?" she faltered.

"Don't be frightened," he said swiftly and low. "It's Stephen. I couldn't wait till tomorrow."

"Mister Heftral . . . you . . . you startled me. What is it? Oh, I hope my father. . . ."

"Don't speak so loud," he interrupted. "There is nothing wrong. I simply could not wait till morning. I had to wake you."

"Why, may I ask . . . if all's well?" she queried, trying to give her voice some fitness to the words.

"Cherry, it was no dream," he went on with deep feeling. "You were right. You have found *Beckyshibeta* for me."

"Of course. Did you wake me to tell me that?"

He hesitated, and then went on explosively. "No . . . but it . . . they . . . you all go together."

Cherry maintained a silence, the cause of which evidently he took very differently from what it actually was.

"Cherry, please don't be . . . be . . . ," he added hastily.

"What?" she asked not encouragingly.

"Why, cold," he burst out. "At least don't freeze me to death. Let me tell you . . . let me unburden myself."

"It's quite unconventional, to put it mildly. But I haven't ordered you out of my boudoir, have I?" she replied, and put a hand out to lift her pillow.

Heftral possessed himself of that hand and held it tightly. He bent over her. Cherry could see fairly well in the dim light.

"Thank you," he said huskily. "I'll be relieved and happy to get this off my mind. . . . Cherry, you've made my fortune. *Beckyshibeta* is marvelous. I have not had time to gauge its scope, but, from what I've discovered already, it is vastly larger and more important than I ever dreamed it would be. In fact, *Beckyshibeta* is one of the great ancient buried cities. It will take years to excavate, and in a scientific way is a priceless discovery. The fact that Elliott discharged me from the museum staff is particularly fortunate for me. I am all on my own. I can dictate terms. I can raise any amount of capital, but I believe I'll accept your father's aid. It will be a fine thing for him, too."

"Mister Heftral," Cherry replied as he paused, "you told me all this before. When you explained what it would mean to you *if* you discovered the ruin."

"Yes, but I never dreamed of its magnitude. . . . Cherry, I've tried more than once to make you see how my heart was in this work. It appeals to me in so many ways. I like delving into the musty past. But I could not advance because I had neither capital nor luck. Now I have the luck. You have made my fortune. I'll be famous. I'll make money writing, lecturing, and I'll have a big position offered to me. Expeditions in foreign countries, if I want, or research work all over this desert. I simply cannot think of all the advantages that will come to me."

"I am glad. You know I always wanted you to succeed, even if I didn't appear interested. And I can feel that I returned some little good for the . . . the evil you did me."

"Cherry!"

"You have ruined my good name," she went on gravely. "It's Dad's fault, but that does not excuse you."

"Oh, Cherry, it really all amounts to nothing . . . nothing," he whispered hoarsely. "In this age! Why, even if the kidnaping had been real, it could not have hurt you vitally."

"I can't agree with you, and we needn't discuss that."

"Listen. I loved you from the first moment I saw you. But I had no hopes or delusions. You remember when I saw you in New York. . . . Well, I don't think I'd ever have gotten over it. I'd never have cared for any other girl. But my heart would not have broken. This trip of yours out here . . . your father's crazy plan . . . the wonderful hours in the desert . . . and lastly, your finding *Beckyshibeta* for me . . . I can never stand them. I can never get over them. I loved you before, but I worship you now. . . . Cherry, will you marry me?"

Cherry tried to withdraw her hand from his warm clasp, for fear that it might betray the true state of her heart.

"I will no longer be a nonentity," he hastened on. "Nor a poor beggar. I can offer you a home . . . good enough for any good girl. I can make you happy, Cherry. Oh, you never fooled me. That gay idle luxurious life never brought out the best in you. There's a lot in you, Cherry. What a wonderful girl to help a man make something out of himself! To make a real American home!"

"Not long ago you thought me all that was bad," she replied scornfully.

"I did not. I never even took you for what you appeared to be on the face of it."

"I remember what you said, Mister Heftral," she returned sadly.

"I don't care what I said. God knows I had provocation enough for anything. I don't care *what* I thought, either. The inspiration of your discovery of *Beckyshibeta* has given me vision. I see clearly. I know you as you are in your heart. You are deceiving yourself, not me. . . . I beg you, listen to me. I'll never importune you again. I love you. I worship you. If you will only rise to the beauty and splendor of what I see!"

"Stephen, you don't allow for a woman's feelings," she returned earnestly. "I respected you . . . liked you. And I proved it by letting you alone. If you had refused Dad's miserable advances. *If* you had told me. *If* you had borne with me and been my friend. . . . *¿Quién sabe?* But now it's too late!"

"Cherry, you can't be so little as that," he pleaded, in torture. "If you liked me at all, it must be lasting."

"You forget you . . . you beat me," she whispered, and felt the hot blood move up to her cheeks.

"No, I don't forget," he said stubbornly. "I'm sorry, of course. But I'd do it again under the same circumstances. Only I want you to understand, I didn't beat you. I *spanked* you. There is a very great difference."

"I don't care about the difference. . . . Mister Heftral, do you honestly believe I oughtn't hate you for that?"

"Hate me? Good heavens, no! My love for you robs that terrible humiliation of any hate."

Cherry knew that was true, and just then hated herself for the passion that held her to her pride and revenge. She knew also that she must end this talk abruptly or yield to him.

"Mister Heftral, any moment you may awaken the others," she said, managing a *hauteur* that must have been sickening to him. "But take my answer. It is all too late for the beautiful thing you vision. Too late, alas! I shall insist that you take me to Flagstaff at once . . . and give me the protection of your name. I shall go to New York, and free you there."

"Oh, Cherry!" he cried in passionate disappointment, and threw her hand from him.

"You will . . . do that much . . . for me?" she asked unsteadily.

"Yes, I'll make you Missus Stephen Heftral," he answered bitterly, and went silently down the ledge, disappearing in the shadow.

Chapter Fifteen

Cherry lay back with a long sigh. The ordeal was over. She realized that in a few moments she would be gloriously happy. Just the instant she had satisfied her insistent modern mind. As she settled back and drew the blankets close about her shoulders, she felt the quivering of her body. She was cold and exhausted. But for the darkness she could never have carried on that intimate talk with Stephen to the climax it had attained. She had deceived him. She had tortured him with the hint of what might have been. The assurance of his love had been what she craved. Her breast swelled and her conscience flayed her as she recalled his words, his emotion, his faith. She would take exceeding great care that no word or act of hers would do anything but increase his remorse and love. Nevertheless, she would go clear to the very last minute with her revenge. No longer revenge, but fun, simply love itself, something to enhance her surrender to him with the sweetest and most unforgettable turning of the tables.

A thought flashed by—was this trifling with her happiness—going too far, risking too much? No! If Stephen worshiped her—and how thrillingly she believed it—dared not yield to it!—a few more days on the desert and then that marvelous climax she must devise to follow their marriage in Flagstaff would make him more miserable, more lovelorn, more wholly hers. How she must rack her brain to make her victory complete—something for which he could only love her more!

And when that last thought swiftly passed, Cherry let herself go. She scarcely divined it, but that was the moment of her change. Long she had guessed its proximity. Would it not be a receding of the flesh? But when she succumbed to love, when she descended from selfishness, egotism, independence to the humble grateful adoring woman she climbed immeasurably. She had a long sweet hour of revel in Stephen's love, in his manliness, his honesty, his ambition, and lastly in his faith that not even she could destroy. How glorious that was to Cherry! Never had she been anywhere so good and worthy as he believed her, but she would attain that height in this very hour of submission, of humanity, of gratitude.

Following that best and happiest hour of Cherry's life came a flashing illumination to her mind. And it took only a flash to see where she had been wrong, and what was wrong with the life she had led. In the tumult of her heart and the transition of her character she saw hope for all her friends, for everyone. Modern life and materialism, with their leaning to the fleshpots of Egypt, could not destroy wholly the best thing in any woman—love

Cherry lay long awake. Sleep would have robbed her. The night wore on. The silver gleam on the walls paled, darkened, vanished. And the cañon grew black, mysterious, silent as a tomb. But by intense concentration Cherry heard a very faint murmur of running water and then the faintest of mournful winds. How wonderful the night, the darkness, the loneliness and wildness, the meaning of these old walls, the echo of past life there, the living powerful love in her heart, and the intimation that nothing died!

Then, as if by magic, the gray dawn came, the brightening of the cañon.

Cherry lay in bed and thought and dreamed and smiled and pinched herself to prove she was awake. Presently she became aware of sounds of camp stirring below. They were early this morning. But she was loath to leave the warm blankets, and would rather have lingered there with her thoughts.

Then her father appeared on the ledge, carrying her riding habit and boots.

"Hello, you're awake," he said.

"Good morning, Father," she replied, demurely peeping from behind the edge of her blanket. He did not look happy and the smile he usually had for her was wanting.

"We're breaking camp. Heftral acquainted me with your wishes and intentions. We will leave for the post and Flagstaff at once."

"So soon! Leave *Beckyshibeta* today?" she exclaimed in dismay.

"Assuredly. I daresay you will appreciate this place . . . and some other things . . . after you have lost them. Hurry and dress yourself. Breakfast is waiting."

Cherry stared after his retreating form rather blankly. "Well," she soliloquized. Then she laughed. What could she have expected? He was tremendously disappointed in her. All the better! Things were working out magnificently. She would certainly teach him a lesson that would last for life. Yet she was very glad indeed that he was so disappointed. She could endure a little longer that he and Heftral should continue to be sad about her and the mess she was going to make out of her life.

Cherry got into her riding habit and boots with extraordinary pleasure and satisfaction. What a transformation! The scant garb she had been wearing did not harmonize with dignity, and certainly had not enhanced her good looks. All the same she would keep that shrunken skirt and torn blouse and the soiled stockings. She rolled them in the blankets. The worn shoes, too. Some distant future day she would don them to surprise and delight Stephen.

Her little mirror showed a golden-tanned face, with glad eyes and a glorious smile, and shiny rippling hair, all the prettier for being wayward and free. Cherry did not need to hide her feelings any longer. She would let Heftral and her father make their own deductions regarding her happiness.

As she descended the ledge she heard Mrs. Sarland squeal with delight. Something had excited her. Heftral and Linn were busy packing. Breakfast steamed on the fire. The Indians were coming up with the horses. A pang tore Cherry's heart. Only an hour more, perhaps less, of these gleaming cañon walls! But she would come back. The gentlemen were not blind to her changed attire and mood, though they did not make any demonstration over her. Indeed she could not catch Heftral's eye.

Mrs. Sarland came up almost running, breathless, triumphant, and radiant. "Oh, my dear, how different . . . you look," she panted. "What do you think? That villain Black Dick forgot to take our money . . . and jewels. My bag was hanging . . . on a cedar twig. Imagine! I was simply overcome . . . and here's your diamond ring."

"Well, of all the luck!" cried Cherry, surprised and pleased, as she took her ring. "I'm very glad for you, Missus Sarland. Of course my loss would have been little. . . . So our desperado forgot to take what he stole? Well, he was a queer one."

"I can almost forgive him now," replied Mrs. Sarland fervently.

Chauncey came up and tipped his sombrero to Cherry. But his sour look did not fit his graceful gesture. Cherry did not need to be told that her father had passed on the important news. The Sarlands might be civil, but Chauncey, at least, would never forgive her. Cherry reflected that it might not matter how they felt or what they did. She would be careful, however, to make it plain to Heftral and her father that she feared the Sarlands and desired to placate them.

Cherry had her breakfast alone. One of the Indians left his task and stood nearby, apparently fascinated at the sight of her.

Heftral kept his back turned and worked hard on the packs.

"Stephen, please get me another cup of coffee!" she called.

He hurriedly complied, and fetched it to her.

"You make such lovely coffee," she said, looking up at him. "I'll miss that, at least, when I'm home again."

"Linn made this coffee," replied Heftral brusquely.

"Oh." But nothing could have hurt Cherry this wonderful morning. Nothing except leaving her cañon. She went aside by herself so that she could feel and think, unaffected by Heftral or her father. The gleaming walls spoke to her. The great red corner of rock that led off toward *Beckyshibeta* beckoned for her to come. And she went far enough to peep around. How wild and ragged and rocky! It was a wilderness of broken stones. Yet for her they had a spirit and a voice. The stream murmured from the gorge, the cañon swifts darted by, their wings shining in the sunlight, the sweet dry sage fragrance filled her nostrils.

Cherry gazed all around and upward, everywhere, with deep reverence for this lonely chasm in the rock crust of the earth. She would return soon, and often thereafter while Stephen was at work on the excavation of the ruined pueblo. She would like to plan her future, her home, her usefulness in the world, here under the spell of her cañon.

How soon could that be? Not yet had she planned any further than Flagstaff. No further than the hour that would make her Stephen's wife! The tumultuousness of that thought had inhibited a completion of her plan. But was not that the climax—the end? It did not satisfy Cherry. It entailed confession, total surrender, both of which she would be glad to give, yet. . . . Suddenly she had an inspiration. It absolutely dazzled her. It swept her away. It was a perfect solution to her problem, and she could have laughed her joy to these watching jealous walls. But—was it possible? Could she accomplish it? How strange she had not thought of it before. Easy as it was wonderful. Whereupon she gave herself up to a mute reverent farewell to *Beckyshibeta.*

A lusty shout interrupted Cherry's rapt mood: "Come on, Cherry! We're off!" called her father.

Very soon then Cherry was astride a horse, comfortable and confident in her riding outfit, going down the trail through the cedars. She was the last of the cavalcade. Heftral and the Indians were ahead, driving the pack animals. Linn was looking after the Sarlands. Winters rode ahead of Cherry. They crossed the boulder-strewn streambed, climbed the dusty soft red trail, and wound away through cedars. Cherry did not look back. It would not have been any use, for her eyes were blinded by tears. They did not wholly clear until she rode out of the rock walls, up on to the desert.

Cherry rode alone all day. And surely it was the fullest and sweetest day of all her life. Forty miles of sage to traverse to the next camp—purple color and wondrous fragrance all around—red and gold walls beckoning from the horizons—the sweep and loneliness of vast stretches—sometimes all by herself on the trail, far behind the others—these were the splendid accompaniments of her happy dreams and thoughts, of long serious realizations, of the permanent settling of convictions and ideals, of consciousness of a softened and exalted heart.

Sunset fell while they were yet upon the trail—one of the incomparable Arizona sunsets that Cherry had come to love. A black horizon-wide wall blocked the west. The red and golden rays of sunlight swept down over it, spreading light over the desert. Above masses of purple cloud with silver edges hid the sky. And it all gloriously faded into dusk.

A flock of black and white sheep crossed the trail in front of Cherry. The shepherds were a little Indian boy and girl both mounted on the same pony. How wild and shy! The dogs barked at Cherry. The sheep trooped over the ridge top. And lastly the little shepherds and their pony stood silhouetted against the afterglow. Cherry waved and waved. The little girl answered—a fleeting shy flip of hand. Then they were gone.

Soon after that a bright campfire greeted Cherry from a bend in the trail. She rode into camp and dismounted, to discover she felt no fatigue, no aches, no pains—and that the exhilaration of the morning had not worn away in that long ride. Mrs. Sarland was bemoaning her state; Chauncey limped to his tasks; Winters showed the effect of long sitting in a saddle. The Westerners were active.

The camp was in the open desert, in the lee of some low rocks. Coyotes were wailing and yelping out in the darkness. A cold wind swept around the rocks and pierced through Cherry. How good the blazing bits of sage. She was ravishingly hungry.

Cherry ate her supper sitting on an uncomfortable pack, and she had to eat it quickly while it stayed warm. Firewood appeared to be scarce, and the desert wind grew colder. There was little or no gaiety in the company. Linn tried to make a few facetious remarks to Mrs. Sarland, but they fell flat. Cherry edged so close to the fire that she almost burned her boots. Heftral kept back in the shadow. She felt him watching her, and needed no more to keep her spirits high. Winters huddled on the ground on the other side of the fire, and his head drooped. Chauncey was silent and dejected. Mrs. Sarland complained of the awful effects of the ride, the food, the cold, the wind, and everything.

"Are those terrible wild creatures going to keep that din up all night?" she queried.

"Wal, I reckon so," replied Linn. "Coyotes are noisy an' they'll come right up an' pull at your hat, when you're in bed."

"Heavens! And we must sleep on the flat ground!"

"You might bunk up on the rock. It'll be tolerable windy. . . . Miss Winters, aren't you scared and frozen stiff?"

"Both," laughed Cherry. "But I think this is great. I love to hear those wild coyotes."

"No more desert for me," sighed Mrs. Sarland.

"Chauncey, surely you will come back to Arizona someday?" Cherry asked curiously.

"What for?" he queried, fixing her with gloomy eyes.

"Of course, Miss Winters, you'll be coming back often to see your husband digging in that heap of stones?" added Mrs. Sarland.

"Y-yes, but not very soon," replied Cherry. "Father is coming back shortly to start the excavating of *Beckyshibeta.* Aren't you, Dad?"

"Sure. I'm going to dig a grave for myself out here," growled her father.

"Haw! Haw! Haw!" bawled the trader. "Did you heah that, Heftral? Wal, folks, you'll all come back to old Arizona. I've yet to see the man or woman who'd slept out on this desert an' didn't want to come back."

"You all better turn in," said Heftral. "Firewood scarce, and you'll be called at dawn."

"Gracious, I forgot about bed!" exclaimed Cherry, giving her palms a last toast over the red coals. "Stephen, where's my downy couch?"

"Here," he replied, and led her a few steps.

"Ugh, it's windy. I hate to think of bed on the cold rocks," returned Cherry, trying to see in the dark.

"Yours won't be windy or cold or hard," he replied briefly. "Here. There's a foot of sage under your blankets, and a thick windbreak. You'll be comfortable."

"Oh! You found time to do this for me?" she asked, looking up at him. The starlight showed his face dark and troubled, his eyes sad.

"Certainly. It was little enough."

"Thank you, Stephen. You are good to me," she said softly, and held out her hand.

Heftral gave a start, clasped her hand convulsively, and rushed away without even saying good night.

Cherry gazed a moment at his vanishing form. Then she plumped down on her bed. "Gee," she whispered, "I want to be careful. He might grab me . . . and then it would be good night."

Removing only her boots, Cherry slipped down into the bed. How soft and fragrant of sage! Her pillow was a fleecy sheepskin, one she had seen in Heftral's pack. Then her feet, bravely stretching down, suddenly came in contact with something hot. It startled her. Presently she made it out to be a hot stone wrapped in canvas. Heftral had heated this and put it in her bed. Let the desert wind blow! The white stars blinked down at her from the deep blue dome above. Had she ever thought them pitiless, indifferent, mocking? The wind swept with low moans through the sage; the coyotes kept up their wild staccato barks; the campfire died out and low voices of men ceased. Tranquil, cold, beautiful night enfolded the scene. And Cherry lay there wide-eyed, watching the heavens, wondering at the beauty and mystery of Nature, at the glory of love, marveling at the happiness that had been bestowed upon her unworthy self.

Next day about midafternoon they rode across the wide barren stretch of desert to the post, the pack train far ahead with Heftral in the lead, and Linn trying to hold Mrs. Sarland in the saddle to the last. Cherry brought up the rear, so late that, when she reached the last level, all the others had disappeared in the green grove that surrounded the post.

Mojave met Cherry at the gate, bareheaded, respectful, but with a face of woe.

"Why, Mojave, have you lost your grandmother . . . or something?" ejaculated Cherry.

"I reckon it's worse, Miss Cherry," he replied meaningly.

"Oh, goodness! For a moment I felt sorry for you. Mojave boy, you keep shy of Eastern girls after this. They're no good."

"Most of them aren't, I reckon. But I know one who's an angel. An' she's gonna be married to a. . . ."

"Mojave, who told you?" interrupted Cherry as she slipped out of the saddle.

"Thet big-mouthed, lop-eared, hard-headed Linn. He came a-roarin' it to everybody, an' no winter cyclone could have knocked us flatter."

"Mojave, honest now, aren't you glad . . . for my sake?" asked Cherry sweetly. She liked this frank clean-cut cowboy.

"Wal, Miss Cherry, since you ask me . . . yes, I am, seein' I cain't have you myself," he replied with reddening face. "I never liked thet kidnapin' stunt an' didn't understand. Shore, if we'd known you was engaged all the time, there'd never been such a mix-up. Poor old Wess, he was the hardest hit, I reckon."

"How about him, Mojave?" Cherry asked anxiously.

"Gone. An' mighty shamed of himself. Asked me to tell you he'd plumb lost his haid. An' wanted you to know it wasn't the first time."

"Well! What did he mean?"

"I reckon Wess figgered thet if you knowed he'd made a fool of hisself over a gurl before, you wouldn't feel so bad aboot what you did to him."

"He was man enough to confess his weakness. I call that square of him, don't you, Mojave?"

"It shore is. Wal, Wess was a good sort, when he wasn't loco over a gurl, or full of licker."

"How are the other boys?"

"They wasn't so bad, till this news came. Reckon now they're down at the bunkhouse drownin' their grief. They shore left the work to me an' the boss."

"How funny! What did they say?"

"Wal, I can't recollect all, but one crack I'll never fergit. Tay-Tay busted out like this. 'W-w-w-what the h-h-hell you think of thet grave robber? He's s-s-sstole our gurl an' he's got a face like a sick c-c-cow!' "

"Well, I never," laughed Cherry. "Mister Heftral ought to look well and happy, oughtn't he?"

"He shore ought. I reckon, though, he feels turrible bad aboot your goin' East an' him havin' to stay on account of *Beckyshi-beta*. Linn told us. You can jest bet, Miss Cherry, no cowboy would let you go off alone."

"I fancy not," she said, quickly. "But you mustn't think ill of Mister Heftral. The discovering of the pueblo has upset all our plans. It's very important. I'm hoping to persuade him to go East with us for a few weeks, but I have some very urgent business reasons for going back immediately with Father. Please regard that as confidential, Mojave. And tell the boys we'll be leaving early in the morning. I wouldn't want to miss saying good bye."

When Mojave had left, Cherry breathed a sigh of relief. Her excuse had been a lame one, but the honest cowboy had apparently swallowed it without a second thought.

Cherry then went on into the house, first encountering Mrs. Linn, to whose warm greeting she responded. The Indian maid showed shy gladness at Cherry's safe return. Linn came bustling in with Winters, both of them blushing and coughing. Cherry thought her father looked much better and she guessed why. The Sarlands were evidently in their rooms, and Heftral was not in sight.

"Mister Linn, we shall want to leave early in the morning," said Cherry.

"Aw, Miss Cherry. One more day," he entreated.

"I'm sorry, but we must go. Some other time we shall come

and stay longer. Dad, I'll change and pack now. Will you please tell Stephen I want to talk to him presently. Say in an hour. Tell him to knock at my door."

"All right, star-eyed enigma," returned her father, with puzzled glance upon her.

Cherry rushed to her room, and lost no time in bathing. She put on her most fetching gown, one of those scant creations that Heftral had hated, yet could not resist. How swiftly her blood ran! What a glow on her face! Indeed her eyes were like stars. Would Heftral see—would he be proud and wretched at once—would he betray himself? While she packed, her mind whirled, keeping pace with her racing pulse. If she had not conceived a grand finale to this desert romance, she was a poor judge of wit and humor. Her father would be completely floored and, best of all, won forever. Heftral? But no stretch of imagination could picture Heftral as she hoped to see him.

A tap sounded on the door. It startled Cherry. She caught her breath and her hand went to her breast. She glanced at her mirror and the image she saw there quickened her agitation. But as quickly she recovered her composure.

"Come in," she said.

But the door did not move, nor was the rap repeated. Cherry went swiftly and opened it. Heftral stood there. She had not seen him like this.

"Oh, it's you, Stephen. I'd forgotten. Come in. I want to talk to you."

He did not make any move to enter and apparently he was dumb.

"Well, you're very reserved . . . and considerate, all of a sudden," she said sarcastically. "Pray don't be shy about entering my bedroom now. . . . Please come in."

Heftral entered reluctantly. There was no bully about him now. "What do you want? Was it necessary to ask me here?"

"Yes, I think so. The living room is not private. And I want to ask a particular favor of you. Will you grant it?"

He went to the window and looked out. Then presently he turned with an almost grim look. "Yes . . . anything."

"Thank you, Stephen," she went on, going close to him, quite closer than was necessary. Every moment made Cherry more sure of herself. There was a strange and magical sweetness in this sincerity of deceit. Yet was it deceit? She risked a great deal, trusting to his mood, his humility. It was a woman's perverse thrilling desire to tempt him. But if he should seize her in his arms. . . . Even so, she would carry out her plan.

"Before I ask the favor, I want to tell you that I would rather have had this otherwise."

"Ha! Maybe I wouldn't!" he exclaimed. "But what do *you* mean?"

"It's hard to say. Partly I'd like to have spared you this."

"Never mind about me. What's the favor you'd ask?"

"Stephen, you are going to marry me . . . aren't you?"

"Certainly. Unless you change your mind."

"Everybody knows it. Everybody thinks we've been engaged."

"That appears to be the way Linn and your father have spread it on," he replied in bitterness.

"What is the object of this marriage?" she asked, proudly lifting her head.

"Your father says . . . and *you* say . . . to save your reputation."

"Yes. My honor. . . . And I fear your sacrifice will fail if you continue to look and act as you do. You are no happy bridegroom to be. Tay-Tay said you had a face like a sick cow. You certainly look wretched. If you don't cheer up and change . . . act and look like a lover . . . the Sarlands will guess the truth. So will the cowboys. Not to mention those in Flagstaff with whom we come in contact. It is a tremendous bluff we are playing. I can do my part. You see that I look happy, don't you?"

"Yes, I do," he answered miserably. "And so help me God, I can't understand you. Always you seem a lie."

"All women are actresses, Stephen. I shall not fail here. And I ask this last favor of you. Look and play the part of an accepted lover. For my sake."

"My God! Cherry Winters, you can ask that of a man whose only crime has been to love you so well? And who must lose you!"

"Stephen, if you loved me that well, you could die for me."

"I could, far more easily than do what you ask. It is almost an insupportable ordeal you set me. I was never much at hiding my feelings."

"Stephen, the Sarlands and the cowboys must not guess this marriage is a . . . a fake."

"I grant that. And I know I look like a poor lost devil. But I thought that'd seem natural to everybody. They all heard I was not going East."

"You don't know women, my desert friend. Missus Sarland is keen as a whip. If you can deceive her . . . make this engagement seem real and of long standing, you will stop her wagging tongue. Then after I get to New York, I can find ways socially to please her. Right here is the danger."

"Perhaps you see it more clearly than I," Heftral said mournfully. "Anyway, I'll accept your judgment."

"Then you will grant my favor?" asked Cherry, beginning to succumb to repressed emotion.

"Favor? I call it the hardest job ever given me. Marrying you will be nothing, compared to this damned hypocrisy you ask."

"I do ask, Stephen. I beg of you. Now at the last I confess I'm not so brazen. I'm afraid of scandal. Nothing bad ever has touched my name yet. All this modern stuff about freedom, independence, license is rot. Face to face with the truth, I beg of you . . . do this thing for me. At any cost."

"Yes . . . Cherry," he gulped, and leaned against the window.

Cherry's reserve strength had oozed out in expression. She waited in suspense. She saw his lean jaw quiver and the cords set in his neck. He turned to transfix her with accusing eyes.

"On one condition," he said.

"Condition. What?" she whispered.

"This, then, is the last time you and I will ever be alone together?" he asked huskily.

She was past falsehood and could only stare mutely at him.

"Of course it must be. Well, my price for your favor is that you let me. . . . No! I will not bargain. . . . You lovely heartless thing . . . you'd only refuse. I'll *take* what will give me strength to do your bidding."

Cherry backed against the wall, her hands against her breast, as if to ward him off. But when like a whirlwind he seized her in his arms, he never knew those trembling hands locked around his neck. Mad with grief and unrequited love, he crushed her to his breast and pressed wild unsatisfied kisses upon her closed eyes, her parted lips, her neck. And releasing her as suddenly, he staggered to the door, like a blinded man, and leaned his face against it, sobbing: "Cherry! Cherry! Cherry!"

He did not turn to see her outstretched arms, her convulsed face. And as Cherry could not speak, he bolted out in ignorance. Cherry closed her eyes, slowly recovering.

"I thought . . . that was . . . my finish," she whispered pantingly. "Poor boy . . . he never looked at me. Well, it'll only be . . . all the sweeter."

Chapter Sixteen

The sun had set when the car entered the heavy forest of pine that skirted the mountains. Snow was blowing. The wind was bitter cold, and moaned in the trees. How the car hummed on. Night fell, and the forest was black. The headlights cast broad gleams into the forest at the curves of the road, making specters of the dark pines.

Soon, then, the street lamps of Flagstaff terminated that wonderful ride.

In the hotel lobby, Cherry, indifferent to loungers there, held frozen ungloved hands to the open fire. She had learned the real good of fire, its dire necessity, as she had begun the learning of many other things.

As Cherry turned, she saw a tall stoop-shouldered man, rather lean and scholarly, rise from a chair to accost Heftral.

"How do you do, Mister Elliott," Heftral said constrainedly. "How are you? This is my friend . . . and patron, I may add . . . Mister Winters, of New York."

"Ah! How do you do, Mister Winters," returned Elliott rather slowly, extending his hand to meet Winters's. "Patron? Of what, may I ask?"

"Hardly patron, just yet," Winters replied. "Heftral is a little previous, naturally."

"Yes, he is, indeed," the doctor returned, not without sarcasm. "Overzealous, I may say, in estimating things. Dreamy when he should be scientific. Witness the ridiculous rumor just phoned in from Cameron."

"Rumor? What was it?" asked Heftral tersely.

Cherry liked the lift of his head, and grew interested. No doubt this was the museum director who had discharged Stephen.

"Some nonsense about your having discovered *Beckyshibeta,*" replied Elliott with a dry laugh. "It was telephoned in to the newspaper by a chauffeur. Annoying to me, to say the least."

Heftral glanced at Winters and said: "We stopped at Cameron for gas."

"Must have been the driver, Bill," Winters replied sprightly, with a shrewd eye upon Elliott.

"Yes, Doctor Elliott, it was . . . rather previous," said Heftral in as dry a tone as the director's. But there was fire in his eye.

"Ahem. I'm waiting here for two of our men due from New Mexico. Expect to put them on the job from which I removed you. I trust Mister Linn, the trader, informed you of this move."

"Yes, Linn told me you had fired me. Mister Winters here will corroborate it."

Winters nodded in reply to the doctor's questioning look, but he did not speak. Cherry knew the gleam in her father's eye. He would say something presently.

"Heftral, I was very sorry indeed to remove you," Elliott went on blandly. "There's no need to repeat my reasons. You've been advised often enough."

"Doctor Elliott, you need not distress yourself over doing what you considered your duty," rejoined Heftral. "It certainly doesn't distress me. In fact it was the only lucky thing that ever happened to me since my connection with the museum."

"Indeed. Excuse me if I fail to see any good fortune in that for you," replied Elliott stiffly.

"You never could see much about me. Perhaps you will when I tell you that *after* you removed me I discovered *Beckyshibeta.*"

"What!" Elliott exclaimed incredulously.

"I discovered *Beckyshibeta,*" Heftral repeated forcefully, truth clear in his paling face and piercing eye. "Probably the greatest of all pueblo ruins. I have my proof. Mister Winters and his daughter can substantiate my claim. Linn, the cowboys, and a Missus Sarland with her son were all there."

Speechlessly Dr. Elliott turned to Winters for corroboration of this astounding assertion.

"Fact," Winters said shortly. "I'm about to wire Doctor Bushnell, head of the museum. Also Jackson, a good friend of mine. Want them to know that I stand behind Heftral. It remains to be decided whether we shall let the museum in on the excavation work."

"Doctor Bushnell! Jackson!" ejaculated Elliott weakly. "May I ask . . . are you Mister Elijah Winters?"

"The same, sir," returned Winters, bowing, and abruptly left the astounded director to join Cherry beside the fire.

"Cherry, old girl, did you get that?" he whispered. "I'm simply tickled pink, as you say. . . . Now listen to Stephen lay him out cold."

Dr. Elliott seemed to be in the throes of amazement and consternation.

"Ah! Indeed! So it's true," he began, floundering to retrieve himself. "Most remarkable. Incredible, I may say. But of course, I understand . . . a fact. You are most fortunate, Heftral, in your discovery and to have gained the interest of Elijah Winters. I congratulate you. And I . . . *er* . . . ahem . . . perhaps it is I who is somewhat previous. Pray forget your hasty dismissal. It really was not authentic . . . going through a third party. Somewhat irregular. We can adjust the matter amicably. In fact I . . . I'd consider it a favor if you will not mention the matter to our New York office."

"I've accepted my release, Doctor Elliott, thank you, and

shall wire the museum to that effect," Heftral replied with cold dignity, and bowed himself away.

The director looked a dazed, beaten, and frightened man.

"Say, Cherry, didn't Stephen look great?" crowed Winters with gleeful pride. "What a coup for him. That will cost Elliott his job. And by gad, I'll see that it's offered to Heftral."

"Daddy, you like Stephen, don't you?" Cherry asked softly.

"Love him, you icicle. And you bet I'll push him for keeps."

"You're kind and good. I'm glad you . . . you care for him," responded Cherry, and turned to gaze into the fire. "It's too bad you . . . Stephen . . . I. . . . Oh, words are idle and useless."

"Cherry, darling, just then you reminded me of your mother," said her father with feeling. "It's a long time since you've done that."

"Mother? I'm glad, Daddy. Perhaps . . . after this . . . this lesson of yours I will grow more like her."

"Cherry," Winters whispered, bending over her, "you mean to go on with this cruel marriage and. . . ."

"Yes," she returned, dropping her eyes.

"It will kill Stephen."

"Nonsense. Men don't die of unrequited love."

"If your mother had led me to the altar . . . and left me . . . I'm sure I'd never have lived to face it."

"Stephen Heftral is made of sterner stuff. Besides, he has a brilliant future. . . . I'm tired now, Dad, and very hungry."

The sunshine poured in at Cherry's window, telling her that she had slept late, though this was to be the day of days. She lay watching the gold shadows on the curtain, aware of the fresh cool dry air on her face. Her active mind took up the development of plans where the night before she had left off. Her father had secured a Pullman drawing room on the Limited. The securing of this, or at least a compartment on the train, was of paramount importance. Only one more detail to arrange—the strongest link in the chain to her climax.

Cherry arose, conscious of inward excitation and suspense. After all, she could not be sure of anything until she was Stephen's wife. That would be the consummation of hopes, the allaying of fears. The rest would be like the denouement of a good play.

She looked out of her window. How blue the sky. The mountain peaks stood up like dark spears. Patches of snow shone in the sunlight, running down to the edge of the vast green belt of forest land. She could see into the fields adjacent to town. Horses were romping with manes flying in the wind; red and white cattle were grazing on a grassy hill; the scattered pine trees seemed to call to her to come and ride. Cut-over timberlands led her gaze to distant foothills and these to far-off black bluffs and hazy desert. Arizona! There was no place in the world so full of romance and beauty, and the natural things that stirred the soul.

Cherry went into the little open parlor of the hotel, where her father sat before a cozy fire, reading a newspaper.

"What a lazy bride-to-be," he said good-humoredly. "We had breakfast long ago."

" 'Mawnin', Dad," drawled Cherry. "Reckon I'll have a cup of coffee and some toast up heah."

"You look very sweet and lovely for a prospective murderess," he said. "Cherry, old dear, I give up forever trying to figure women."

"Fine. Now you will be the best of fathers. Where's Stephen?"

"He was here a moment ago with the marriage license. Lord, but he's funny. Like a sleepwalker. I have made a ten o'clock appointment with a minister . . . Doctor Cardwell. Nice old chap. He's from Connecticut. Came here years ago with lung trouble. His life had been despaired of in the East. But he's hale and hearty now. I tell you, Cherry, this Arizonie, as Linn calls it, is a wonderful country."

"Arizona. Mellow, golden, sustaining, beautiful, clean with desert wind," murmured Cherry, gazing down into the fire. "Presently I shall tell you what it has done for me."

"I'll fetch your coffee and toast," returned Winters with alacrity.

The moments passed with Cherry musing. Presently her father entered, carrying a small tray. Heftral also came in. He wore a dark suit that showed his stalwart form to advantage. Cherry admired again the clean-shaven tanned face, lean and strong.

"Good morning, Miss Winters," he said with courtesy, but his steady gaze made Cherry almost feel a little uneasy in spite of herself. She gazed at him over her cup of coffee.

"Howdy, Stephen. Are the horses ready?"

"No," he flashed. "But the taxi is."

Cherry laughed, her composure restored. How eager Heftral was to get this awful business settled. "Dad, you said our train left at seven something, didn't you?"

"Seven-ten. It's the Limited and always on time," he replied.

"So long to wait. I wish for Mister Heftral's sake it left hours earlier."

"Don't worry about Stephen, my dear," returned Winters. "We've got a lot to talk over and won't bother you."

"Thank you. I'll get my things on and be back *pronto*," Cherry said, and hurried away to her room.

Heftral showed that the strain was wearing upon him. Cherry thought it would be wise for her to see as little as possible of him after the wedding up until nearly train time. She felt nervous and tense herself. It wanted but a few minutes to 10:00. She put on her coat and hat, and a veil, which she carefully arranged. How white her face and big her eyes. Then she hurried back to join the gentlemen, who rose at her entrance.

"I'm ready," she said rather tremulously. "Is . . . everything arranged?"

"Why, I'm sure it is, Cherry," replied her father, turning to Heftral. "There's not so much. Minister, license, taxi. What else?"

"Mister Heftral, did you purchase a wedding ring?"

"No," he replied with the strangest of glances at her.

"Then you must do so at once. I'll go with you. Surely there's a jeweler here."

"I have a wedding ring," Heftral interrupted. "It was my mother's. It hardly matters whether it fits or not."

"Doesn't it? That's all you know," said Cherry. Her hands were trembling while she tried it on. "Oh, it's a perfect fit. . . . What a pretty ring! I like old-fashioned wedding rings best."

"Old-fashioned weddings, too," added her father. "Lord, Cherry, I always dreaded one of those swell weddings for you. Might have saved myself a lot of worry. Come on. We'll have this over in a jiffy."

He led her downstairs, through the lobby, and out to a waiting taxi. Heftral had evidently stopped behind for something. Presently he came out, and, squeezing into the taxi, he laid something on Cherry's knee without a word. She tucked aside a corner of her veil and opened the loose paper package on her lap. Flowers of some kind. Then she thrilled. The tiny bouquet was composed of bits of cedar and juniper foliage, with their green and lavender berries, several wild roses, and a sprig of sage with the exquisite rare purple blossoms. Cherry was so deeply touched that she could not speak, and she quickly dropped the corner of veil, lest Stephen should see the havoc wrought by these sweet symbols from the desert.

★ ★ ★ ★ ★

The short ride, the simple brief ceremony, and the return to the hotel were like changing moments of a trance to Cherry. She would not have exchanged the simplicity of her marriage for all the pomp of royalty.

Once more safe in her room she laid aside the bouquet, flung her gloves, tore off the veil, and threw aside hat and coat. And she did not recognize the face in the mirror. Cherry had never raved about her looks, but she gloried in them now.

"It's over. I'm his wife," she whispered, kissing the slim band of gold on her finger. "Now. Now I'm safe . . . and oh, so unutterably happy! How can I wait to tell him? Suppose he ran off to his desert before I could. Oh, my bursting heart!"

Cherry wept in the exaltation of that hour. It was long before composure returned, and then it was such composure as she had never known. No one would have guessed that she had cried like an overjoyous girl.

Her father knocked at her door and called: "Cherry, we've arranged a lunch over here at a restaurant! Will you come?"

"Indeed I will. Just a minute, Dad, and I'll join you." She dispensed with the veil this time. Let them be mystified at the glow on her face and the light in her eyes. They were only men who knew nothing of the wondrous strength and generosity of a woman's heart. Then she went out.

"My word, Cherry, but you look great!" Winters exclaimed with conscious pride.

Heftral stared at her as if she were an impenetrable stone image hiding the truth of woman. Nevertheless, once seated at table, the constraint eased, and they enjoyed a capital luncheon.

"Well, that was fine," Winters said with satisfaction. "Now, Cherry, we'll take you back to the hotel, where Stephen and I must go into an important conference over plans for work at *Beckyshibeta.*"

"I shall not be lonely. I'll visit the stores . . . and look out for cowboys," replied Cherry gaily.

"You'll find cowboys on every corner," warned Winters. "Be careful, Cherry," he grimaced.

"Wait, Dad, please," Cherry replied, catching his sleeve. "I've something to tell you and . . . my husband."

Heftral winced at the first use of that word between them. Winters dropped back in his chair, sure of catastrophe.

Cherry transfixed them with a glance in which long-past resentment and pain blended now with some emotion they could not name. "Gentlemen, do you recall one late afternoon at Linn's trading post when you planned to kidnap me?"

Heftral looked stricken and Winters gulped: "No. Can't say I do."

"Tax your memory, Dad," Cherry went on dryly. "It never was good. But this was a special occasion."

Heftral coughed uneasily. "I remember, Miss Winters."

"I am no longer Miss Winters," corrected Cherry.

"Pardon, Missus Heftral," he corrected himself mockingly.

"Dad, I was lying out in the hammock beside the open window when you made your infamous offer to Stephen Heftral," said Cherry.

"My God, no!" her father cried, thunderstruck. "I don't believe you."

"Listen. You'll believe your very own words," replied Cherry, and went on to repeat many things that had been burned indelibly on her memory.

"That's enough," suddenly interrupted her father, very red in the face. "I can see you were there."

"All the time you knew!" Heftral exclaimed, wide-eyed and ashamed.

"All the time," replied Cherry, smiling at them.

"Lord save me from another daughter," burst out Winters helplessly.

"I'll run along now," Cherry added, rising. "Thanks for the luncheon. I'll remember it. . . . Dad, we will wait for dinner on the train. . . . Mister Heftral, you will go to the train with us to say good bye? Please. It will look better. Must I remind you . . . ?"

"No, you needn't remind me of anything," Heftral interrupted almost violently, dark and passionate pain and reproach in his eyes. "I'll be at the train to bid . . . good bye . . . to my wife . . . forever."

"Ah. . . . Thank you. Then all is well," replied Cherry, averting her eyes. "*Adiós* till then."

As she glided away from them, out into the main restaurant, she heard her father say: "Stephen, my God . . . I need a drink."

Heftral's reply followed with a sudden scrape of a chair on the floor. "Eli, you old villain, I'll need two," he said weakly. "And we'll drink to all that's left to me . . . *Beckyshibeta.*"

Cherry went out, tingling, blushing, glowing. It was even more fun, more satisfaction than she had anticipated. How flabbergasted her father had been. And she had dared only one fleeting look at the stricken Heftral. "All the time you knew," he had cried. Cherry reflected that when he had returned to sanity, he would recall many things that might embarrass her. But she would take good care he never recovered his sanity. Then she went about the last few tasks needed to insure this blissful future for Heftral.

First she engaged the hotel porter to fetch Heftral's bag to the train with hers and her father's. She made it clear to the bright-eyed colored lad—as well as remunerative—that Heftral was not to see this removal of baggage. Next she set out to look for some cowboys.

But not until actually embarked on this quest did she realize its absurdity and risk, not to consider embarrassment. It was an early afternoon hour on Saturday. Flagstaff appeared full of cowboys and those she passed on the street were certainly not unaware of her presence. Finally, near the post office, Cherry located three typical cowboys standing beside a motion-picture advertisement that graced the corner of the block. It happened to be a vacant lot, which accounted, perhaps, for the cowboys being comparatively alone.

Cherry walked slowly by, calmly appraising them. How like Mojave, Zoroaster, Wess. Cowboys all resembled one another. Cherry expected to be noticed and commented upon. She was not disappointed.

"Andy, did you see what I seen?" broke out one.

"Wal, I reckon. An' I'm shore dizzy," was the reply.

"Some looker, pards," added the third.

The encounter ordinarily would have ended there, but these cowboys, or some cowboys, at least, were indispensable to her plan. She had to have them. She was prepared to go to the limit of making eyes at them to carry her point. Thinking hard, Cherry decided to walk by them again, down the street, then return, and ask them to come into the post office. To that end she turned back. As she neared them, she was afraid she was smiling. What a warm feeling she had for these lean, hard-faced cowboys. She passed, with ears acute to catch any whispers.

"My gawd . . . Andy, look at them legs," hoarsely whispered one. "Wimmin ought to be arrested fer wearin' them short skirts."

"Only seen her eyes, but thet was aplenty," came the reply. "My pore little Susie! I'll never love her any more."

Cherry did not hear the third man's remark, and was glad she had not. Her face burned. What keen devils these cowboys. Right then and there Cherry's plan, so far as they were concerned, went into eclipse. Still she would not give up. Crossing the street, she went into the department store, made a few purchases, and, going out, crossed the street again, at the other end of the block, and came down to enter the post office. She was cudgeling her brain. If those cowboys saw her and followed her into the post office, she would risk speaking to them. Most cowboys were chivalrous gentlemen at heart, for all their coarseness and deviltry.

There appeared to be only two men in the post office. One was huge and dark, the other small and fair. Suddenly Cherry stood transfixed. She recognized bold black eyes in the giant and sly twinkling ones in the other. She knew these men.

"Black Dick! Snitch!" she exclaimed in astonishment. "Oh, I'm glad to meet you."

"Same hyar, Miss Winters," Dick replied, smiling broadly as he removed his ragged sombrero. "How about you, Snitch?"

"Me? I never was so tickled in my life," Snitch said, gallant and bareheaded. "It shore is fine of you to speak to us . . . after the deal we gave you."

"Never mind that. But aren't you afraid to be in town? Aren't you in danger of being arrested?"

"Wal, miss, not that we know of. You see I'm not exactly the fellar you took me fer."

"Oh, then you're not Black Dick, the outlaw?" Cherry asked in disappointment.

"I'm awful sorry, miss, but I ain't. Honest. Didn't your father tell you aboot us?"

"My father! No," Cherry replied ponderingly. "Wal, he shore ought to have. Fer he hired me an' Snitch to give you a scare."

"Ah, I see. . . . And it was no accident that you left Missus Sarland's jewel bag behind?"

"Accident? I should smile not. I jest hung it on a tree where she'd bump her haid on it."

"Well! Well! My Dad's the limit, isn't he?"

"If you want my idee, miss, I think he's a prince," Dick replied heartily.

"You'll always be Black Dick and Snitch to me. But I'm indeed glad you're not real desperadoes. What a trick you played on us." Suddenly a thought like a bright flash struck Cherry into radiance. "Come here, both of you," she whispered, and drew the grinning men away from the door into a corner. Here they were out of sight of the post office employees. No others had yet entered. What luck! Cherry felt a gush of riotous blood heat her veins. "Will you do me a favor? Do you want to make fifty dollars apiece?"

"Well, Miss Winters, your voice is sweet music," whispered Dick.

"Lady, I'll lay down my life fer you fer nothin'," Snitch declared.

"Listen," began Cherry hurriedly, "I am no longer Miss Winters. I was married to Mister Heftral today. Never mind congratulating me. Listen, Father and I leave tonight on the Limited. Mister Heftral . . . my husband . . . I'm afraid he doesn't want to go East with me very bad. But I want him to go. I want him terribly. Will you help me kidnap him?"

"Wal, we'll hawg-tie the cold-hearted scoundrel an' throw him on thet train," Dick declared, his eyes rolling.

"I never heard of the like," added Snitch most forcefully. "The lucky son-of-a-gun! But them archaeologists are plumb queer ducks. Lady, we'll shore do anythin' fer you."

"Splendid. Can you get another trusty man . . . a friend . . . one who is big and strong? Heftral will fight."

"Shore. I know a fellar who's bigger'n a hill. He can throw a barrel of flour right up into a wagon. Reckon the three of us can put Heftral on thet train in less'n a couple of winks."

"Very well. Then it's settled," went on Cherry, now calm and serene. "Here are your instructions. The three of you be at the station when the Limited comes in. Keep sharp look-out for me. I'll be with father and Mister Heftral. Follow us a little behind . . . not too close . . . and when we reach our Pullman, you wait a little aside. I'll stop at the car entrance nearest the drawing room. I'll wait until the conductor calls all aboard. When I step up, that will be your signal to seize Heftral and carry him after me. Be quick. And don't be gentle. Remember, he is powerful and will fight. I want this to go off just like that." And Cherry snapped her fingers.

"Lady, say them instructions over," Dick replied earnestly.

She repeated them word for word.

Black Dick lifted his shaggy black head. "Jest like thet," he said, snapping huge fingers. "Lady, it's as good as done."

"Then here's your money in advance," Cherry said, producing some bills. "You won't fail me?"

"I wish my chanst fer heaven was as good," Dick rejoined fervently.

"Lady, you shore picked the gentlemen fer thet job," added Snitch warmly.

"You are my very good friends," concluded Cherry, all smiles. "You are helping me more than you can guess. I'll never forget you. Good bye."

She left them there, rooted to the spot, and swept out of the post office in a state of supreme bliss. The gods had favored her. Suddenly she saw the three cowboys not far ahead, standing expectantly. They had seen her come out. Cherry checked a wild impulse to break across the street in the middle of the block, so she would not have to pass them. Then, very erect, with chin tilted, she went on and by, as if she had never seen them.

"Say, Andy, did you feel a cold wind round heah?" asked one in disgust.

"Huh? I been stabbed with a pitchfork of ice," came the reply.

"Pard, she's a goddess, an' I like 'em hard to win," said the third.

If they could have seen Cherry's convulsed and happy face, when she reached the corner, they would have had more cause to wonder about the female species.

The afternoon passed like a happy dream. Cherry spent most of it trying to think of things to say to Stephen when the revelation came. She changed it a hundred times. How could she tell what to say? But every moment that brought the climax closer found Cherry's state more intense. She must hold out. She must stay to the finish. When the porter knocked, she leaped up with a start.

"Mister Winters is waiting," he announced. "The Limited is in the block."

"Where is . . . Mister Heftral?" Cherry asked with lips that trembled.

"He's waiting, too. I'll fetch your baggage . . . all of it, right after," he replied, and he winked at her.

Cherry hurriedly got into hat and coat, and omitted the veil. How white she was. Her eyes looked like great dark gulfs. She went downstairs. Her father looked exceedingly uncomfortable. Heftral had not a vestige of color in his face. She joined them, and they went out in silence. Dark had fallen. The street lamps were lit. The air had mountain coolness in it. On the moment the Limited pulled into the station, and slowed down to a stop, steam blowing, bell clanging.

It was only a brief walk from the hotel to the broad platform where the Pullmans stood. Cherry had the glance of a hawk and saw every group of persons there. Not until she spied Black Dick and his comrades did the tension in her break. What a stupendous man the third one was. He made Dick look small. Cherry knew Dick had seen her, though he seemed not to notice. He and his allies kept outside the platform, where Heftral was oblivious of them. Indeed he seemed oblivious of everything.

"Here's our car," Winters spoke up with an effort.

"See if our drawing room is at this end," replied Cherry, and she stepped to face around. That made her confront Heftral. Over his shoulder she saw her three accomplices scarcely a rod away, and Black Dick was watching. It was going to be a success. Cherry felt a blaze within her—an outburst that had been smothered.

Her father touched her arm. He looked miserable, shaken. "Drawing room at this end. I'll go in. So long, Stephen." And he fled.

Cherry edged nearer to Heftral, close, and peered up at him, knowing that a blind man could have read her eyes. But he was more than blind. She pulled at a button on his coat, looking down, and then she flashed her eyes into his again. "Stephen, I'm sorry. Promise me you'll never . . . *never* kidnap another girl."

"God! I'd do it tomorrow if I thought it'd hurt you," he returned hoarsely.

The engine bell rang, to echo in Cherry's heart.

"All aboard!" yelled the conductor somewhere forward.

Cherry wheeled and ran up the car steps and, turning, was in time to see three dark burly forms rush Heftral, and literally throw him up the steps, onto the platform. Cherry ran into the hallway, shaking in her agitation. She heard loud exclamations, the tussling of bodies, the thud of boots. Then the men appeared half dragging, half carrying the fiercely struggling Heftral. Cherry fled to the door of the drawing room. They were coming.

"Soak him, Bill. He's a bull," Dick said, low and hard.

Cherry heard a sodden blow. The struggle ceased. The men

came faster. They were almost carrying Heftral. Cherry's heart leaped to her throat.

"In . . . here," she choked, standing aside.

They thrust Heftral into the drawing room, and rushed back toward the exit. Black Dick turned, his big black eyes rolling merrily. Then he was gone. The train started—gathered momentum. Outside the porter was yelling. He slammed the vestibule doors and came running.

"Lady . . . what's wrong?" he asked in alarm. "Three men upset me. I couldn't do nothin'."

"It's all right, porter," replied Cherry. "My . . . my husband had to be assisted on the train."

"Aw, now, I was scared."

Cherry's father appeared from down the aisle. "What was that row?" he asked nervously.

Cherry barred the door into the drawing room. "Dad . . . I've kidnaped Stephen," she said, very low and clear.

Winters threw up his hands. "Holy Mackerel!" he gasped.

Cherry closed and locked the door. The drawing room was dark. She turned on the light. Heftral was breathing hard. He had been dazed, if not stunned. There was grime on his face and a little blood. The bruise Wess had left over his eye, and which had not wholly disappeared, had been raised again. Cherry darted to wet her handkerchief. She wiped his face—bathed his forehead. She had told that ruffian Dick not to be gentle. Remorse smote her. Suddenly she touched Stephen's face.

He was staring with eyes that appeared about to start from his head. He grasped her with shaking hands. He gaped at the car window and the lights flashing by. Then he seemed to realize what had happened.

"They threw me on the train," he burst out incredulously.

Cherry rose to stand before him.

"You . . . you. . . ."

"Yes, I've kidnaped you," she interrupted.

"My God! Cherry, could you carry revenge so far? Oh, how cruel. You pitiless woman!" He fell face down against the cushion.

"Stephen," she said, trying to stay the trembling hands that leaped toward him. When he did not look or speak, she went on softly: "Stephen." No response. Her head fluttered to his shoulder. "Husband."

At that, his haggard face lifted and his terrible eyes stared as those of a man who knew not what he saw.

"I have kidnaped you . . . yes . . . forever!"

He fell on his knees to clasp her blouse with plucking hands. "Cherry, if I am not drunk or mad . . . make me understand," he implored.

She locked her hands behind his head. "Indeed you are hard to convince. Have we not been married? Are you not my captive on this train? Is this not the eve of our honeymoon?"

"It's too good to be true," he replied huskily. "I can't believe it."

She bent to kiss the bruise on his forehead. "Will that do?"

"No!"

She kissed his eyes, his cheeks, and lastly, as he seemed rapt and blind, his lips. "Stephen, I love you," she said.

"Oh, my darling, say that again."

"I love you. I love you. I love you. . . . It was what you did to me. Oh, I confess. I deserved it. I *was* no good . . . and, if not actually bad, I was headed for bad. Oh, Stephen, you spanked some sense into me in time, and your desert changed and won me. I bless you for making me a woman. I will give up what was that idle, useless, wasteful life . . . and work with you . . . for you . . . to make a home for you. Forgive this last little deceit. Oh, you should have seen Dad's face. . . . Kiss me! Come, let us go tell him I'm your *Beckyshibeta.*"

ABOUT THE AUTHOR

Zane Grey was born Pearl Zane Gray at Zanesville, Ohio in 1872. He was graduated from the University of Pennsylvania in 1896 with a degree in dentistry. He practiced in New York City while striving to make a living by writing. He married Lina Elise Roth in 1905 and with her financial assistance he published his first novel himself, *Betty Zane* (1903). Closing his dental office, the Greys moved into a cottage on the Delaware River, near Lackawaxen, Pennsylvania. Grey took his first trip to Arizona in 1907 and, following his return, wrote *The Heritage of the Desert* (1910). The profound effect that the desert had had on him was so vibrantly captured that it still comes alive for a reader. Grey couldn't have been more fortunate in his choice of a mate. Trained in English at Hunter College, Lina Grey proofread every manuscript Grey wrote, polished his prose, and later she managed their financial affairs. Grey's early novels were serialized in pulp magazines, but by 1918 he had graduated to the slick magazine market. Motion picture rights brought in a fortune and, with 109 films based on his work, Grey set a record yet to be equaled by any other author. Zane Grey was not a realistic writer, but rather one who charted the interiors of the soul through encounters with the wilderness. He provided characters no less memorable than one finds in Balzac, Dickens, or Thomas Mann, and they have a vital story to tell. "There was so much unexpressed feeling that could not be entirely portrayed," Loren Grey, Grey's younger son and a noted psychologist, once recalled, "that, in later years, he would weep when re-reading one of his own books." Perhaps, too, closer to the mark, Zane Grey may have wept at how his attempts at being truthful to his muse had so often been essentially altered by his editors, so that no one might ever be able to read his stories as he had intended them. It may be said of Zane Grey that, more than mere adventure tales, he fashioned psycho-dramas about the odyssey of the human soul. If his stories seem not always to be of the stuff of the mundane world, without what his stories do touch, the human world has little meaning— which may go a long way to explain the hold he has had on an enraptured reading public ever since his first Western novel in 1910. His next Five Star Western will be *Panguitch.*